"I SHOULDN'T DO THIS."

"Do what?" Eden asked without turning to face him.

Sullivan sighed. "I really shouldn't."

Eden snapped her head around. "Mr. Sullivan, are you talking to yourself or do you intend to answer—"

She stopped speaking, her breath literally stolen away as Sullivan placed a large hand at the back of her head and slowly began to pull her toward him. She trembled all over, but he seemed calm, relaxed, steady as a rock as he laid his lips over hers.

It was not her first kiss. But not one of those other, meaningless kisses had felt anything like this. Sullivan's lips were warm and soft, but not *too* soft. There was a tender urgency in the way he pressed his mouth to hers, a very gentle demand. He moved those lips as if he were tasting her, as if he savored the flavor of her mouth.

Then his mouth left hers, barely, briefly, and she whispered his name. "Sinclair."

He kissed her again, his touch more demanding, and her heart thudded in her chest. And when he took his mouth from hers once again, she whispered simply, "Sin."

Dear Romance Reader,

In July last year, we launched the Ballad line with four new series, and each month we'll present both new and continuing stories set everywhere from medieval England to the American West—the kind of passionate, romantic stories you love best, written by the most gifted authors. At the back of each book, we'll tell you when you can find subsequent books in the series that have captured your heart.

First up is the second entry in Lori Handeland and Linda Devlin's wonderful *Rock Creek Six* series. This month Linda Devlin introduces **Sullivan**, a half-breed bastard with no place in the world—until he finds his fate in a special woman's arms. Next, Maura McKenzie continues the *Hope Chest* series with **At Midnight**, as a modern-day newspaper reporter tracks a murderer into the past, where she meets a Pinkerton agent determined not only to solve the case, but to steal her heart.

The passionate men of the *Clan Maclean* return in Lynne Hayworth's spectacularly atmospheric **Winter Fire**, as a widow with a special gift meets the laird of the proud but doomed clan. Will her love bring about his salvation? Finally, Kelly McClymer offers the fourth book in the charming *Once Upon a Wedding* series, introducing **The Infamous Bride** who begins her marriage on a rash wager—and finds that her husband's love is the only wedding gift she wants. Enjoy!

Kate Duffy
Editorial Director

The Rock Creek Six

SULLIVAN

Linda Devlin

ZEBRA BOOKS
KENSINGTON PUBLISHING CORP.

http://www.zebrabooks.com

Chapter 1

1871

"Aunt Eden, why are they hitting that man?"

Eden frowned as she pulled on the reins and halted the buckboard. "I don't know, but it doesn't seem fair at all," she said softly. "Six against one." Millie slid across the seat, closing the short distance that separated them. The little girl was clearly afraid, her eyes wide as she watched the scene unfolding in the middle of the street.

To Eden's way of thinking, such fear in a child wasn't right. Millie was only six years old, and yet she'd seen more than her share of injustice. It wasn't the child's fault that her mother had had the poor sense to become pregnant without benefit of marriage, or that the unfortunate woman had died so young. The little girl really should be in the care of a loving family, with a mother and a father and perhaps even brothers and sisters, but as not one of the families of Spring Hill, Georgia, had come forward to offer such an arrangement, Millie had become Eden's traveling companion. Goodness, she couldn't possibly have left the child behind.

Eden placed an arm around Millie and pulled her close. Millie's pale, curling head rested against Eden's side, and the little girl looked down so she wouldn't have to watch the melee that blocked their progress through the crossroads called, according to the weathered sign Eden had seen at the edge of town, Webberville. She hadn't even planned to stop here. They really should pass straight through the little town and travel for several more hours before setting up camp.

But in front of her eyes there unfolded an annoying complication to her simple plans. Six ruffians pounded on some poor man who could barely stand. One of the thugs would hold their victim up while another hammered his face and then his midsection. Then they would practically throw the beaten man across an open space and into the arms of an impatient hooligan who would start the nasty process all over again.

The man being thrashed no longer fought back. Eden had seen him attempt to throw a punch, just once, as she brought the buckboard to a halt, but since then he hadn't so much as lifted his arms. She suspected he was incapable of defending himself at this point. Goodness knew how long this had been going on.

Quite a while, apparently. Long dark hair covered much of the underdog's face, but what little she could see was cut and covered with blood, as if this beating had been going on for some time.

"Teddy." Eden turned to the child who rode in

the back of the buckboard only to find the boy as terrified as Millie, who continued to cling to Eden's side. Teddy Cannon was a few years older than Millie, nine years old, the exasperated sheriff who had handed him over had informed her. He hadn't said a single word since his uncle had died several months before, according to the same sheriff. Teddy's parents had both passed away two years back, and after the uncle's death there was no more family. Teddy had apparently resisted the alternative living arrangements that had been offered, running away from the blacksmith who had agreed to provide room and board in exchange for help around his place. The sheriff and the blacksmith had both seemed relieved to be rid of the child.

Teddy's gaze was riveted on the beaten man, and his dark brown eyes shone with unshed tears.

"Teddy," she called again, and this time the child turned his fragile face to her. "Would you please sit up front with Millie for a moment and hold the reins?"

He scrambled over and took the reins she offered. Eden closed her hands over his, wrapping her gloved fingers over his small, trembling hands. "Don't be afraid," she said softly.

He refused to look directly at her, as he often did. Wondering what had happened to Teddy drove her to distraction and made her so angry she tried not to dwell on the possibilities. Something had made him silent and more horribly frightened than any child should ever be. Children should *never* be afraid.

"I'll take care of it," she assured him.

With that, she climbed down from the wagon, unhurried in her movements, determination in her mind. No one would scare *these* children, not while they were in her care.

Eden brushed some of the trail dust from her blue calico skirt as she advanced toward the thugs. A hand to her hair confirmed her suspicion that it behaved as expected, as it had since she'd begun this rough leg of the trip, which meant her fair hair fell in disarray from the bun she had attempted to fashion this morning.

She stopped several feet from the brawl, straightened her spine, and waited for a moment. When it became obvious that the ruffians either did not notice her or intended to ignore her presence, she cleared her throat. And then again.

Finally, they stopped pounding the poor man who was now slumped, practically unconscious, between two thugs who held him upright by the arms. Even if he had been physically able to defend himself, his arms were immobilized.

"Excuse me, gentlemen," Eden said with a smile. "Your fracas is blocking the roadway and I must pass."

They all breathed with great effort and perspired profusely, flexing bloody fists as she finally claimed their attention. Was it such hard work for six men to beat up one poor soul? Apparently so. It looked as if the outnumbered man had gotten in a few licks of his own, in the beginning. The six men who were able to stand without assistance sported their own battle scars: a couple of swollen lips, a seeping cut just beneath an ear, a freely bleeding gash. One fellow favored his left leg and held his side with one hand. Breathing was obviously an effort for the man, but she could not feel sorry for him. They all looked at her like she was daft and said nothing in response to her request.

A potbellied balding tough badly in need of a bath turned away from her, balled his fist, drew his arm back, and hit the victim in the stomach. The beaten man didn't even make much of a sound. He just expelled a whoosh of air as he fell forward and then was yanked back up again.

"What did he do to deserve such a beating?" she asked calmly.

The man with the paunch turned to her, exasperation on his red, fleshy face as he quickly looked her up and down. He was definitely no gentleman! "Lady, this is none of your business."

"I'm sure that's true," Eden said quickly. And then she waited for a response.

"This damn breed kissed my woman," the same man seethed.

Eden cocked her head to the side and dipped down slightly, trying to get a better look at the battered face. She couldn't see much, with long strands of dark brown hair and drying and fresh blood obscuring her view.

"Well, it doesn't look as if he'll be kissing anyone anytime soon," she said lightly. "Don't you think he's had enough? The punishment does seem rather severe, when you consider that his crime was nothing more than to kiss the wrong woman." The thugs lost some of their steam, as she had hoped they would, and took a good look at the man who had to be propped up to stay on his feet.

"Drop him," the potbellied man ordered tiredly.

Those who held the so-called breed did just that; they loosened their hold and allowed the fellow to fall to the ground. He crumpled and landed face first on the dirt road.

The ruffians who had beaten him so badly turned away and headed into the saloon, the very place where the fight had no doubt begun. They studied their battle scars and wiped away streaks of blood and patted one another on the back.

Eden returned to the wagon, flashing a smile for the children. The fear had faded, though she could still see remnants of terror on their faces. Faces so young should be innocent and bright, not afraid and wary.

"You made them stop," Millie said.

"Yes, well"—Teddy clambered into the bed of the wagon to sit with her trunk and their supplies, and Eden climbed into the driver's seat—"it needed to be done."

She set the horses in motion and they progressed slowly, passing by the prone, motionless, beaten body in the street.

Millie's wide, clear eyes stayed on the man, and she bit her lower lip in consternation. "Will he be all right, do you think?" she asked in a small voice.

Eden reluctantly brought the buckboard to a halt in the middle of the street, sighing softly and refusing to look down. It was one thing to take responsibility for two children who had fallen on hard times. But a full-grown man? She knew nothing about him, but that he had the poor sense to kiss another man's woman.

She turned to Teddy and found that the boy studied the beaten man as intently as Millie did. Mercy.

"Hold these very firmly," she instructed, handing the reins to Millie. "Teddy, I'll need your help."

When she stood over the fallen man she had another gut-wrenching flash of doubt. He was huge. Bigger than she had realized. He remained facedown in the street, and she had a chance to study broad shoulders beneath a once-white shirt that was now covered with dust and dirt and smudges that could only be his own blood. His legs were incredibly long, and they were covered in worn denim that had been tucked into large black boots.

She'd lived all her life among large men, overly protective males who'd sheltered and adored her and called her *Little Bit* or *Shorty*. Most of the big men she'd known had big hearts, but it was impossible to tell about this one.

She lifted her head to find Teddy right beside her. He stared at her with wide dark eyes, waiting for her to proceed. Those thugs had called the man on the ground a breed. One look at Teddy was enough to confirm that he was of mixed blood himself; she would've known even if the sheriff hadn't revealed that his late mother's name was Rosario. With deep brown eyes, long black hair, and beautifully warm brown skin, Teddy was a lovely child. And he looked up at her as if he expected her to *do* something.

"Well"—she sighed—"we can't just leave him here."

He was dead. The air on his face felt cool, the surface beneath his back soft. To his ears there was only blessed silence all around. And so Sinclair Sullivan knew he must be dead.

But as he woke the pain in his face and his stomach grew. Sharp pain and dull, constant and fleeting, deep and superficial. On some part of his body, he felt it all. Surely a dead man wouldn't feel such pain.

He managed to open one eye just slightly. The

other refused to cooperate. Night had fallen. All was dark, but for a hint of pale light to his right. The glow of a small campfire, perhaps. To his left there was a . . . a very large chest surrounded by a few smaller pieces of baggage.

It took a moment, but Sullivan finally realized that he was lying in the back of a wagon. The softness beneath his back was a layer of blankets. The coolness on his face was the night breeze. And the silence was broken by a gentle, caressing voice.

"You're awake."

He tried to lift his head and found, to his frustration, that he couldn't.

"Be still," the soft voice urged, and the wagon moved just slightly, dipping with the addition of weight near his feet. He could feel her moving cautiously past him until her face hovered over his. "We were so worried."

From what little he could see she was still worried. The soft light of the fire illuminated one half of her face and a dismayed, forced smile.

"Who are you?" he asked, but the words were garbled. The lady who bent over him leaned a little closer, and for a moment he had a clear view of her face and a halo of silky, pale hair. He wanted to watch her, to study her, but found he couldn't keep that one eye open.

So he closed his one functioning eye and took a deep breath. She smelled so good. Clean and sweet, but not perfumed. Not like that saloon girl who had draped herself all over his arm and shoulder and then kissed him just as an ardent suitor walked into the saloon. He felt like he'd been set up, but it could just be his suspicious nature. The calico might have simply been trying to make her lover jealous.

"Is he awake?" a child's voice whispered. The soft question came from nearby—from the driver's seat of the wagon, most likely.

"He was for a moment," the woman who remained with him answered in a whisper. "Don't worry, Millie. He'll be fine. We'll take good care of him."

Why? He wanted to ask, but neither his lips nor his brain would cooperate. *Why* would they take good care of him? And where was her husband, the little girl's father?

She stayed beside him and lightly brushed a cool cloth over his battered face. The tender ministrations felt good, until she touched the corner of his mouth. He jerked his head to the side, away from the cloth.

"Sorry," she whispered.

He wanted to answer her, to ask her a hundred questions, to get a better look at her face. But he contented himself with a deep breath of her comforting smell, and then he drifted away.

Eden placed the gown across the ground and poised above it with a sharp pair of shears. She hesitated for just a moment before she cut the full skirt from the bodice. Pink muslin and lace slipped beneath her fingers, and once she had begun she didn't have another doubt. Millie needed a new and proper dress, something pretty, and Eden had several suitable gowns in her trunk. More than she needed.

The bodice of this particular dress had been stained with bacon grease. She'd tried to remove the stain, but found it impossible. There was more than enough fabric in the skirt of this dress to fashion a nice shift for Millie. If she'd had more time, she would have bought a few ready-made dresses in Spring Hill. But traveling to Texas had been a spur-of-the-moment decision, and bringing Millie along had been a last-minute impulse. She had so wanted to find Millie a proper home before leaving on her journey. She'd been unable to do so, however, and now Millie was her responsibility.

They should be on the road, she knew. Every moment wasted was a moment she wasn't closer to Rock Creek. She was days from her destination, and she didn't want to waste a single minute, much less hours.

Before she'd packed up and left home, it had been several weeks since she'd heard from Jedidiah. More than two months, in fact. It wasn't that he'd been the best of correspondents in the ten years since he'd left home, but she could usually count on a short missive from him at least once a month. They came from all over, from small towns and large, and rarely from the same town twice. He liked to keep on the move, Jedidiah did.

He'd found trouble again, she was certain. She could *feel* it; she'd been having dreams of her brother lately. Just like she had during the war, when he'd been hurt or in danger and she'd felt it, sensed it in her sleep and her quiet moments.

A familiar and insistent tapping began at her shoulder. Teddy might not speak, but he was learning to assert himself in other ways.

"Just a moment, Teddy."

The tapping didn't stop, but increased in speed and in strength until she was sure he would put a hole in that one spot.

Eden dropped the scissors and lifted her face to Teddy. "What is it? Is something wrong?"

He pointed to the wagon, and Eden turned her head.

The man she had rescued stood in the back of the wagon watching her, and for the first time since she'd driven the buckboard away from that awful little town, she wondered if she hadn't made a terrible mistake.

Huge and angry and frightful, he stared at her. His beaten face did nothing to alter the menacing image she had of him; it only enhanced the notion. Which wasn't fair, she knew.

"Good morning," she said sweetly, feeling and dismissing the unsteady beat of her heart in her throat.

"Who are you?" he asked through gritted teeth.

"Eden Rourke." She laid the shears aside and stood slowly. Perhaps if she stood he wouldn't seem so imposingly tall. She reminded herself that he stood in the back of the wagon, after all, which gave him an unnatural advantage. And besides, she stood barely five-foot-one. Almost everyone was tall by comparison. "Teddy," she added, turning to the boy, "would you fetch Millie from the stream? We will be able to travel this morning, after all."

Eden turned back to the man, trying to convince herself that she had nothing to fear. She had saved his life, for goodness' sake. Facing him, that fact didn't reassure her in the least.

"And you are?" she prodded.

He mumbled something unintelligible, and at the questioning lift of her eyebrows he repeated himself more slowly and with evident pain. One word. *Sullivan*.

"Would you like some breakfast, Mr. Sullivan?" She turned to what was left of their campfire. "Some coffee, perhaps?"

Eden busied herself over the pot, pouring out the last cup of lukewarm coffee. When she turned with the cup in her hand he stood right *there*, not a full foot away, and the cup flew out of her hands to soak the front of his shirt. She hadn't heard him leave the wagon, hadn't heard a warning squeak, or even the soft sound of his footsteps on the hard ground.

"Oh, dear," she muttered, faced with a wide chest soaked and stained with coffee. The shirt, which was stained with dried blood and torn in a couple of places, had already been ruined. Still, she was sure he didn't appreciate a dousing with the last cup of coffee.

He didn't move, didn't even flinch. Eden spun around and reached down, grabbing the bodice of the dress she had just cut in half. She wiped away the coffee as best she could, dabbing and scrubbing with pink muslin and lace. Sullivan didn't move. He was like a rock beneath her hands, and, blast him, every bit as tall and overpowering as she had suspected he was as he lay unconscious in the Webberville street.

When he was as dry as he was going to get, she drew her hands away and studied her work.

"Thank you, I think," he mumbled, "Miz . . ." His eyes narrowed suspiciously. "Did you say Rourke?"

Eden smiled and lifted her eyes. Just her eyes. Dark hair fell past Sullivan's wide shoulders, and his face was even more battered looking this morning than it had been the night before. That poor face was blue and purple and red, cut and distended and bruised. One eye had swollen shut, and the other was little more than a narrow slit that revealed a piercing dark eye. Not brown, as she'd suspected it would be, but a lovely hazel green.

"Yes, Eden Rourke, Mr. Sullivan," she said as she turned away from him and gathered up the skirt she would eventually transform into a dress for Millie.

He mumbled something, but she didn't bother to ask him to repeat himself.

Millie burst through the brush, with Teddy right behind her. She immediately latched on to Eden's leg, peeking out from behind the full skirt. "He's awake."

"Yes, he is," Eden said firmly and with a reassuring smile. "Isn't that marvelous?"

"Why?" The question Sullivan muttered was muffled, but it was clear enough.

"Why what?" Eden felt stronger with the children beside her, for some reason. The sentiment was nonsense, she knew. Millie had been with her for two months, since her mother's death. Teddy had been with them for two days. They were children, lonely children who had no one else and who needed her. She knew in her heart that she needed them just as much, but she made the silent admission reluctantly.

"Why is it *marvelous*?" Sarcasm colored Sullivan's garbled voice. Sarcasm and distrust.

"Well . . ." Eden hesitated. Why was it marvelous? She did not know Sullivan at all. For all she knew the beating was well deserved. No. No one deserved to be treated that way, outnumbered and pounded until he could not stand. It was an injustice.

"Aunt Eden stopped those men from beating you up," Millie said in a soft, high voice, still presenting no more than a corner of her face to

Sullivan. "Because it wasn't fair that there were lots and lots of them and only one of you and because Aunt Eden doesn't like anything that's not fair." Millie stopped and took a deep breath before she proceeded. "And we weren't sure if you would wake up or not, and if you didn't wake up we would have to bury you in the ground. . . ."

"Millie!" Eden interrupted.

"Well, it's true," Millie continued, her voice overly bright. She'd obviously been truly distressed about the possibility of burying this stranger. Children shouldn't have such fears. Ever.

Eden's own childhood had been unusual, but she'd never been subjected to violence or hate. She'd had her gruff and overly protective older brother, Jedidiah, a mother who loved her, a father who'd died too young, a stepfather who'd raised her as his own even after her mother's death. She'd been sad, at times, and confused, but she'd never been afraid or alone.

"I could use a hug," Eden said softly, dipping down to Millie's level. The child obliged her enthusiastically.

"Now," Eden said as she pulled away, "would you like to ride in the back of the wagon with Teddy today? I think Mr. Sullivan might prefer to travel up front."

Eden lifted her face to Sullivan, expecting a scowling frown to be directed her way. But his face was strangely passive, less threatening than it had been moments ago. "Unless, of course, you prefer to go on." She nodded to where the horses grazed. "Teddy and I tried to get you into the wagon ourselves, but I'm afraid you were too heavy for us. We had to solicit help from the saloon." She wrinkled her nose at the memory of her brief time in that establishment. "I decided as long as I was there I might as well ask about your horse."

In spite of his size and his harsh and battered face, Sullivan was not such a threatening man after all. Her imagination must have been working much too hard earlier, when she'd felt almost afraid of him.

"I promised them that if they let me take you and your horse I'd do my best to keep you out of their less-than-friendly town." She gave him a small smile.

"Those sons of bitches," he muttered. "I've got a good mind to head back there right now and . . ."

"Please don't curse in front of the children," Eden said in a lowered voice. He did not look at all chastened. "Perhaps in the future you'll be more selective about the women you kiss." Her tone was light; the face he turned to her was not. "I asked one of those horrible men why they were beating you," she explained. "I don't suppose you remember that part."

He silently turned and began to tend to the horses, checking his own fine steed, a tall black stallion, before leading her team to the front of the wagon.

"So, where are you headed, Mr. Sullivan?" she asked as she gathered up the pink skirt and the coffeepot.

"Rock Creek," he mumbled.

His attentions were elsewhere as he hitched the horses to the wagon, and so he couldn't see Eden's face, her fading smile, the flicker of fascination in her eyes. For that she was grateful. Jedidiah had always told her she'd make a lousy poker player, with every thought so clearly displayed on her face.

As he moved to hitch his own horse to the back of the wagon, she said, "How very interesting. So am I."

He grunted something that sounded obscene, but since she couldn't be sure, she didn't reprimand him. The only word she was certain she understood was *Rourke*.

Suddenly she smiled. Sullivan was heading for Rock Creek, himself, and the way he'd mumbled her last name . . . "You know Jedidiah, don't you?" she asked.

Sullivan turned slowly to face her. "Yeah, I know him." It was impossible to tell from the expression on his face whether he and Jedidiah were friends or enemies or casual acquaintances.

"Is he well?" she asked. "I haven't seen him in five years, and lately . . . Well, lately he's been on my mind quite a lot."

Sullivan didn't ease her mind or satisfy her curiosity. In fact, he was turning out to be a confoundedly closemouthed man. He looked at the children in the back of the wagon, studying them closely, thoughtfully.

"I don't think he's there," he did say, finally. "At least, he wasn't there three weeks ago, when I left. But I imagine he'll be back before too much longer. He always turns up sooner or later."

Her spirits fell. She hadn't realized how much she had her heart set on riding into Rock Creek and finding Jedidiah. "Well," she said, determined not to show her disappointment, "perhaps you're wrong."

Sullivan took her hand and assisted her into the wagon seat; then he vaulted, carefully on account of his recent beating, to the seat beside her. "Can

I ask why you're so all-fired set on seeing Jed?" he asked as he set the horses into motion.

"He hasn't been home in years," she said. "But I know he hasn't forgotten about me. He usually writes regularly, but lately . . . Lately he's been writing less and less, and he doesn't really tell me anything about his life. His last two letters were posted in Rock Creek, and he mentioned the place with some fondness. He also said I could write to him there, in care of the Rock Creek Hotel. That made me hope that perhaps he'd made a place for himself there, and I decided that if he won't come home, then, by golly, I'll go to him."

"By golly," he said softly, and with more than a touch of sarcasm. "I didn't even know Jed was married, much less that he had a pretty little wife willing to track him to the ends of the earth when he doesn't come home on time."

Eden broke into a huge grin as she realized Sullivan's mistake. "Wife? Don't be silly. I'm Jedidiah's *sister.*"

He cut her a suspicious glance—one-eyed, still. "Sister?"

"Yes. My stepfather died last year, and now I have no family left but for my brother." Her heart leaped a little. She still missed the man she'd called Daddy. The past few months had been lonely and frightening. She hated living alone, positively *hated* it. "A person should be with family, if at all possible. Don't you agree, Mr. Sullivan?"

He didn't answer.

"So, if Jedidiah won't come home to Georgia, I'm moving to Rock Creek."

Sullivan studied the road silently for a while, lost in thought, sullen and battered. When he finally spoke, his voice was clear at last. "So, Jed's sister just happens to be riding through that shit-hole Webberville while I'm getting my ass whupped for the first time since I got outta short pants. What a coincidence.''

Eden watched his profile, wincing at the injury to his face, damage that looked uglier and more obviously painful by the light of the sun. Her smile faded. She really should reprimand him for using coarse language in front of the children again, but she couldn't find her tongue. His final disdainful, mocking comment stayed with her, instead. Coincidence?

Eden Rourke didn't believe in coincidence.

But she did believe in fate.

Chapter 2

As the horses silently trod along the rutted road, Sullivan held the reins and cast the occasional furtive glance at Eden Rourke. She wore a permanent look of enchanted satisfaction, lost in her own world. She watched the desolate land they traveled through as if she saw something that wasn't there.

He didn't have much use for beautiful women, mainly because they'd never had any use for a half-breed bastard like him. And this one was truly beautiful. Jedidiah Rourke's sister? Jed had mentioned a sister, once, but Sullivan had never dreamed she was anything like this lady sitting beside him. There wasn't a gruffer, meaner, more ornery son of a bitch in Texas than Jedidiah Rourke. Jed was tall and wide and crude, and Eden was short and slender and refined. Sure, they both had blond hair and blue eyes, but he couldn't believe that Jed and this delicate, sunny woman who would rescue a stranger off the street because what she saw wasn't *fair* were related.

The kids weren't hers; he knew that. At first glance he'd thought perhaps they were, but she looked too young to be the boy's mother, and the little girl with her own blond hair and blue eyes had called her Aunt Eden, not Mama.

More Rourkes. Just what Texas needed.

"How do you know Jedidiah, Mr. Sullivan?" she asked, trying once again to make light conversation. So far she'd asked about Rock Creek and tried to begin a civilized discourse on the weather, but Sullivan had never been one for idle chitchat. He preferred peace and quiet, and he usually kept to himself. When they stopped for the night, in just a few hours, he'd set up his own camp as far away from the others as possible. Close enough to keep an eye on Eden and the kids, but far enough away to be alone.

"We worked together a few times," he finally answered. A safe enough answer.

He glanced at her as she smiled widely. Dimples. Blue eyes, golden hair, and *dimples*. What had he done to deserve this?

"Then you know him well, I imagine," she said sweetly. "What jobs were you on with him? He's always been such a drifter," she added before he could answer. "A drover, a miner, a bartender, even a sheriff's deputy once." She looked at him with wide eyes, awaiting her answer.

"We both hire our guns out, on occasion, to towns in trouble or local law officials who get in over their heads. We've found ourselves on the same side a time or two." He saw the wonder in her wide eyes, the unasked questions. "We also served in the war together," he added softly.

Eden's smile faded. "Oh. Jedidiah never said much about those years." She turned her head so she no longer looked directly at him. Just as well. "I had nightmares about him then." He could swear he saw her shudder slightly. "They were more than nightmares; they were almost like visions or premonitions. Like I was there," she whispered. She turned those wide blue eyes on him once again. "Was it terrible?" she asked softly. "In my nightmares it was terrible."

Nothing about Sullivan's life had ever been soft. Not his childhood, not his life as a soldier, not his time with women. But there was such softness in Eden Rourke's eyes he wanted to fall in, headfirst, and get lost there. He recognized the danger, noted it, dismissed the unexpected longing.

Approaching horses, far in the distance behind them, gave him an excuse not to answer her probing question. He'd handed his Colt, holster and all, over to a bartender in Webberville, as had all the other customers. He felt quite certain the barkeep hadn't volunteered to hand the revolver over to Eden Rourke when she'd rescued him and his horse.

"Do you have a weapon?" He kept his voice low so as not to disturb the kids who rode quietly in the bed of the wagon. He glanced back and found them both asleep, curled up, bouncing slightly and obliviously with every turn of the wheels.

"Of course," she said. "There's a six-shooter under your seat and a Winchester rifle behind it, both loaded. And I have a derringer in the pocket of my skirt."

Three loaded weapons within reach; perhaps she was Jed's sister, after all. "Someone's coming."

She sighed. "I know."

With that, she slipped down onto the floorboard and reached beneath the seat. It was a tight fit, but she was so small the maneuver seemed no effort at all for her. Soft arms brushed against his leg as she reached around him, and her warm breath actually penetrated his denims and touched his thigh. He gritted his teeth and concentrated on the pain in his battered body to take his mind off of the soft, attractive woman at his feet.

She laid her hand on his thigh as she rose and retook her seat, the move innocent and unthinking. *Jed's sister,* he reminded himself. If ever a woman was off-limits . . .

"Would you like to hold on to this?" she asked sweetly.

Sullivan glanced at Eden and saw that she offered the six-shooter to him.

"I imagine they're just travelers like us, but as Jedidiah always told me, you can't be too careful."

He took the six-shooter from her and slipped it into the waistband of his denims. Her eyes met his, and she attempted a small, reassuring smile.

Didn't she know any better than to look at a man that way? Damn. *Jed's sister,* he reminded himself as the travelers to their rear grew closer. Jed's damn *sister.*

A full day of healing had done little to remedy the evidence of Sullivan's beating. The blood was gone, washed away at the stream before they set out, and the second eye had opened a while back. Still, he was cut and bruised and swollen in a way that made her heart lurch when she looked closely at him. It just wasn't right.

He might be a handsome man, but it was hard

to tell at the moment. With a haircut and a change of clothes, and when his face had a chance to heal . . . perhaps. Still, she didn't expect he looked any softer or safer even when he hadn't been recently beaten up. He was definitely not what one might call an upstanding citizen.

She'd known full well the dangers of a woman traveling in this wild country, with only young children for companionship. Being well armed eased her mind a little, as did her caution and the fact that since she'd left the railway in San Antonio and started out in her own wagon, she hadn't run across a single other traveler.

The three men who approached from behind didn't appear to be threatening, but the hairs on the back of Eden's neck stood up all the same.

"Good afternoon," the one in the lead said affably. "Where you folks headed?"

The man pulled up alongside, but Sullivan didn't slow the progress of the wagon. "West," he said simply, without so much as turning his head to glance at the stranger.

"Us, too," the man said cheerily. "Mind if we ride along with you?"

Sullivan mumbled a reluctant consent.

The man on the horse turned his eyes to Eden, then spared a glance for the sleeping children. "Afternoon, ma'am," he said cordially. "My name's Curtis Merriweather, and these are my brothers Will and George."

Will and George drew closer, one on either side of the wagon. They tipped their hats absently, as if playing at being polite.

Curtis looked down at Sullivan, and if Eden wasn't mistaken, his eyes hardened. "What's your name, mister?"

"Sullivan," he muttered.

Curtis grinned. He had thin lips and a slash of a mouth, and his smile was somehow odd, forced and much too wide. "Fine Irish name. Funny, Sullivan, but you don't *look* Irish."

Sullivan glanced up, and Curtis's smile faded. "Damn, mister. What happened to you?"

Sullivan didn't answer, just continued to stare at the man on the horse.

"Please watch your language," Eden scolded softly, leaning forward. "There are children present, and just because they happen to be sleeping doesn't mean you should pay less mind to your manners."

"Sorry, ma'am," Curtis said with a touch of a condescending smile. "So," he continued, setting his eyes on Sullivan again, "where are you and the missus and the kiddies headed again?"

In an instinctive response, Eden opened her mouth to tell the man that she was *not* Sullivan's missus. A sharp, warning glance from the battered man stopped her, his eyes ordering her to remain silent. Well, perhaps it would be less complicated if the men believed her to be Sullivan's wife, since they were traveling together. For the moment, anyway.

"We're going to see my brother," she said brightly.

"Do tell," Curtis said, apparently happy to turn his attention to her and away from Sullivan. "Well, this is rough country. Me and my brothers, we'll ride along and make sure your journey through this county is a safe one."

"Great," Sullivan mumbled.

The men spread out, effectively surrounding the wagon. One of the brothers, Will or George, rode ahead, and Curtis and the other Merriweather brother flanked the wagon. After a while their attention seemed to drift away from the occupants of the wagon, and they stared straight ahead, deadly serious and lost in thought.

Eden scooted across the wagon seat to sit close to Sullivan, thigh to thigh. She lifted her chin and arched up to whisper in his ear, "What's your name?"

He looked down at her. "Sullivan," he said softly.

She smiled slightly. "Your given name. If we're supposed to be married . . ."

"Just call me honey," he interrupted, and she could swear she detected a touch of humor in his voice.

"Really, Mr. Sullivan"—she leaned on his hard arm and looked up into his hazel eyes—"that would hardly be appropriate."

He squinted at her, his gaze hard. He wrinkled his nose and a muscle in his cheek twitched. "Sinclair," he finally whispered.

Her smile bloomed. "What a lovely name. Sinclair." She rather liked the way the name rolled off her tongue. It was an unusual name for an unusual man. Yes, she liked it. "I don't trust them," she added in a lowered voice.

"Neither do I," he muttered through battered lips.

Curtis looked back at them, and one eye narrowed. To ease his evident suspicions, she quickly kissed Sinclair Sullivan on the cheek just above one particularly nasty bruise. Her lips barely brushed his skin, but he tensed and turned his head to glare down at her. The ruse worked; Curtis returned his attentions to the road.

Millie rolled onto her knees and, yawning,

leaned over the seat. "Where are we? Who are those men?"

Eden gave the little girl a wide smile. "Millie, sweetheart, we're going to play a game."

He'd be better off if he were still sprawled in the middle of the Webberville main street, facedown and unconscious.

Curtis Merriweather and his *brothers* had decided to camp close by. The seven of them had eaten supper, beans and bacon and dried fruit, together. Millie had quickly and easily fallen into the "game," calling Eden Mama and looking up into Sullivan's face with wide, blue eyes and calling him Papa even when the Merriweathers were not within hearing distance.

The little boy Eden called Teddy remained, thankfully, silent.

Eden got the kids bedded down for the night in the back of the wagon on a bed of blankets, nestled together under a thick, well-worn quilt. She kissed them both good night, wished them sweet dreams, and then came to the campfire, where Sullivan sat on the ground wishing he was far away and facedown in the dirt.

Not because of the Merriweather brothers, he decided as Eden lowered herself to sit close to him. But because of *her*.

"Who are they?" he asked softly, nodding to the wagon where the children slept.

Eden pulled up her knees and locked her arms around them, and then she looked at him, wide-eyed and serious, soft and pretty. A lady through and through, but every bit as much a woman.

"Millie has been with me for two months," she

said in a soft voice. "Her mother died and . . . and no one else wanted her. It seemed best that she come to Texas with me. Maybe a fresh start is just what she needs."

"And the boy?"

Taking a deep breath, Eden hesitated. She looked at him as if she wondered why he was so curious about the children who traveled with her. He wondered if he'd get a straight answer.

"When Millie and I left the rail, I purchased my own wagon and set out for Rock Creek." She pushed back a strand of pale hair that had fallen from the bun long ago. Soft and silky, it brushed against her face. "I suppose we could've taken the stage and shipped my baggage separately, but the route by stage was so unnecessarily roundabout, and the accommodations seemed less than comfortable, so I decided this would be a more sensible way to travel." She looked him square in the eye. "Do you believe in fate, Mr. Sullivan?"

"No," he answered in a lowered voice.

She almost smiled. He could see it, in a new sparkle in her eyes and a slight crook of her mouth. "I do. Two days after I left San Antonio, I stopped in a small town to purchase supplies. And there was Teddy, filthy and hungry and being chased by a fat deputy who obviously was not accustomed to dealing with children." Her nose wrinkled in distaste at the memory. "Teddy ran right into me, and, of course, when the sheriff arrived on his heels I insisted on knowing why a small child was being chased about the streets like a criminal."

"Of course," Sullivan muttered.

"Teddy had been pretty much living on his own for months, since his uncle passed away, and they were going to ship him to an orphanage." She turned her eyes to the dying fire. "It was clear to me that no one there had his best interests at heart, that no one cared what happened to that frightened, lovely child."

"So you took him?"

She looked into his eyes again, as if testing him. "I couldn't just leave him there. No one minded. Not the sheriff, nor the blacksmith who was supposed to be caring for him, nor the gaggle of women who gathered to watch us take our leave. I feel quite sure they were glad to be rid of him.

"He hasn't spoken, but he does understand." She stretched her legs out and leaned back slightly to look up at the sky as if she'd never seen it before. Her expression softened, turned dreamy and hopeful. "I think I was meant to find these children, to take them in and care for them."

"Fate," he said softly.

Eden shot him a quick glance. "I take it from the tone of your voice that you really don't believe."

He shook his head.

"What do you believe in?"

"Nothing."

She didn't like that answer, not at all. "You must believe in something."

"I believe that before sunup we're going to have trouble with the Merriweather brothers." He turned his eyes to the second campfire not too far away. Coarse, lowered voices drifted their way, but he couldn't tell what the brothers said. If Eden weren't sitting beside him, he'd head over that way to listen, but then if Eden weren't there he wouldn't be, either.

"Perhaps it's fate that I found you, too, Sinclair Sullivan," Eden said softly. "Why, think of the trouble I might've had handling the Merriweathers on my own."

He looked at her, hard and unflinching. She was naive, sweet, so damned gentle . . . She didn't belong here, and she definitely didn't belong in Rock Creek. "If Jed is half as smart as I think he is, he'll escort you back to Georgia before you get the chance to spend a single night in Rock Creek."

She smiled at him as if the thought had already occurred to her. "Oh, don't you worry about Jedidiah. I can handle him."

Most nights she slept in the back of the wagon with Millie and Teddy. It wasn't the most comfortable bed she'd ever slept in, but it was tolerable. There were blankets and a few pillows and even a tarp in case of rain. She had not yet had to use the tarp, thank goodness.

Last night they'd given Sullivan exclusive use of the wagon bed, and tonight . . . Well, climbing into that wagon bed with the Merriweathers close by didn't seem wise. They'd be like fish in a barrel, wouldn't they? The children were safe there, but if she or Sullivan joined them and the Merriweathers made their move, well, it wouldn't be safe at all.

Eden lay on her side, facing the few remaining embers from their campfire. Sullivan lay close behind her, his head propped up in his hand as he kept watch. They hadn't heard a sound from the Merriweathers' camp in a good while. Maybe they were wrong. Maybe the brothers were innocent travelers after all. She wanted to believe that. With all her heart she wanted to believe. Unfortunately, she didn't. Those men were definitely trouble. She saw it in their eyes.

She rolled over to face Sullivan. "I don't think I can stay awake all night," she whispered.

"I can," he whispered back. There was reassurance in that emotionless voice, and she was reminded that without Sullivan at her side she might be in a real fix. Jedidiah would skin her hide when he found out she'd traveled all this way on her own. Well, no. He wouldn't ever lift a hand to her, but he would have his say in the matter and it wasn't likely to be pleasant.

"Sinclair," she whispered. "That really is a lovely name."

"Everybody calls me Sullivan."

"Sullivan is a fine name, also," she said, scooting slightly closer so there was no need to raise her voice. "But I like Sinclair. May I call you Sinclair, even when we're not pretending to be married?"

He tensed, his entire body going rigid. She noticed the instant change, even though she could not see him at all well by the light of the half-moon. "Call me whatever you want, lady. I don't care."

Sullivan's voice was gruff, his eyes set unerringly on the other camp, and yet she didn't buy the tough act he was putting on. She reached out and laid her fingers softly on his jaw. She got the feeling that he wanted to flinch, to draw away from her hand, but he didn't.

"I believe the swelling is already going down. Does it still hurt?"

"No," he said through clenched teeth.

She smiled. He was such a terrible liar! A breeze, cool enough to remind Eden that autumn had arrived, washed over them. The wind ruffled Sinclair Sullivan's long hair and brought goose bumps to Eden's arms. "Are you cold?" she whispered.

"No."

"Well, I am." She brought the thin blanket to her chin and edged closer to Sullivan. His body heat warmed her. His length buffered the wind. Edging a little bit closer, she felt oddly comforted by his closeness.

Sullivan was a stranger still, and yet she knew without a doubt that she could trust him with her life. It was more than the fact that he was Jedidiah's friend. She looked into his eyes and felt nothing but goodness and warmth, and she always trusted her instincts.

"I'm going to sleep a little while, Sinclair," she said softly. "Wake me if you hear anything suspicious."

As she drifted off to sleep she could've sworn she heard him mutter, "Jed's *sister.*"

Even if he hadn't been waiting for the Merriweathers to make their move, he wouldn't have gotten any sleep. He'd never given the matter much thought, but in all his twenty-nine years he hadn't actually slept with a woman before. He'd screwed plenty, prostitutes and loose women who thought it might be fun to hook up with a half-breed for a night or two, but he'd never *slept* with one.

Eden Rourke continued to edge closer and closer through the night, as she slept, until she finally ended up with her nose buried in his chest. One small foot slipped between his calves and settled there for the duration, and one dainty hand rested on his side.

Once again he had a sneaking suspicion that

Eden was not who she claimed to be. She was much too trusting to be any relation to Jedidiah Rourke.

Sullivan shifted slightly, but his movements did not disturb the woman who slept against him. He cursed beneath his breath, but she didn't move.

Damn it, this woman made him as nervous as the Merriweathers. Eden Rourke was clearly a lady through and through, and *ladies* usually didn't waste much time on a half-breed who carried a gun and dared anyone to get in his way. They turned away; they crossed the street; they pretended they did not see. How many times in his foolish youth had he looked at a woman and seen the frightened shift of her eyes, the way she lowered her gaze and turned away? Often enough that he didn't bother even looking anymore.

But this one didn't cast down her eyes, did she? She looked her fill and flashed heartfelt smiles as if . . . as if he were just a man and she was just a woman.

It was near dawn when the Merriweathers made their move. He heard them first, then saw them in the gray light as they crept upon the camp. Revolvers in hand, they headed slowly and cautiously for the place where Sullivan waited and Eden slept.

The rifle was behind him, the six-shooter close at hand.

"Wake up," he whispered in Eden's ear. "They're coming."

She stirred, but she didn't open her eyes.

"Miss Rourke," he whispered again. "Eden."

She smiled and opened her eyes slowly, setting them on him in a way that was warm and trusting and sweet. When she was fully awake and realized exactly where she had slept, that her foot was wedged between his legs and her arm was around his waist, her smile faded and she slowly, carefully, scooted a few inches away from him. Even though it was dark, he was sure he could see her blush. He hated to ruin the moment with the news.

"They're coming."

She nodded once. Her soft body went rigid, but there were no tears, no sign of panic that he could see.

Without words, he told her to stay put. He rolled over, into the dark shadow of a copse of trees, and eased up with the six-shooter in his hand. He headed around the perimeter of the campground, staying in shadow, hoping to take the brothers by surprise. Eden didn't move.

Moving soundlessly, quickly, and with ghostlike grace was his gift. That was the reason he'd been the scout with Reese's elite Confederate unit in the war. He could sneak up on a man eating his supper, take his knife and spoon, and be gone before the man knew what had happened. The others assumed it was his Comanche blood that gifted him with the ability, but he knew better. A lifetime of trying to be invisible had the same result.

The brothers had spread out and approached from three directions in the faint light of dawn. They kept their eyes on the dark lump that had been Sullivan's bed as they sneaked forward. Eden didn't move or make a sound. If he didn't know better, even he would think she was still asleep.

Sullivan approached one brother, staying in the darkness of the trees, making not a single noise, not a whisper or a scrape or an audible breath, until he could almost smell his adversary, until he could reach out and touch the man who crept toward Eden. He made his move quickly and

silently, surprising the tall, thin Will, disarming
him, and knocking him to the ground with such
force that the man lay very still in the dirt as he
tried to catch his breath. There was no more need
to be silent as the other brothers turned, startled,
in his direction. Surprised, they twitched and raised
their weapons.

"I don't think so." Eden's soft but firm voice
startled them all, and the three armed men turned
in her direction.

She had come to her feet and held the rifle as
though she knew exactly what she was doing. Steady
and calm, she aimed at Curtis Merriweather. When
she dropped the lever and brought it back up
swiftly, the sound echoed like thunder in the silent
morning. Well, he no longer doubted that Eden
was Jed's sister.

"I'm very disappointed in you, Mr. Merriweather." She sighed. "What on earth must your
mother think, that all three of her sons have fallen
into a life of crime, bless her heart?" She sounded,
to Sullivan's ears, as if she were truly distressed.

"She won't shoot," Curtis said, taking a step
toward Eden.

Without warning, she did. The dust at Curtis's
feet danced and swirled as he came to an abrupt
stop. The crack of the rifle split the quiet air. She
cocked the lever again.

The man on the ground stirred, sitting up slowly.
Maybe Eden did know what she was doing with
that rifle, but they were still outnumbered. Three-
to-two odds weren't bad, but damn it, he didn't
know exactly what to expect from Eden Rourke
next.

Curtis shook his head in what appeared to be
reluctant appreciation. "Good-lookin' and handy

with a rifle to boot. What's a woman like you doing married to a goddamn half-breed?"

Eden's lips pursed and she squinted slightly, as if taking aim. "Watch your language, Mr. Merriweather."

He ignored her. "Ain't it enough that the Injun dresses like a white man and tries to pass himself off as a *Sullivan* without going and marrying one of the rare pretty white women we got in these parts?" His grip on the six-shooter changed, tightened; his entire body tensed as he got ready to fire. The six-shooter snapped around quickly.

Eden didn't respond but to shoot again, and Curtis Merriweather's revolver flew out of his hand. He squealed and grasped his fingers; he tried to take a breath and squealed again.

Two reluctant heads appeared from the back of the wagon, rising slowly to peek over the side. "Good morning," Eden said softly, her voice shaking slightly. "Teddy, would you be so kind as to collect the Merriweathers' horses and hitch them to the back of the wagon?"

The boy moved without question to do as he was asked.

"We'll take your horses to the next town and leave them there," Eden said, "along with a message for the local law officials." She had begun to shake, just a little. The reaction was so subtle, Sullivan wondered if any of the three bandits noticed. If they did, if they sensed a weakness in her now . . .

George Merriweather looked at his brother Will, who still sat on the ground, and at his other brother Curtis who grasped his fingers and cried in pain. Sullivan saw the desperation, the panic, in George's eyes. Men did stupid things when they were cornered, and this one was about to do something incredibly stupid. He knew it in his gut.

The one remaining armed Merriweather popped his weapon up, taking aim at Eden. Without a single second thought or moment's hesitation, Sullivan fired. One shot to the heart. George fell to the ground without getting a chance to fire at Eden.

Eden's eyes widened and her shaking got worse. Sullivan cursed beneath his breath. Had she thought it would be so easy? That she could threaten these men and chastise them and then ride away without seeing anyone die? Hellfire, she did not belong here.

Something in her changed dramatically. Something in her weakened. Her confidence dissolved. She'd been so self-assured facing the Merriweather brothers, insisting that they back down. Right now she looked like she might faint at any moment—just like a woman.

Sullivan dismissed his fleeting concern for a woman who should not have even been there. Using a length of their own rope, he bound the remaining two brothers, if they were indeed related at all, together and to a tree. He hitched up Eden's horses to the wagon, and checked to see that Teddy had done a good job of securing the bandits' mounts with his own stallion. He had.

He loaded them all, Eden and Teddy and Millie, into the wagon and left the two bandits pleading for mercy. Damn it, he didn't like the look that crept over Eden's face, as if she was scared, as if the encounter had drained the life out of her.

"What will happen to them?" she asked without looking back.

"We'll stop in the next town and send the sheriff back for them, like you said."

She nodded as if she agreed that was an acceptable plan. They were a good ways down the road before she spoke again.

"I've never seen a man killed before." Her voice was low, soft as the wind. "I'd never even seen a man shot, until I shot Curtis Merriweather's hand." She looked at him then. He didn't look back, but watched her from the corner of his eye. "Jedidiah put a rifle in my hands as soon as I was old enough to hold one. He'd take me out and we'd shoot at targets. Bottles and cans, mostly. Mother would never let me go hunting with him; she said it wasn't a ladylike pastime. But Jedidiah convinced her that I should know how to defend myself, so even after he was gone I practiced several times a week. I promised him, before he left for the war . . ."

She shuddered. "What happened this morning was nothing at all like shooting at a target that doesn't shoot back, that doesn't . . . bleed. It all happened so fast, before I even had a chance to *think*, and now a man is dead and another one is injured. It was so . . . so horribly violent. And so quick," she added in a lowered voice as she shuddered again. "It happened so fast. I hope I never see anything like that again as long as I live."

Sullivan kept his eyes straight ahead and his mouth shut. He didn't think now was the time to tell Eden that he'd seen so many men die violently he could no longer remember the number.

Chapter 3

Ranburne was an even smaller town than Webberville, but it did have a decent general store and a sober sheriff. As it was the closest town to Rock Creek, Sullivan had met Sheriff Tilton before and trusted him. He told Tilton where he could find what was left of the Merriweathers, handed over their horses, and learned some disturbing information about the brothers.

Tilton knew better than to ask a single question about Sullivan's battered face.

While Sullivan was with the sheriff, Eden was in the general store buying a few more supplies. Walking in that direction, he considered sending her on her way and heading back to Webberville to reclaim his Colt and the hat he'd left hanging on the hat tree near the swinging saloon doors. A knot of anger twisted in his gut. He liked that hat. It fit just right and was well broken in. Besides, he felt he owed a few residents of Webberville a rematch. If they hadn't caught him off guard, if they hadn't sucker punched him . . .

But he couldn't go back, not now. Jed was one of the few men in the world he called his friend, and he couldn't abandon the man's sister to travel alone. She was a fool woman for attempting it in the first place, but he couldn't go back and change the fact that she was here. All he could do was see that Eden reached Rock Creek safely. After that, she was Jed's problem, and he could see about getting to Webberville to reclaim his hat.

Teddy stood, solemn and silent, on the board-walk outside the general store. The kid lifted his eyes and peeked through strands of straight, dark hair that hung too long about his face. He waited, nervous and so anxious he seemed not to breathe at all. Sullivan forgot all about his hat.

The boy was afraid of something, of everything. The fear was in his eyes, in the way he flinched when anyone got too near him. Eden, in her own little world, didn't always notice. Sullivan not only noticed, he remembered what it was like to live that way, always afraid, constantly waiting for the next backhand. Or worse.

"Are the ladies inside?" he asked as he neared the boy. Teddy nodded, and Sullivan reached out to lay a hand on the boy's head. The kid didn't move away, but he tensed so hard his neck corded and his hands balled into little fists. Sullivan's hand didn't linger on Teddy's small head. Trust didn't come easy or fast, he knew.

Eden placed her purchases on the front counter as Sullivan entered the general store, and she turned her head to smile familiarly. Millie had been exploring, and when she saw him standing in the doorway, she shouted "Papa!" and ran to him with a smile on her pretty face.

He didn't live in this town, but there were a few people here who knew him by reputation and by sight. They knew what had happened in Rock Creek last year; they recognized and respected or feared him. More than a few eyes widened as Millie reached up her arms to him.

He stared down at her, not knowing what to do or say. "You and Teddy get settled in the wagon," he said softly. Her little arms fell, but her smile never faded. "We're almost finished here."

Eden paid for her purchases, and Sullivan went to the counter to carry them for her. He could feel people watching him, and he knew what they were thinking—Sinclair Sullivan, domesticated? Tamed? Cowed? *Married.* He thought about correcting all the unspoken thoughts with a few gruff words, but was sure anything he said would come out sounding defensive and meaningless. Let them assume whatever they wanted. Besides, no one would give Eden any trouble if they thought she was his.

The shopkeeper gave Sullivan a sly "you-old-dog" grin as he handed over Eden's purchases. "Well, Mr. Sullivan, you're certainly full of surprises." He turned his much too interested eyes to Eden. "Will you be settling in Rock Creek, ma'am?"

"Yes, I will," she said brightly, a subdued, alluring smile on her face. "And I'm very much looking forward to it."

"It's a rough place," the man said, "but with Sullivan there to look out for you, you won't have any problems a'tall."

Eden looked up and gave Sullivan a smile that was sure to confirm the suspicions that they were married. That smile was full of sunshine and promise and wonder. Hell, it made his own insides do a dance.

"I'm sure you're right," she said. "He's been quite capable up to this point."

The shopkeeper's wide grin faded a little. *Capable* wasn't exactly a romantic or thrilling description.

"Let's go," Sullivan said as he turned away. "We've got a long way to travel today."

"Of course, Sinclair," Eden said sweetly. "The sooner we get started, the sooner we'll get to Rock Creek."

He tossed Eden's purchases into the back of the wagon with the kids. They had a three-day trip ahead of them, at the pace they'd been traveling. Three days. On horseback he could be there in a matter of hours, but the way this wagon lurched an inch at a time down the road made the trip interminably long. As he made sure the purchases were secured where they wouldn't fall over in the wagon, Millie reached out both hands and patted him on the cheeks. Softly, since he still sported a number of cuts and bruises on his face.

"Papa, Papa, Papa," she said softly. He was about to correct her when she continued. "I never had a papa before, not even a pretend one. I like this game."

It was going to be a damn long three days.

Perhaps the excitement of the early morning hours had dampened her spirits somewhat, because Eden was quiet for the remainder of the day. She spoke to the kids, and to him when it was necessary, but there were no more attempts at casual conversation; they were well past that point.

He liked the quiet, and he liked sitting beside Eden in the wagon's hard seat. He liked looking at her, when she didn't know he was watching, studying the curve of her cheek and the curve of her breasts and the curve of her hip. If not for the kids, if not for the fact that she was Jed's sister, he might be tempted to reach out and touch one or all of those tempting curves.

That would never happen, of course. He remained with her because he felt an obligation to her and to her brother. She'd likely saved his life in Webberville, and besides . . . If he left Eden to her own devices, if he allowed her to continue to travel alone, Jed would be pissed.

After they stopped for the night, she fed the kids beans and jerky and ate a few bites herself. She picked at her food, as if she had no appetite. He'd think she was simply tired of beans and jerky if he didn't already know her so well. The killing still bothered her, more than a little.

When the kids had crawled into the back of the wagon and Eden was preparing to join them, Sullivan broke the silence. "He would've killed you," he said softly, so the kids wouldn't hear.

"Maybe," she whispered, uncertainty clear in her voice. "We'll never know for sure."

"No maybes about it, Miss Rourke," he said sternly. "Those men intended to kill you and me and even the kids."

Her head snapped up, and he could see the fire in her eyes. "They wouldn't have," she whispered.

He nodded once. "I'm afraid so. The sheriff in Ranburne told me a little bit about those three when I told him where to find them. They really are brothers, and we weren't the first travelers they joined up with and ambushed. They've done it several times before, and every time but one they killed everybody. The only time they didn't kill everyone it was a mistake. One of the kids hid under their wagon and watched as they killed his entire family. In the past three years the Merriweather brothers have murdered women and children, young men and old." It was a harsh reality, but one she had to face up to. He would not pretty facts up for her, try to make things nice and easy.

Her stubborn chin lifted, and by the firelight he could see the sheen of unshed tears in her eyes. She was a little thing, but *damn it* there was strength in her heart. She didn't back away from anything. "A man who would kill a child deserves to die."

"Yes, he does."

Eden paced on the other side of the fire, thoughtful and restless. Perhaps she was wisely deciding she'd made a terrible mistake coming here.

"If you'd like, I'll take you back to San Antonio and put the three of you on the next train heading East."

She stopped pacing and set her eyes on him. "I have no intention of going back to Georgia."

"Jed isn't waiting in Rock Creek, and he won't be happy to find you there when he does show up."

She gave him her haughtiest look, but it didn't quite work. Maybe it was the delicate cut of her cheek or the almost childish quality of her cute little nose. Maybe it was the softness in her eyes. Whatever the reason, *haughty* didn't work on her. "He *will* be happy to see me," she insisted.

"You don't belong here."

"Maybe not yet," she said. "But I will. Eventually."

"What about the kids?" If nothing else, she had a soft spot for those children. She'd do whatever was best for them. He didn't mind using that soft spot against her. "What are you going to do with two orphans in Rock Creek? It's a small, hard place. People aren't exactly lining up to take in other people's kids."

"They'll live with me, of course," she said, as if she'd never considered any other option. "I'll enroll them in school. There is a school in Rock Creek, isn't there? If not, I'll teach them myself," she continued without waiting for an answer.

"They're not yours," he insisted, wondering why anyone would willingly take on two unwanted kids.

"They are now."

He looked into the fire. Hell, there was no arguing with this woman. She was completely irrational, had a misguided answer for every logic he presented to her, and like all women, she intended to have her way.

While he stared into the fire, Eden rounded it slowly. He didn't move, but he sure as hell sensed every step she took as she came near and then sat on the ground beside him.

"I never thanked you," she said softly. "Those men might've ... might've ..." She didn't want to talk about what might've happened anymore than he did.

"No need to thank me," he said gruffly.

Eden Rourke had no reservations at all when it came to touching. He saw her do it with the kids all the time, a hug, a slender hand on a shoulder, fingers on a smudge of dirt. It was as if she touched without even thinking about what she was doing.

She did it to him now, reaching out to tuck the strands of hair that hid his face from her behind his ear. "Your face looks so much better already," she said softly, her finger tracing a small cut. "The swelling is down, and nothing seems to be infected.''

Sullivan held his breath, and a strange lump formed in his chest. He fought the urge to grab her wrist and push her away, just as diligently as he fought the urge to reach out, grab her, and pull her body against his. He told himself he wanted to hold Eden because he'd never known anyone like her, because she symbolized a goodness he had never known. He reasoned with himself as he held his breath. She was simply too naive to know that she should not be touching him, not even innocently. Eventually her hand fell away.

After her hand was gone he felt her, still. He smelled her; he heard her breathing softly. Something inside him whispered that he could kiss her and she wouldn't protest. Not much anyway, and not for long. Eden Rourke was not the kind of woman to give herself freely to a man; she was definitely not an easy woman. He'd bet his life she was a virgin. Still, that something whispered that if he said and did everything right he could lie with her tonight.

But he wouldn't. This tempting, soft woman who kept touching him was Jed's sister, and Sinclair Sullivan wasn't ready to die for a woman.

"Good night," she said, walking away slowly, with an unconscious sway in her hips and a discreet backward glance.

No, he wasn't willing to die for a woman—not yet, anyway.

They stopped frequently during the day, to rest the horses and to stretch their own legs. Eden was always grateful for the chance to get down from the wagon's hard seat and walk around, even if the respite was brief.

The children used the opportunity to expend some of their seemingly endless energy. Millie usually picked whatever wildflowers she could find and presented them to Eden with great fanfare. Eden always made a fuss, no matter how wildly untidy the bouquet might be.

Today Millie and Teddy ran down a small slope to the trickle of a stream and back up again. Millie giggled. Teddy remained quiet, but he seemed to be having fun. Oh, she so wanted him to have fun, to behave like a child.

Sullivan walked down to the stream himself, dropped to his haunches by the edge, and splashed a handful of water on his face. Eden kept her distance and watched, wincing as she imagined how his poor face must hurt.

He carefully pulled his shirt over his head, and Eden winced again at the bruises on his back and sides. She really should turn away and give him some privacy, but found she couldn't bear to take her eyes from him. The sight of his long hair against his muscled back, the way his wide shoulders looked so strong and utterly masculine made her certain, at the moment, that he possessed a beauty like no other. Silly thought.

He dipped a length of fabric, part of the shirt he'd been wearing when he'd been beaten, into the water, and brought it carefully to his midsection. Eden sauntered casually down the hill.

"Are you all right?" she asked. "If you need to rest for a while . . ."

She stopped speaking when he stood and turned to face her. "I'm fine. I don't need to rest."

She started to reach out to touch the blackest

bruise on his midsection, a horrid-looking mark against muscled flesh, but pulled her fingers back before she could be so foolish.

"Why do people do things like this to other human beings?" she asked softly, her eyes on the horrid bruise. "I will never understand."

"Some are just born mean, I guess," Sullivan said, sounding as if that fact didn't bother him at all. He pulled on his shirt, carefully, his muscles dancing softly with each move. "And some," he said, setting his eyes on her as the shirt fell into place, "are too damn softhearted for their own good."

Before she could argue or tell him not to curse, Millie ran down the hill with a fresh batch of wildflowers grasped in her little fist. "Mama," she shouted joyfully, "this is for you."

"What beautiful flowers," Eden said, taking the raggedy bouquet. Several of the stems had been broken, and the already wilting flowers fell over her hand. "You are so sweet to pick them for me."

Teddy was right behind her, a single flower in his own hand. He watched the flower as he walked down the hill, and when he reached the threesome he lifted his eyes to Eden. Almost nervously, he raised the orange bloom.

"Oh, Teddy," she said, trying not to cry. The sweet gesture was his first tender overture to her. To anyone in a long while, she suspected. "This is beautiful, too."

With his free hand, Teddy motioned for her to lean closer, and when she complied he cautiously tucked the flower behind her ear.

"Papa needs a flower," Millie said, excitement making her voice high. "He has beautiful hair, too."

She plucked one of the flowers from the bouquet in Eden's hand, and with her wiggling fingers waved Sullivan down. Eden wondered if Sullivan would be so cruel as to laugh or refuse the offer, but of course he didn't. He bent slowly forward, and Millie placed the flower behind his ear.

Obviously delighted with the results, the children ran up the hill. Eden set her curious eyes on Sullivan, and she couldn't help but smile. Before her stood the most vital, masculine man she had ever met, and he had a bright yellow flower tucked behind his right ear.

"Don't you dare laugh," he said quietly.

Eden smiled widely. "Of course not. That would be rude."

"How long do I have to wear this before I can take it out without hurting the kid's feelings?"

"Until it's dead, I think."

Sullivan grumbled something that sounded vaguely obscene as he headed up the hill. Then he added, "That's what I was afraid of."

Eden was quite sure she'd never met a man like Sinclair Sullivan. He was tall and strong, like Jedidiah, but that's where the similarities ended. Sullivan went about the duties he took on himself without complaint or comment, whereas Jedidiah always had something to say. Sullivan had worn that yellow flower behind his ear until it was well and truly dead, whereas Jedidiah would have surely refused to wear it even for a moment.

He allowed Millie to continue her game, calling them Mama and Papa, even when the Merriweathers were a full two days behind them, and he was developing a strange and silent relationship with

Teddy. Sometimes when they stopped for a midday meal or at the end of the day, the two would sit silently side by side, by the campfire or a stream or in the shade of a tree. Teddy helped Sullivan with the horses, and they worked well together. It warmed her heart to see the big man go out of his way to be nice to the children.

More than his kindness warmed her heart. There was something utterly fascinating about Sinclair Sullivan's face. As the swelling faded, she could see that he was, indeed, quite handsome. His Indian heritage was clear in his features, but she saw the Irish in him, too. It was an appealing combination, attractive but completely masculine, hard but tender.

Ah, he would likely argue with her if she confessed that she saw tenderness on that healing face.

The cool night air was refreshing—sweet and chilly without being icy. She liked the feel of it on her face, the way a gentle breeze ruffled her skirt and her hair. Millie and Teddy were sound asleep, hunkered down in the back of the wagon. In a short while Eden would join them there. Sullivan would not. He had to sleep sometime, but so far she had not seen him succumb to such a trivial need. He watched over them, he protected them, and when he was sure all was safe, then, perhaps, he slept.

Sullivan sat on a fallen log beside the fire, staring into the flames. She wanted, so much, to know what he saw there, what he thought.

"Will we be in Rock Creek tomorrow?" she asked.

"Tomorrow afternoon," he said, glancing up at her. "We'll try to get an early start in the morning, so you might as well get to sleep."

She ignored the suggestion and sat beside him, perching herself carefully on the log. "In a few minutes. I'm not very tired tonight. I guess I'm too excited to sleep."

"There's nothing in Rock Creek worth getting excited about," he mumbled. "Trust me."

She wondered if she'd see Sinclair Sullivan at all after their arrival in Rock Creek. She wouldn't really need him anymore, and he wouldn't have any excuse to stay with her. For some reason, she was reluctant to see their partnership come to an end. Oddly enough, she would miss him.

"Millie and Teddy adore you," she said casually. "Once we get settled, you'll have to visit them."

"I probably won't be there that long. I have to go back to Webberville to get my hat."

Her heart lurched. "You are not going back to Webberville," she snapped. "And certainly not for anything so . . . so inconsequential as a *hat*. They almost killed you last time."

"They caught me by surprise last time," he said lowly. "That won't happen again. Besides, they've got my Colt and holster, too."

"I'll buy you a new hat," she said quickly, almost desperately. "And I'll give you my six-shooter. I don't think I can use it again, anyway." It had been used to kill a man, after all. Yes, George Merriweather had been a very *bad* man, but still . . .

"I want my own hat," Sullivan said stubbornly, "and my own six-shooter."

A surge of something unpleasant rose within her, and she tasted a fear unlike any she'd ever know. The fear led to anger.

"If you'd refrain from kissing strange women," she said, trying for a prim, reprimanding tone of voice, "perhaps you wouldn't have to worry about angry beaus defending their honor." For some reason, the idea of him kissing one of those awful saloon girls made her angry and a little sad. She wondered if the woman he'd kissed was the red-head she'd seen when she'd asked for assistance in the Webberville saloon, or the dark-haired woman who'd watched from the corner, or another of the coarse and colorful women who'd inhabited that awful place. "I think your judgment in such areas needs improvement."

"What . . . areas?" he asked softly.

Good thing it was dark and he could not see her blush. She turned her head away from the firelight, to be sure he couldn't see. "Really, Mr. Sullivan, you shouldn't go around kissing just anyone. Such intimate matters should not be taken lightly, and to kiss a saloon girl who's obviously involved with another man is . . ."

"I shouldn't do this," he muttered.

"Do what?" she asked without turning to face him.

He sighed. "I really shouldn't."

She snapped her head around. "Mr. Sullivan, are you talking to yourself or do you intend to answer—"

She stopped speaking, her breath literally stolen away, as Sullivan placed a large hand at the back of her head and slowly began to pull her toward him. She trembled all over, but he seemed calm, relaxed, steady as a rock as he laid his lips over hers.

It was not her first kiss. Bobby Joe Bowers, when he'd asked her to marry him, had surprised her with a wet and rather chilly meeting of their mouths. William Cooper, on the afternoon of his proposal, had tried to stop her instant "no" with an impulsive kiss that had surprised and dismayed her. Seymour Mayfield had kissed her once, after she refused his offer of marriage, and that particular kiss had been mildly pleasant, she supposed.

But not one of those kisses had felt anything like this. Sullivan's lips were warm and soft, but not *too* soft. There was a tender urgency in the way he pressed his mouth to hers, a very gentle demand. He moved those lips, as if he were tasting her, as if he savored the flavor of her mouth.

She closed her eyes and found herself tasting back, sucking gently against his mouth, moving her own lips in a rhythm that matched the beating of their hearts to the flow of the wind to the trembling in her hands, as if everything, *everything*, were linked by the meeting of two mouths.

His mouth left hers, barely, briefly, and she whispered his name. "Sinclair."

He kissed her again, his touch more demanding. Her heart thudded against her chest. "Sin," she whispered as he took his mouth from hers. She wasn't quite capable of saying his entire name, and Sin seemed to fit, so she whispered it once more just before he kissed her again.

His lips lingered possessively over hers, and she couldn't get enough. There was an unexpected power in the kiss, a power that drained and rejuvenated her at the same time. She could smell and taste and feel Sin all around her, and without thinking she reached up to lay her hand on his neck. Her fingers felt his steady pulse, delighted in the feel of his skin the way her mouth delighted in his kiss.

She felt his strength; she was encompassed in it. But she felt his tenderness, too, and it was that tenderness that swept her away.

Kissing sapped her energy, leaving her wonderfully weak, strangely wobbly. She draped her arms over his shoulders for support. He pulled her close and slipped his tongue inside her mouth—just a little, as if he were testing her, waiting for her response. A jolt of energy shot through her body, and she knew this was now much more than a simple kiss.

She slowly pulled her mouth from his and dropped her arms, and he didn't argue or try to pull her back. There was nothing to say. There was no way to take back a kiss like that one, and at the same time she couldn't acknowledge it, either.

"Good night, Sin," she said. "I mean, Mr. Sullivan." Her knees shook.

"Good night, Miss Rourke," he said with a touch of bitter humor in his low voice. "Sleep well."

As she walked away she heard a fragment of a sentence in a whisper so low she wouldn't have heard it if the wind hadn't carried it to her,

". . . worth dying for."

Chapter 4

"This is it?" Eden asked as her eyes swept down the main street of Rock Creek.

Sullivan heard the disappointment in her voice. He wasn't surprised.

"It doesn't look much different from Webberville or Ranburne," she added. "It's very . . . small."

"What did you expect?" Sullivan asked as he drove the wagon down the street toward the hotel. Rock Creek was like hundreds of other towns in Texas—small, rough, looking as if it had been thrown up overnight. It was little more than a single main street of crude buildings with a few homes straggling beyond. The river ran just to the west, and there trees and grass grew green and abundant. Here in town, though, all was dry and brown and rugged. The church, with its tall bell tower, added the only touch of civilization to the scene.

"I'm not sure what I expected," she confessed, casting him a glance and a small smile. Her smiles came so easily, so naturally. "Something grand, I suppose."

Well, the job was done. Eden was safe and sound in Rock Creek; Sullivan figured what Jed did with her now was none of his business. "There's nothing grand about Rock Creek," he said. "It's a rough town, only partially tamed, and it's no place for a lady."

People on the boardwalk stopped and stared as they passed. A jaw or two dropped. He knew what kind of picture the four of them painted, and how inconceivable the people of Rock Creek would find the idea of Sinclair Sullivan as a family man.

Eden stared ahead at the dusty street. "Don't try again to convince me to leave," she said succinctly. "You'll just be wasting your breath."

"I know."

The Rock Creek Hotel was a three-story dilapidated monstrosity of a building at the south end of Main Street. Grady McClure, a crotchety old man if ever there was one, owned and operated the less-than-magnificent establishment. The rooms were nasty, the food in the restaurant was all but inedible, and complaints were met with a sour "If you don't like it you can sleep somewheres else!" Of course, there was no other hotel or boarding house in Rock Creek.

After *El Diablo* had been taken care of, Sullivan and the other five men who'd fought side by side on the battlefield and on this very street had made Rock Creek a home, of sorts.

Cash slept in a room over the saloon, an abandoned business he'd taken over as his own. Reese and his wife, Mary had their own place, now, and a baby girl to boot. Nate slept wherever his head happened to fall—sometimes in a room over the saloon, sometimes in the Rock Creek Hotel. Rico, Jed, and Sullivan himself stayed at the hotel when they were in town. There was no other place to take Eden and the kids.

She wasn't going to like it.

He brought the wagon to a stop in front of the hotel, and almost immediately the hotel door opened and Rico stepped onto the plank walkway. Across the street bat-wing doors swung open and Cash walked out, straightening the ruffled cuffs of his lucky shirt as he stepped into the street. A few brave souls sauntered down the boardwalk, their steps a bit quicker than normal. They stopped a good distance away, but close enough to hear what was said, if they listened hard enough. Sullivan had a feeling they were all listening pretty damn hard.

Rico looked up with a grin on his face. "Did you catch those *banditos*?"

"They were rustlers, Kid," Sullivan said as he left the wagon. "And yeah, I got 'em."

"Did the rustlers beat you up or were you caught in a stampede?" Cash asked as his eyes lit on Sullivan's battered face.

Sullivan ignored the question and assisted Eden from the wagon. Strangely enough, she felt natural in his hands, light as a feather and warm as a spring morning. He could practically feel Rico and Cash watching her as she drifted to the ground, his hands on her waist, her hands on his shoulders. Let 'em enjoy looking while they could. As soon as they found out whose little sister she was, the leering would come to an abrupt end.

"Me too, Papa," Millie called sweetly. "Me, too."

Eyes were no longer on Eden. They were, raised eyebrows and all, squarely on Sullivan.

"The game's over, sugar," he said as he swung Millie from the back of the wagon.

"That's right," Eden said. "You will have to call him Mr. Sullivan, now."

Millie pouted, sticking out her lower lip as he placed her on her feet. "I like Papa better."

"Yeah," Rico said. "So do we. *Papa?*"

He expected Teddy to scramble over the wagon himself, but the child silently offered his own arms over the side of the wagon, and Sullivan lifted him down, as well. Millie went to Eden to hold on to her skirt, but Teddy stayed firmly beside Sullivan.

Rico and Cash looked quickly over the foursome with calculating eyes.

"Papa," Cash said softly, "you've been keeping secrets from us. Big ones," he added accusingly.

"I know how this must look," Eden said, "and it's really a very funny story. Isn't it, Mr. Sullivan?" She flashed a dimpled smile guaranteed to win over Rico, and maybe even Cash, no matter what story she told.

"Hilarious," he muttered.

"You see, I was traveling to Rock Creek, and I met up with Mr. Sullivan in Webberville. . . ."

"So you two are not . . ." Rico interrupted, "married?"

"Good heavens, no," Eden said with a widening smile.

Sullivan could see the immediate change that came over Rico and Cash, and he didn't like it. He didn't like it at all. Rico sized up Eden like she was a blackberry pie and he hadn't had dessert for months, flashing his most charming grin in her direction. Cash openly studied her from head to toe, as if judging whether or not she'd make a tasty addition to the girls he already had working in his saloon.

"Fellas," Sullivan said calmly, "this is Miss Eden Rourke, from Georgia."

Rico's smile dimmed slightly. Cash took a step back toward his beloved saloon and said, "Rourke?"

"Yes," Eden said brightly. "I imagine y'all know my brother, Jedidiah. Is he here?"

"Not at the moment," Rico said cautiously. "I expect he'll be back in a couple of weeks."

Eden's smile faded. She looked disappointed, even though Sullivan had warned her not to expect her brother to be waiting.

"Well"—she sighed—"I guess I'll just have to wait, won't I?"

The Rock Creek Hotel was a dismal place, but Jedidiah's friends were very nice. Rico Salvatore, a handsome flirt if ever she'd met one, was eager to help move her things into her room. Where Sullivan was given to silence, Rico was not. He told her a little about the hotel, talked to the children, and winked at her every now and then. If not for the very large knife on his belt and the obvious Mexican heritage on his face, he might've been a real Southern gentleman—the kind Jedidiah had always warned her about.

Cash was initially friendly, too, in his own way, but when it came time to start unloading the wagon he disappeared into the saloon. Just as well. With his piercing eyes that looked right through her and that dark, well-trimmed mustache and goatee, he looked like the devil himself. Yes, now she knew the devil wore a dark suit and a white ruffled shirt, and a matching pair of six-shooters, as well.

The room she and the children would share was on the second floor. Rico told her, as he carried the largest of the trunks into the room, that he and Sullivan, and sometimes another friend named Nate, stayed on the third floor. Jedidiah stayed there, too, when he was in town.

Eden tried not to be dismayed as she surveyed her room. Dust covered every surface, and the window was so filthy the afternoon sun was dimmed. The quilt on the bed was stained and torn, and the chest of drawers had a cracked mirror mounted above it. One drawer was missing.

And Rico assured her this was the finest room available. The hotel owner, referred to more than once as "that old crank Grady" was apparently ill, so Rico did the honors of offering her the guest book to sign and assigning her a room.

She wanted to thank Sullivan properly, but as soon as the wagon had been unloaded and her things were placed in her room, he'd disappeared. Literally disappeared without a sound. One minute he stood right behind her in the hotel's dusty lobby; the next he was gone.

"So you are Jed's sister," Rico said.

Eden spun to face the young man who stood in the hotel doorway. "Yes. I was so hoping he'd be here."

Rico stepped into the lobby and gave her a broad grin. Like Sullivan, he was dark and handsome, but beyond that they looked nothing alike. Rico wore his hair short. His build was more on the slender side, though he was far from skinny. And while Sullivan was often sullen and hard to read, Rico had an easy, friendly smile. As a matter of fact, he looked very sweet, but for the fact that he wore that very large knife.

"He will be back," Rico said, trying his best to assure her. "I am sure if he had known you were coming he would have been here to greet you."

She gave Rico a friendly smile of her own. He was an easy man to like, brotherly warnings aside. "If Jedidiah knew I was coming, he would've met me halfway and escorted me promptly back to Georgia. He seems to think me too delicate for Texas."

"You have survived this far," Rico said with a wink. "If Jed tries to drag you back to Georgia against your will, you call on Rico. Rock Creek doesn't have nearly enough *senoritas bonitas* to suit me. I see no reason to forcefully remove our newest beauty." He bowed crisply to her.

Rico wasn't just friendly, he was an outrageous flirt. "You're kind to offer, but I can handle Jedidiah on my own." After all, she'd had plenty of practice.

Sullivan led his stallion to the hotel stables and handed the animal to the boy whose father kept the place running. He carried his saddlebags and the contents back to his room, and like a coward he peeked into the lobby to make sure Eden wasn't still standing there. The coast was clear.

Now that Eden had been safely delivered to Rock Creek she was no longer his responsibility, right? He could return to Webberville tomorrow, if he was of a mind, and reclaim his hat and his Colt. He could put Eden Rourke out of his mind for good.

If only he hadn't make the mistake of kissing her.

He made it all the way to the third floor without running into anyone.

The door of the room next to his was open, and Rico sat on the edge of the bed, sharpening a small silver knife. Sullivan could slip past anyone—but Rico.

"Eden Rourke is *muy bonita*," Rico said without lifting his head from his task.

"Yep."

"She likes you very much, I think."

"I doubt it." His voice was just a little bit too gruff.

"If a *senorita bonita* looked at me the way Eden looked at you, I do not think I could make myself slip out the door while she was not looking." He held the knife up to study the sharp edge.

"The *senoritas* look at you plenty, Kid, and it's brought you nothing but trouble."

"*Senoritas* have brought me the greatest pleasures of my life," Rico said with a grin.

"Well, they've brought me nothing but grief," Sullivan snapped. "Did you get a good look at her?"

"*Si,*" Rico said lowly, his grin never fading.

"Do you really think . . ." he stumbled. "She's not the kind of woman . . . She's a lady for God's sake, and she's Jed's little sister."

"I never took you for a coward."

Sullivan moved one door down and almost violently tossed his saddlebags onto the bed.

Dinner in the hotel dining room was served by a cheerless woman in a dirty apron. When Eden introduced herself, the woman sullenly gave her own name as Lydia. The beef was so tough the children couldn't eat it and Eden didn't want to try. The beans were passable, but not exactly tasty, and the biscuits were burned.

Eden tried to strike up a friendly conversation with Lydia, but the woman obviously wasn't interested. She served the almost inedible meal and then disappeared into the kitchen. Well, she did look tired, and Eden told herself it was possible Lydia was a lovely young woman who was simply having a bad day. Tomorrow she would surely be friendlier.

But when Lydia stuck her head out of the kitchen to snap at Eden, "Aren't you done yet?" she had her doubts about tomorrow.

By the time she settled Teddy on a pallet in the corner of the room and tucked Millie into the bed they would share, her own bedding replacing the hotel's unsatisfactory linens, she was thoroughly dejected. The hotel was not exactly what she'd expected. Rock Creek was not what she'd expected; Jedidiah wasn't here, and Sinclair Sullivan . . . Sinclair Sullivan had all but vanished.

With the lamp out, she went to the window and looked through filthy panes of glass out over the main street. The view was indistinct, with the sun gone and the clouded glass obscuring her view, but below her, the street was more lively now than it had been that afternoon; there was a great deal of traffic into and out of the saloon across the street.

For the first time, she considered that coming here might've been a mistake. Jedidiah wasn't in town, and Sullivan was right about one thing. He wouldn't be happy to see her when he did arrive.

Eden took a deep breath and fortified herself. She was here now, and it was too late to go back.

The trip had been hard, but she would make this place her home. True, Rock Creek was not what she'd expected, but perhaps things would look better tomorrow.

Yes, tomorrow.

A tall figure with a familiar head of long dark hair crossed the street from the hotel to the saloon. The walk was unmistakable, the set of the shoulders and the thick brown hair unique.

She couldn't help but think of the way Sullivan had kissed her last night. Goodness, she'd never felt anything like it, had never imagined that a kiss could be so wonderful. If she tried hard enough, she could feel his lips on hers, still. She moved closer to the window, so close her nose almost touched the glass.

Why did she have this deep, gut-wrenching feeling that Sinclair Sullivan was somehow hers? That he *belonged* to her? It was nonsense, really. She hadn't known him long, and he was certainly not the kind of man she expected to marry, when the time came for her to take that momentous step. He was rather rough around the edges, not at all a gentleman. Not at all the kind of man who would make a suitable husband. She shouldn't be experiencing such feelings for any man other than the one she would marry. It just wasn't right. Was it?

Besides, maybe Sinclair Sullivan wasn't a gentleman in the traditional sense, but he was definitely honorable and decent and good. And he kissed like an angel.

Her strong and unexpected emotions stemmed from more than just the kiss, she reasoned. She'd felt something for Sullivan the moment she'd looked into his eyes. Well, *eye,* actually, since only the one had been visible when she'd first seen him face-to-face. She felt like she'd known him forever, like he'd be a part of her life from here on out, no matter what.

Last night's kiss had been their first, but she didn't think it would be their last. It had been much too special to ignore. Hadn't it? Was she imagining something that didn't exist?

"Look at me, Sullivan," she whispered, her eyes on Sinclair Sullivan's form as he reached the swinging doors that would lead him to goodness knows what for an evening's entertainment.

"Sinclair," she whispered, liking the sound of his more intimate given name. "Sin," she said, so softly she could barely hear the sound of her own voice. "Look back. Just once, just for a split second." If he looked back and up, she'd know that he was, at least, thinking about her, that maybe somewhere deep inside he thought of her as *his* and remembered their kiss.

Just as Sin stepped inside the saloon, he glanced over his shoulder and up, his eyes landing, perhaps, on this very window she was peering out from.

And Eden went to bed with a smile on her face.

Sullivan stepped up to the bar and ordered a glass of whiskey from Yvonne, the only female bartender in these parts, hoping for a few minutes of peace before the vultures descended. No such luck.

"Well, if it isn't *Papa*," Cash drawled.

Sullivan turned his back to Yvonne and leaned casually against the bar. Cash was, as always, dressed in a fine suit and a fancy shirt. The diamond stickpin he'd won in a poker game a few months back was prominent in a black silk tie, and he wore the fancy shoes and flat-brimmed hat he'd ordered from a New York City catalog. His face was downright pretty, his mustache and goatee were always neatly trimmed, and his smile was quick, but Sullivan knew a little of what went on behind those eyes. Cash was not a man you'd want to ignore or turn your back on, but he was a helluva man to have beside you in a fight.

Yvonne set his whiskey on the bar without saying a word and moved away. Damn, the war widow made a fine bartender. She knew when to smile and talk and when to disappear.

"Let's get this over with here and now," Sullivan said calmly. "Go ahead. Have your say."

"Jed's going to kill you," Cash said with a smile. "You come riding into town with his baby sister in tow, a little girl who calls you Papa, and a kid that would pass as yours on a quick glance. Quite the happy-looking family." The words were light, but Cash's eyes went hard.

Sullivan explained, as curtly as possible, how he had met Eden Rourke. He told Cash about Webberville and the run-in with the Merriweather brothers.

Cash's smile died quickly; his eyes darkened, turning almost black. "Webberville, you say. What say we pay them a visit, you and me and Rico and Nate? A surprise visit. Hell, it wouldn't take more than a few minutes to set those rubes straight."

"No," Sullivan said softly. "I'll handle it myself."

Cash shrugged his shoulders. "If you need someone to watch your back, give me a holler."

Sullivan knew if he rode into Webberville with Daniel Cash at his side, the men who'd been so quick to jump him would piss their pants and run like hell. While it was an entertaining and tempting picture, he wanted to take care of those men on his own. And he wanted his damn hat back.

"She's an attractive lady," Cash said, changing the subject. "Reminds me of the girls back home. Innocent, respectable, so sweet you just want to lick them all over and see if they taste like penny candy. They have the world at their feet and paradise between their legs and they don't even know it yet." His voice was hard, cynical. His eyes darkened.

Sullivan turned his back to Cash and took a sip of his whiskey. Daniel Cash was as fast and loose with his women and his mouth as he was with his gun, and Sullivan found he was in no mood to hear the gambler and gunslinger talk about *licking* Eden.

Not that he had any right to feel possessive, not that it made a damn bit of difference to him *who* licked Eden, when the time came. She'd taste good, though, wouldn't she? She'd smell good, too, with his nose right against her skin, with his tongue . . .

"You got a claim on her?" Cash asked softly.

"Nope," Sullivan answered without hesitation and without a hint of emotion in his voice. "If you want her, she's all yours."

A soft, harsh bark of laughter was Cash's answer. "Jesus, I wouldn't touch Jed's little sister with a ten-foot pole if you gave me a dozen saloons like this one to do it. Do you know what happens to men who trifle with women who have brothers like Jedidiah Rourke? I do," he said without waiting for an answer. "And I *like* my nuts."

Sullivan looked Cash in the eye.

"If you like yours," Cash added in a lowered voice, "you'll quit daydreaming about little Miss Rourke."

Nate came in, stumbling over an invisible obstacle near the swinging doors. His citified suit was rumpled; his hair was cut so short it couldn't possibly be mussed. His eyes were bloodshot and he needed a shave, as usual. He looked like he'd been drinking all day, maybe all week. The ex-preacher claimed a table in the corner and ordered a bottle.

Sullivan ordered his own bottle from Yvonne and joined him. At least Nate wouldn't preach. He'd given up that calling long ago.

Chapter 5

Breakfast in the hotel dining room had been as glum and unappetizing as dinner the night before. Lydia was just as antisocial, but Eden refused to allow herself to be dismayed. She had plans for the day. Perhaps she couldn't do anything about the condition of the hotel, but she could certainly do something about her room.

The children helped with the enterprise, Millie sweeping and Teddy washing the windows. The door and the window Teddy was not washing remained open, in hopes that a bit of fresh air might carry away the odor that permeated the room. She did not want to spend another night in a room that smelled like someone else's sweaty feet. They'd just been working a few minutes when a raspy voice in the doorway startled Eden.

"What the hell are you doing?"

She spun around to see a thin old man leaning against the doorjamb. His skin was so wrinkled he looked a hundred years old, his eyes were sunk in his head, and his sparse white hair looked as if it had just left the pillow; it stood out in all directions.

"C-c-cleaning," she said, her nervousness making her stutter. "Isn't that all right?"

The old man rolled his eyes. "If this room is clean, *everyone* will want a clean room," he mumbled, his voice weak, watery.

"Oh, you must be Mr. McClure," she said with a wavering smile. "I understand you've been ill." In truth, he looked like death warmed over. "I do hope you're feeling better today."

"No," he snapped, "I am not feeling better."

"You'd best get back to bed, then," she said firmly. "Why, whoever is looking after you will be worried if they find your bed empty."

"No one's taking care of me, missy. I can take care of myself."

Eden's heart went out to the old man. It was terribly sad to be old and alone, sick and without someone to care for you, and too stubborn to admit that you need help. She couldn't possibly allow him to continue in this way.

"My grandmother had a home remedy that was sure to cure any ailment," she said in her most sensible voice, giving Mr. McClure a warm smile. "It's just a simple tea with a few secret ingredients, and I promise you it's quite tasty. Perhaps you'd allow me to make it for you."

"I don't need any damned tea," he rumbled.

Eden's smile faded. "Please don't curse in front of the children," she said in a lowered voice. "It isn't proper."

Mr. McClure didn't argue with her; in fact, his sunken eyes filled with tears and his lips trembled slightly. "You sound just like my mama, God rest her soul."

Eden couldn't bear to see the old man make the effort to stand there any longer, so she escorted him from her room, offering her arm for support and leading him down the dusty hallway to his own room. Impossibly, the room was in worse shape than her own, with a broken chair by the single window and an odor of illness that would probably never wash out.

He crawled into bed, and Eden opened the window. "It's a lovely day," she said. "The fresh air will make you feel better."

"I don't like fresh air," Mr. McClure grumbled.

"Well, you're going to get it anyway," she said with a smile. "When was the last time you ate?"

"I had some beef yesterday about lunchtime."

If it had been prepared by the same woman who'd prepared her own dinner and breakfast, Eden was quite sure he hadn't eaten much. And he looked so weak! "I'll make you some tea and soup."

He made a face that was, impossibly, more sour than his normal expression. "I hate Lydia's soup."

"I'll make it myself," she said.

"I don't want any damned soup," he grumbled. "Get out of my room."

Eden sighed and made her way to the kitchen. Some people, and perhaps all men, just didn't know what was best for them.

It was nearly noon when Sullivan left his room. His head pounded, a consequence of drinking too much whiskey last night, and the bruises on his body ached in a way they hadn't when he'd been on the road. He felt like everything had caught up with him at once.

He descended to the second floor slowly, each step calculated. In a couple of days the ache would be gone, and he could head back to Webberville for a short visit.

Lifting his head, he caught sight of a vision in blue, and he ached all the more. Eden Rourke, a smile on her face, her pale hair piled loosely atop her head, a slight, feminine sway in her walk, came toward him with a tray in her hands. The bowl on the tray she carried steamed enticingly.

"Surely you're not just now rising?" she asked, her smile widening. "Really, Sinclair, how decadent of you."

Decadent? When he looked at her, he felt nothing *but* decadent. He wanted to take that plain blue dress off of her, take down her hair, and forget all his aches and pains. He did his best to put that fantasy aside.

"I didn't get much sleep on the trail," he said.

Her smile faded as they met in the hallway and each came to a halt. "Of course you didn't," she said in a voice that was intimately soft and inviting. "You were much too busy watching over us to get much rest. How could I have forgotten that? Did I ever thank you?"

"I'm sure you did," he said softly.

"Well, in case I forgot in all the excitement, thank you, Sinclair Sullivan." Her fetching blue eyes widened. "What would I have done without you?" Gentle and sweet and almost unbearably tempting, she looked up at him. And he was a goner.

"Did I ever thank you for saving my skin in Webberville?" he asked.

"I don't believe so," she whispered.

"Thank you, Eden Rourke," he whispered. "What would I have done without you?"

All was silent for a moment, as he looked into blue eyes and remembered the night he'd kissed her. He'd tasted her passion, felt her response to his very bones. Maybe she was a beautiful woman; maybe she was a lady; maybe she was Jed's sister. Right now none of that mattered. The ache in his ribs subsided, but was replaced by a more insistent, more demanding ache in his loins.

She leaned slightly forward, her face tilted up. He leaned carefully forward and down, until their lips met somewhere above the soup.

It was a soft kiss, a thank-you. An impulsive test, perhaps. The kiss didn't last nearly long enough, but it was plenty enough to ruin what was left of Sullivan's day. How was he supposed to think of anything else when Eden was right here before him?

When they both pulled back, he set his eyes firmly on hers, searching for a sign. He saw warmth and a flicker of untested passion. She licked her lips.

"Would you open Mr. McClure's door for me, please?" she whispered, her voice wavering slightly.

"That's his soup?" Sullivan asked.

She smiled up at him again, the kiss not forgotten but lingering in her eyes. "I made a big pot. Go downstairs and get yourself a bowl."

He opened Grady's door and got quite a shock. The room was clean, the windows open to allow a fresh breeze to waft in. And Grady smiled as Eden entered the room.

"That smells good," the geezer said weakly.

"It is good," Eden insisted, "and I expect you to eat every drop."

Grady's smile dimmed as his gaze lit on Sullivan. "Look at what the girl did for me," he said, tears coming to his faded eyes. "She put fresh sheets on the bed, and made me some kind of godawful sweet tea, and fussed at me every time I said goddamn it."

"Mr. McClure," Eden said sternly, "please don't use such language."

"See what I mean?" Grady asked fondly. "She's an angel, come to take care of me while I die."

"I'll have no talk of dying," Eden insisted as she sat beside Grady's bed and lifted a spoonful of soup to his mouth.

In truth, Grady really was dying. He'd been going downhill for months, looking smaller and older with every passing day. Until today, he hadn't grown any less disagreeable. Eden seemed to bring out the best in the old man.

Sullivan watched her feed the ailing man, content, for the moment, just to be in the same room with her. Just to watch her feed an old codger soup. Every move she made was graceful; every word she said so sweet the sound of her voice made him ache.

He wanted her. Jedidiah Rourke be damned, he wanted Eden with everything he had, in a way he'd never wanted anything before. He craved her, he needed her, and another kiss over steaming soup was not going to be enough. Having her would likely cost him everything he held dear: his home, his friends, maybe even what little heart he had left. Surely a woman was not worth such sacrifice. Not even this one.

She lifted her head and smiled at him. She said so much with a smile, with her eyes. No one had ever looked at him this way before, and likely never would again.

"Go get yourself a bowl of soup, Sinclair. You look like you could use a little nourishment, yourself."

Yep, he wanted her bad. He *needed* her, and one way or another he was going to have her.

She hadn't intended to spend her first full day in Rock Creek doing laundry in a tub just outside the hotel kitchen door, and cooking and caring for a sick old man, and cleaning, but as far as Eden was concerned she had no choice. This was her home now, and she was determined to make it a suitable place for the children.

She'd never worked so hard, and by the end of the day she was exhausted. But it wasn't a bad feeling. She had accomplished something today; she'd made this place a little bit her own.

Less than an hour earlier she'd tucked the children into clean beds. Teddy now slept on a small cot instead of a pallet on the floor, and Millie was deep asleep in the same bed Eden herself would crawl into later. Once she was sure they were sound asleep, she'd turned out the lamp and come downstairs for a breath of fresh air.

The front of the hotel faced the saloon, and she had no desire to watch the comings and goings of that sinful place. Besides, watching a saloon was surely no way to find peace and quiet.

Beyond the rear door of the lobby was a small enclosed area. There had once been a garden here, but the area was dry and as untended as the rest of the hotel. A rickety old bench had been placed against the wall, and this is where she sat. The quiet was blissful, and after a long day simply sitting still was a pleasure.

What a shame that the hotel had been neglected for so long. She could imagine this as a wonderful place to sit at the end of the day, if there were roses blooming. With a proper flower garden, there would be morning birds everywhere, she imagined, making it a nice place to have a cup of tea or coffee before a busy day began. Instead the garden area was brown and lifeless, devoid of color and the fragrance that should fill the air.

She leaned against the hotel wall and closed her eyes. It had been an exhausting, trying day, but one small moment had carried her through it on a cloud. Sin had kissed her again. In the hallway, over a bowl of soup, he had leaned forward and taken her mouth with his. He'd kissed tenderly, longingly, sweet with just a touch of wickedness. He must care for her, at least a little, to kiss her that way.

"What are you doing out here?"

She smiled and opened her eyes at the sound of that familiar voice. *Thinking about you.* "Nothing," she said, turning her head to glance at Sin as he stepped through the door and closed it behind him. "Just resting. And thinking," she added, to be honest.

He sat down beside her, making the bench rock slightly. Strange, how comfortable it felt to have him sit so close to her. She felt as if she'd known Sinclair Sullivan forever, not just for a few days.

"Pretty night," he said, looking up to the clear sky. A soft breeze brushed back the long strands of dark hair to reveal his face in moonlight. Why did the sight of that face make her heart leap into her throat?

"Yes," she said. "Very pretty."

"You're probably worn out," he said. "You were busy all day."

"I was," she said. "And I am tired, a little, but I don't mind. I like to stay busy."

She could tell, even in the near dark, that he was nervous, maybe even as nervous as she.

"I'm not complaining," he said. "The soup was good. The best I've had in a long while."

With the cool breeze wafting about, the moonlight shining on them, and the privacy of the enclosed and neglected garden, Eden felt strangely bewildered. She'd traveled for weeks to get to this strange place, and now she was here, in a place she was determined to make her home, and she had no idea what would happen next.

She did know that this man was special to her. Looking at him made her heart beat fast, and remembering the kisses they'd shared made her tingle from the top of her head to the tips of her toes. Sin was unexpected, unplanned, a gift, perhaps.

As she watched him she decided Rock Creek, with its unostentatious appearance and busy saloon and horrid hotel, was a wonderful place. It was wonderful because Sin was in it.

"Aren't you going to kiss me?" she whispered boldly, afraid he'd sit silently beside her all night long without so much as looking in her direction.

He turned to face her, his eyes no longer on the stars. "Do you want me to?"

She nodded, and he very slowly lowered his face to hers. She closed her eyes as his mouth covered hers, wrapped her arms around his shoulders as he put his arms around her, fell against him an instant later.

Her heart beat fast, as she lost herself in the power of a kiss. Her breasts pressed against Sin's hard chest, and it seemed right and true that they hold each other so close and tight that she could barely breathe. He was strong, but what she felt was more than the physical strength in his body. She sensed a strength that came from deep inside, from his heart and his soul. She felt that strength encompass her, and it was a marvelous sensation.

Her fingers speared through his long hair, and she held his lips against hers as his tongue danced in and out of her mouth, the motion so light and fleeting it left her breathless and wanting more.

"Sin," she whispered. "Do you mind if I call you Sin?"

"You can call me anything you want," he said breathlessly, as he claimed her mouth again.

Sin was restless; his body shifted against hers. He lowered one hand and lovingly caressed her hip, a familiar touch that made her shudder all over again. His hand settled on her thigh, and while she knew she should tell him to move it, that it wasn't proper that he rest his hand there, she wouldn't risk taking her mouth from his to deliver the order. Not just yet.

Eventually he moved the hand on his own, raking it up her ribs to barely touch the side of her breast. At her sharp intake of breath he clamped his mouth ever tighter to hers and kissed her so deep she went weak in the knees. Her protest died on her lips, and his.

He began to tilt her backward, slowly but surely, until his long hard body hovered over hers and she was all but lying on the bench with Sin above her.

He took his mouth from hers. With his face in

shadow and his hair falling like a curtain around it, she could see nothing of his features. "I want you," he whispered hoarsely. "More than I've ever wanted anything. Come to my bed. Tonight. Now."

"Oh, Sin," she whispered. She closed her eyes. It would be so easy to say yes . . . easier than she'd ever imagined. "I can't."

"You can," he breathed against her mouth. "I know you want me, too. I can feel it. I can see it."

"Maybe I do, but . . ."

"That's enough," he insisted. "That's all we need. I want you; you want me . . ."

"We're not . . . We're not married," she said, embarrassed to be stating the obvious at a moment like this. "It isn't right."

"Married?" he repeated. They came up a little, out of their almost-lying position.

"Well, people who go to bed together are supposed to be married first, you know."

They were sitting up again. "Some of them are," he agreed.

She didn't want to admit to Sin, or to anyone else, that her knowledge of what happened after the kissing was inadequate, at best. Her mother had died when she was ten years old, long before such information was shared between a mother and daughter. Her stepfather had certainly not offered any such knowledge. And the one time she'd worked up the nerve to ask their cook, Hallie Smithers, for details, the woman had offered no more than a prim, *You'll find out on your wedding night, as is right and proper.*

No one had ever told her she'd be swept away by a kiss, and come very close to making a colossal mistake.

"I know who I am," she whispered. "There's no

use pretending I'm someone else." She reached up to touch his cheek. "I don't take what I shouldn't have because I"—she swallowed hard—"because I crave it."

"I do," Sin whispered. "I see what I want and I take it."

In her current position, she should be frightened by those words. But she wasn't frightened at all. She could never be afraid of Sinclair Sullivan.

"I can't dismiss everything I know and believe in simply because you make me feel so good." Oh, and he *did* make her feel good.

He groaned, but continued to hold her.

"If nothing else, how can I forget what happened to Millie's mother?"

He lifted his head and looked down at her.

"Perhaps she felt just this way when she gave herself to Millie's father, whoever he was. Perhaps she sat outside on a cool autumn night and allowed herself to be swept away by the moon and a kiss and the thud of her heart. For her foolishness she ended up raising a child alone, taking in laundry and doing goodness knows what else to feed her child and keep a roof over their heads. She was younger than I am now when she had Millie. A couple of months ago she died of a bout of pneumonia she should have been able to fight at her age. I think she just gave up, in the end."

Sin's hands dropped, and he slowly moved away.

"I won't put myself, or a child, in that position," Eden whispered. "Millie has had to pay, every day of her life, for her mother's misfortune. It's unfair, but no less true. I can't . . . I won't . . ." she stammered.

"You're saving yourself for marriage," Sin said

gruffly, rescuing her from further inadequate explanations.

"Yes. You can call me prudish, if you'd like, but I don't see it that way." She reached up and allowed her fingers to slip through his hair. "I just think it's important that I live my life properly, the way my mother expected me to." She lowered her voice. "I think it's important that I remember who I am."

Sin leaned over and planted a kiss on her forehead. "Too bad. We coulda been good together. Real good."

Doing the right thing didn't feel so wonderful at the moment. As Sin stood, it felt like a loss of some kind. She expected him to stalk away, to turn his back on her and dismiss her and her annoying morals without another thought. To her surprise, he placed his hand on her cheek and traced it softly.

"This will never work," he said softly. "You're looking for forever, and I'm just looking for a little fun."

Her heart sank, like a stone that settled uncomfortably in her stomach. What had she expected? That he'd ask her to marry him here and now?

"I'm sorry," she whispered.

He gave her a pained smile. "Never apologize for being a lady, Eden Rourke. Never apologize for being who you are. Don't get me wrong. Right now I wish you could forget about what's right and fair and let me take you to my bed and show you that fun I'm looking for. I'm a selfish bastard and I want you more than I've ever wanted anything. I want you so much I can't think of anything else.

"But the truth of the matter is, the world would be a better place if there were more people like you in it."

He turned abruptly and walked away, stepping through the door and into the lobby, returning the way he'd come. And as he closed the door Eden knew, without a doubt, that she loved him.

Chapter 6

Sullivan had an idea he'd be spending a lot of time in Cash's saloon, as long as Eden was in town. It was bad enough to be forced to see her now and again, but to sleep under the same roof and not be able to touch her, well, that was flat-out torture.

His dilemma was a temporary one, he knew. If Eden didn't decide soon enough that Rock Creek was not the place for her, then her brother was sure to toss her over his shoulder and forcibly carry her back to Georgia.

How did she know just what to say to make him back away without a fight? He could've argued, quite well, with her theory that she couldn't take that which was not rightfully hers. He could convince her that they didn't have to be married to share a bed, no matter what her mother had taught her. But the story about Millie's mother had stopped him cold.

Eden couldn't possibly know that he'd paid for

his mother's misfortune all his life, that he knew what it was like to live with an infamy you had no control over, no power to fight.

Just as well. Eden Rourke was a fine woman, and she had no business passing her time with a man like Sinclair Sullivan. Not tonight. Not ever. And still, he wanted her so much he hurt.

"From the look on his face, I'd say things did not go well for Mr. Sullivan this evening," Cash drawled in a low voice as he leaned against the long, polished bar.

"Go away," Sullivan said softly, no insult intended by the remark, and none taken, from the way Cash grinned crookedly.

"Let me guess," Cash said softly. "You foolishly made your move on Jed's sister and she showed you the door."

"Close enough," Sullivan muttered.

Cash made a low noise in his throat and demanded a bottle of the finest whiskey from his well-trained bartender. They waited until the bottle had been deposited before them and Yvonne had moved down the bar before resuming their conversation.

"Women," Cash said, calling on his wisest voice, since he considered himself an expert on the subject, "are fickle creatures. While it is my most ardent suggestion that you keep yourself the hell away from Miss Rourke, if you choose to ignore that advice and move forward you must do so with some considerable caution. She's not a saloon girl, you know. You need a plan."

"What does that mean?" Sullivan asked tiredly.

"Succinctly, it means court her, promise her whatever she wants, screw her, and then get the hell out of town before her brother returns."

Sullivan rotated his head slowly to see if Cash had one of his trademark grins in place. Surely he was kidding! Apparently, the man was deadly serious.

"I can't do that. Eden's a nice girl." Unfortunately for him, that was the truth.

Cash tossed back a half glass of whiskey and then slammed his glass on the bar. "God save us from nice girls," he muttered. "Trust me," he said, his voice just a little bit louder than before, "inside every *nice girl* there is a soul-stealing bitch just waiting to be set free."

Sullivan shook his head. "Eden's not like that."

Cash rotated slowly and leaned against the bar. "You want a woman, Sullivan?" He looked smug, at home, at ease in the saloon that was his home. "You never avail yourself of the local talent. Why is that?"

"I live here." As far as he was concerned, that was explanation enough. Hell, he was in this saloon almost every day when he was in Rock Creek. He didn't want any ties here, any obligations. Not even with a prostitute.

"So you prefer to take your pleasures elsewhere," Cash said, seeming to understand. "I can understand that." He wrinkled his nose. "Well, not really. Where's your sense of community? Don't you think we should do all we can for the local economy?"

"Not really."

"Look around you," Cash said, his smile creeping back, "and pick one. I am very selective about the women I allow to take up residence abovestairs. And I don't take a penny of the money they bring in, so I don't want you to think I have any ulterior motives in pressing you in their direction."

"You know," Sullivan said, anxious to change the subject, "this is not your place."

Cash raised haughty eyebrows. "The coward who owned it ran off when *El Diablo* showed up, and he never returned. What am I supposed to do? Sit around and allow a perfectly good saloon to go to waste?"

"That would never do," Sullivan mumbled.

Cash ignored his sarcasm and lifted a hand to gesture casually, the lace at his cuff swaying. "Laurel's a sweetheart," he said, pointing out the brunette at the opposite end of the bar. "And she's very"—he took a deep breath and exhaled slowly—"energetic. Ethel," he said, turning his head to the table where the blonde sat on a gambler's knee, "is as *nice* a girl as you'd ever want to know. She's new. Showed up one day at the door looking for work, and I simply could not make myself turn her away. She makes a lot of noise, though," he said with a frown. "Likes to talk all the damn time, even when . . . Well, given that you don't usually talk much at all, I'd look elsewhere if I were you. Then there's Kate," he said, his frown slowly transforming into a sly smile as he watched the redhead climb the stairs with another customer. "The woman has got the finest tits I've ever had the pleasure of fondling. And she knows how to keep her pretty mouth shut. Unless of course . . ."

"Enough." Sullivan groaned. "I don't want . . ." he began. "I can't . . ."

Cash set cold eyes on him, and Sullivan shivered. He'd suspected, in days past, that Daniel Cash had no heart, perhaps even no soul. He killed too easily, too quickly, and without remorse. No wonder Cash was such a successful gambler; no one could read those eyes.

He was an unrepentant womanizer, relishing in his pleasures but never getting too close to any one female. He'd smile at a woman and flirt outrageously and get what he wanted from her, but from what Sullivan could see, Cash didn't feel anything for anyone.

Talking to Cash about women was like talking to Nate about God.

"Thanks for the advice," Sullivan said, pushing away from the bar, "but I think I'll just head back to the hotel and turn in."

"Sullivan," Cash said softly, "be careful. I don't have many friends, and I wouldn't want to see one of the few who are left dangling in the wind over a woman. If you won't take my earlier advice, then try this. Get out of town. Tonight, first thing in the morning at the latest. Don't say good-bye. Don't kid yourself that one last kiss will be all right; just leave. And don't come back here until you know she's gone."

Sullivan had to admit that last suggestion made a lot of sense. "Maybe I will." He nodded once, knowing Cash was right. "Yeah, I'll leave in the morning. I need to . . . fetch my hat, anyway."

Hellfire. The day Daniel Cash started making sense about women was a sorry day, indeed.

After an almost sleepless night spent tossing and turning, gently so as not to disturb Millie, Eden was up with the sun. If she couldn't sleep, she might as well get something productive done.

Mr. McClure needed nourishment, and he simply refused to eat Lydia's cooking—with good reason. Eden decided that if she was going to feed the hotel owner, she might as well make enough for everyone. Jedidiah's friends had been kind to her; it was the least she could do.

When she caught sight of a figure in the hotel lobby, she was surprised to find anyone else up and about at this hour. When she realized that it was Sin and that he carried heavily loaded saddlebags over his shoulder, her heart did an unpleasant flip in her chest.

"Good morning," she said from the stairway, interrupting Sin's determined stride toward the door.

He stopped, then turned slowly to face her. "Good morning," he said in a low, somewhat dejected voice.

She stepped quickly to the bottom of the stairs. "Where are you going?"

He sighed before answering. "Webberville." He shifted, redistributing the weight of his saddlebags. "I want my damn hat back."

Her hands balled into fists at her sides. When she'd first seen him, badly outnumbered and being beaten, it had hurt. To see any human being suffer pain was difficult. But now she *loved* Sin, and the idea that he would subject himself to such pain again was too much to bear.

"No," she whispered.

Something resembling a smile began to cross his face, barely tilting the lips, barely lighting his hazel green eyes. "No?"

She had to remind herself that he was a man and would not take kindly to orders from a woman. "At least," she said, calling on her calmest voice, "I wish you would wait a few days. I could use your help," she added. "I . . . I need you here."

His hint of a smile disappeared. "Why?"

Why? Why, indeed? She took a deep breath as she searched for an answer Sin would find suitable. If he thought she was trying to protect him, he would surely run.

"Since Mr. McClure is ill, I thought I might help him out around the hotel. You know, fix the place up a bit. You could help with the heavy lifting and the moving of furniture."

"Rico can help you, and I'm sure he'd be glad to. Nate, too, if he hasn't had too much to drink. Just don't ask Cash to lift anything heavy." He grinned at the mild slur.

Eden clasped her hands before her and moved forward. She wanted to reach up and push those long strands of hair back, so she could see Sin's face. Her hands positively *itched* to touch him. "Well, I suppose it's true that anyone can help me with those chores, but ... but ..." She lifted her eyes to Sin's as the idea came to her. "But I'm going to enroll the children in school today, and I know they'll want you there. Especially Teddy. It might be a difficult day for him, but I don't think it would be right to shelter him completely from the world even though I am tempted to keep him close for a few more days. I worry about him." She took another step forward. "And he does so look up to you."

"I really shouldn't," he said, but she could tell he was having second thoughts.

She glanced at the weight on his broad shoulders. "Why such a heavy saddlebag for the trip to Webberville? It can't be a long trip on horseback."

He hesitated. She could see the reluctance to answer in his eyes and the way his mouth worked slightly before he answered. "I won't be coming directly back to Rock Creek."

"Where are you going?" she asked, being very careful not to sound too disappointed. "Are you going to visit family?"

"I don't have any family," he said curtly.

"I'm sorry."

"I'm not," he said, and she could tell that he meant it.

Eden took another step forward. "It sounds very lonely, not to have any family at all."

"I like it that way."

She finished closing the distance between them. "You know, Sin, that's the main difference between you and me. You enjoy being alone, depending on no one and making sure no one depends on you. And I, well, I'd rather live in the most desolate place on earth, surrounded by people I love, than live alone in paradise."

"If you came to Rock Creek looking for the most desolate place on earth, you found it," he said in a lighthearted voice that rung with insincerity.

He was going to leave, ride off to Webberville and face those horrid ruffians without anyone there to help him. Who would save him this time? Ah, he would surely never accept or acknowledge that he needed saving.

"I can't convince you to stay?" she whispered.

He shook his head.

"Then kiss me good-bye."

She didn't give him a choice, but came up on her tiptoes and laid her mouth over his. As soon as their lips touched, she closed her eyes and savored the taste and feel of Sin's kiss, the rush in her body, as though she'd drunk too much wine.

"Moving furniture," Sin said as Eden pulled her lips from his.

"Ummm-hmmm," she murmured, and then she kissed him again. His lips were soft, sweet, addictive. She couldn't get enough.

He pulled his mouth just slightly from hers. If she wasn't mistaken, he sighed, low and deep, in what could only be resignation. "Maybe it would be best if I took Teddy to school. I could introduce him to Reese, the schoolteacher, and explain the situation."

"That would be so sweet," Eden whispered with a smile, and then she kissed him again. With every kiss she melted a little bit more. And so did he. "You really are a very sweet man," she muttered against his mouth.

"Maybe I could postpone my trip for two or three days," Sin said as Eden pulled her lips from his once again. "Maybe a week or so."

"What would I do without you?" she breathed, and Sin dropped his saddlebags to the floor and took her in his arms for a proper kiss.

Sullivan cast a sideways glance to Eden, who held Millie's hand as the four of them, their little pretend family, walked toward the Rock Creek schoolhouse. There was a deep and complete peacefulness on her face, a serenity he himself had never known and never would.

Why had he agreed to stay so easily? He never backed down, *never,* not at the threat of guns or fists or any other weapons of war. Hell, he could recognize and challenge the threat of a blade or a bullet, but blue eyes and a soft kiss did him in. He hadn't even put up a fight.

Teddy walked beside him, silent as always and more tense than usual. As the schoolhouse came into view, the kid reached out and grabbed Sullivan's hand, little fingers slipping against a large palm and taking hold. Sullivan made a fist and held the kid's hand, firmly but not too tight. Almost immediately, Teddy relaxed.

Sullivan didn't like the fact that this kid had somehow come to depend on him, that he, as Eden said, looked up to him. Half-breed bastards who lived their lives moving from one fight to the next didn't need little kids hanging on to them any more than they needed nice girls popping up to turn those lives upside down.

When Sullivan opened the schoolhouse door, Reese, who leaned over the desk at the front of the room, lifted his head. His eyebrows arched in surprise as he invited the foursome in.

Reese was different these days—a schoolteacher, for God's sake! The man who had led them all in many battles was a husband, too, and the father of a baby girl. He had settled in Rock Creek; he had found peace. But he was the same man in many ways. He was still one of them, and he always would be. The surprise on his face quickly faded.

"Miss Rourke would like to enroll these kids in school," Sullivan said as they approached the desk and his former captain. "This pretty little girl is Millie." He nodded to the child, who smiled brightly. She'd have no problem fitting in, for the duration of Eden's stay in Rock Creek. "And this is Teddy."

Teddy held on to Sullivan's hand tight and took a step back, moving to the side, as if trying to hide behind one long leg.

"Maybe Teddy should wait a few days," Eden

said, looking at the boy with real concern in her eyes. She tensed as much as the kid had. "Perhaps he's not ready. . . ."

"He's ready," Sullivan said sternly but in a soft voice. "Just let me have a word with him."

He and Teddy walked to the back of the room, leaving Eden to introduce herself to Reese. Sullivan heard Millie's bright voice as he reached the doorway and bent down to look Teddy in the face. They still held hands.

"Reese is a good man," he said softly. "He would never hurt you. Do you understand?"

Teddy nodded once, but he did not relax.

"I know you don't want to stay here," he added, "but Eden wants you to get some smarts, so what are we gonna do?" He shrugged slightly, and so did Teddy. "Besides, I want you to keep an eye on Millie for me. She's just a kid, you know. She'll need you to keep an eye on her, so she won't be afraid. It's scary, sometimes, being in a new place with new people."

Teddy nodded again, and his dark eyes seemed less panicked. He still looked fragile, too small, too vulnerable.

"And I'll be here after school to walk you back to the hotel."

Teddy slipped his hand from Sullivan's and faced the front of the room, head high, spine straight, just a little bit afraid. Sullivan gave him a gentle nudge on the shoulder, and Teddy shuffled forward to join Millie.

The door opened, and three older girls walked in, laughing and hugging their books to their chests. Eden left Millie and Teddy with Reese and walked to Sullivan with a weak smile on her face. She only looked back twice.

As she and Sullivan started to walk through the door, Millie called out, her voice bright and clear, "Good-bye Mama. Good-bye Papa."

Sullivan glanced over his shoulder to see that this time Reese's evident surprise was not so quick to fade.

Chapter 7

Eden was ready to dive into her chores, once they returned from delivering the children into the schoolmaster's hands. She missed Millie and Teddy already, but she knew they needed to be in school. An education was important for both of them, and they needed to meet other children. She knew this, and still she missed them.

Mr. McClure had been fed and was sleeping soundly, so it was time to come up with something to keep Sin busy, something that would keep him away from Webberville. There was so much to be done in the old hotel, that wouldn't be at all difficult.

On the ground floor, not far from the foot of the stairs, there was a chamber, not much more than a pantry really, where residents of the hotel could bathe. A dividing wall separated the area from the lobby, so that someone leaving the room did not step directly into the main public room of the hotel. The room was quite small, and apparently, it was infrequently used. There was, however, a large, deep bathtub that, when scrubbed, would do quite nicely.

She had Sin drag the tub out of the small room so she could sweep and dust. When that was done, he carried the tub back in and watched while she wiped it down. As usual, he didn't say much at all.

Perhaps that was just as well. If his mind drifted without warning to improper thoughts, as hers had so often during the day, silence was probably best.

"There," she said, standing when the chore was finished. "Isn't that better? Why, with a few clean towels and some bath oils and special soaps, this will be a wonderful room for bathing. And this tub is in excellent condition." She looked over her shoulder and smiled at Sin. "It's so large, I'll bet it's even big enough for you."

She glanced down into the deep tub, already longing for a nice, long soak. "Why don't you sit in it, just to be sure?"

"You're kidding, right?" he asked softly.

"No. I'd like to know if it's adequate for the guests, before I go to the trouble of gathering towels and all the rest. I know it'll suit me and the children, but since most of the hotel guests are male, it seems only right that I do my best to make sure the facilities are adequate."

Sin cursed as he stepped past her and into the tub, boots and all. She didn't bother to tell him to watch his language.

"Have a seat," she said, when he continued to stand there.

With a sigh, he complied, sitting down, then leaning back, then stretching out his long legs so the heels of his boots were propped up on the edge.

His long hair hung around his face, dark and silky and lovely.

Eden smiled. "Perfect."

She wasn't prepared for what came next, as Sin's hand shot up and grabbed her wrist and pulled her into the tub with him. Her foot caught the edge of the door, and it slammed closed as she fell into his lap with a squeal.

"Big enough for two," he said softly, his mouth so near her ear she shivered.

She really should scramble out, she knew that, but she fit so perfectly she could not make herself leave. She leaned back and relaxed, resting her legs atop Sin's. His chest made a warm and comfortable chair back; his arms were lovely and so tempting to rest her own arms on she couldn't resist.

"It is a lovely tub," she said softly.

"Lovely," Sin muttered, and his arms slipped around to encircle her. His lips found her neck and he kissed her there briefly. Too briefly. She melted against her warm, hard chair. This was surely sinful, decadent, and shocking, and not at *all* proper.

"I really should get out of here and start cooking something for lunch." She couldn't make herself move. "I told Lydia that I'd cook lunch today, and she really didn't seem to mind. . . ."

"Neither will anyone else," Sin mumbled. The fingers of one large hand began to rock against her side.

Eden felt the mild touch through her blouse, and it sent a quiver to her very core. Oh, she could stay here forever; she could rest in Sin's arms, quite happily, and need nothing else.

"I really should . . ." she began, making a weak attempt to rise.

Sin pulled her back into place. "Not yet," he whispered.

She dissolved against him. Goodness, he smelled and felt so good, she didn't ever want to leave the tub!

"Eden," he whispered against her neck, "you know what I want."

"Sin . . ." she began.

"And I know just as well that I can't have it," he interrupted. "But there are other things we can do," he breathed.

Since she had no real idea of what it would be like to lie with a man, she certainly didn't know what *other things* he could be talking about. "Like . . . kissing?" she guessed as he planted another one on her neck.

"Like kissing," he said. "And touching."

Eden gulped. She had no idea if what he wanted was any less improper than going to his bed. "Touching?"

One hand raked up her midsection to settle lightly over one breast. His fingers brushed gently over the tip of her breast, sending a wave of unexpected tingling through her body. Sin moved his mouth to the other side of her neck, and she shivered deeply when he laid his lips on her skin.

While his fingers teased her breast, the other hand moved lower to brush down her thigh and up again. Anxious and quivering, she shifted slightly and landed on something hard. She shifted again, but it was still there.

"Sin?" she whispered.

He murmured his response against her neck.

"Are you wearing a gun?"

He laughed low and dark without ever taking his mouth from her flesh. "No," he murmured.

"Then what . . .", she began, and then, with a sudden startling clarity, she knew what she was feeling.

She turned about so she was not sitting on the evidence of his arousal, and twisted her head so she could see Sin's face. What she saw there startled her. Last night it had been too dark to see his features and the feelings he might have revealed there, but today sunlight came through the high window in the room and she could see the passion in his eyes. That passion was dark and tempting and more than a little frightening.

"We shouldn't be doing this," she said, placing one hand on his cheek.

"I promise not to hurt you, and I promise not to do anything you don't want me to," he said. "All you have to do is tell me to stop, and I will." He tested her, raising his hand to her breast again, cupping it tenderly, brushing his thumb against the tip.

Eden licked her suddenly dry lower lip, but she didn't tell him to stop. These were surely liberties best saved for a husband, but in truth she saw no harm in a little touching and kissing.

"I'd rather have a little bit of you than nothing at all," Sin whispered. "For as long as we're both here, for as long as we both want it."

She knew she should climb from this tub and call a halt to this, here and now. Sin's hands on her body were driving her crazy. His kisses were passionate and tender and only made her want more. This had to be difficult for Sin, too. More difficult than for her, since he was, after all, a man.

But she didn't want to call a halt to what they were doing. She did not want to give up this moment. Not yet. "Can I touch you, too?" she asked.

Pain joined the passion in his eyes. "Yes."

Shy, she touched his cheek and his neck, trailing her fingers over his warm flesh. His hand settled on her hip, and she trailed her fingers down to his chest. She felt his small nipples beneath his shirt, felt him quiver as she raked her hand down his ribs.

She speared her fingers through his hair. "Why do you wear your hair long?" she whispered. "It's lovely," she added, "but . . . different."

"It reminds me of who I am," he said darkly. "Of where I come from. It should remind you, too," he whispered. "I'm a half-breed, Eden, and a mean son of a bitch when I have to be. I don't belong in anybody's world. Not white, not Comanche." He laid a hand in her hair. "I sure as hell don't belong in your life, not even for a little while. You should slap me right now and tell me to get lost."

Eden's heart warmed as he tried to warn her away. "First of all, I don't believe for a moment that you have a mean bone in your body. Perhaps you've done things that needed to be done, unpleasant, terrible things that you don't speak about." When he opened his mouth to respond she laid a silencing finger over his mouth. "But you are not mean. You're good and noble and . . ." *And I love you.* Oh, she couldn't tell him that. Not yet. "And secondly, you belong in whatever world you make for yourself. I'm very glad that at the moment you're in mine." She laid her mouth over his and kissed him deeply. The touch of his hands changed, as he held her tighter than before, and he plunged his tongue into her mouth and took her breath away.

She couldn't get close enough to him, no matter how she tried. Finally she found a position that satisfied her, her breasts pressed against his chest, one leg hiked up so that she lay comfortable and close to him. The kisses continued unbroken, tongues dancing and reaching, lips coming together and parting just slightly before clamping together again.

The ache in her grew. Sin moaned into her mouth. She felt her skirt slipping up and up, and then felt Sin's hand against her bare leg. She moaned a mild protest as his fingers crept slowly up her thigh, and at her very center she throbbed.

He was going to touch her *there,* and she was so lost in sensation she didn't dare to stop him. She didn't want to stop him.

"Sullivan?"

She lifted her head and looked toward the closed door. "Someone's calling you," she said breathlessly.

"I know," he said, unconcerned.

"Damn it, Sullivan, I know you're in here somewhere. Your horse is still in the stable."

"It's Cash," Sin said with a dejected sigh as the man cursed and ran up the stairs. "Don't worry. He won't think to look in here. He'll give up and head back to the saloon when he doesn't find me in my room."

Moments later Cash ran back down the stairs.

"He'll head back to the saloon, now," Sin said softly, kissing her again and smiling. "I think this is as long as he's been out of the place in the past six months."

The door flew open, and the man in question

stared down with disdain and disappointment on his handsome face.

He barely gave Eden a glance, but settled his cold dark eyes on Sin's face. "I thought you were leaving this morning," Cash said calmly. "But I see you were detained."

Eden straightened her clothes, mortified to be caught in such a position. "Mr. Sullivan has agreed to stay a few more days to help me put the hotel in order for Mr. McClure. The poor man's been so ill. . . ."

Cash lit his eyes on her with pure condemnation. It didn't matter that he wore a very nice suit and a ruffled shirt better suited to a dandy than a gunman. With that mustache and small beard and the void in his eyes, again he looked too much like her mental image of the devil. It was the eyes, she decided. She shuddered. There was no warmth there, not one iota.

"I can see for myself how he's helping you out, ma'am," Cash said crisply. "Are you not aware that your brother will kill Sullivan when he finds out what's been going on?"

Eden lifted her chin, determined not to be afraid. "Nothing's been going on."

Cash folded his arms across his chest. "And what do you call this?"

"We were cleaning the tub," she said indignantly.

The gambler grinned lasciviously. "Well, that's a new name for it."

"Get out of here, Cash," Sin said softly. "This is none of your concern."

"None of my concern?" he asked, incredulous. "I didn't watch your back all these years just to see you end up dead because you couldn't keep your hands off a . . . off a *woman*."

"I said," Sin seethed, "get out. Now."

Cash shook his head in dismay, threw his arms in the air, and stalked away.

With Sin's help, Eden left the tub and straightened her hair, her skirt, and her blouse. Her heart still beat too fast, but Cash's interruption and accusations had ruined the moment. Just as well. Who knows when they would have stopped, otherwise?

She was so embarrassed by her response to Sin's touches and kisses, she couldn't make herself look him in the eye. "I really should see to lunch," she said crisply. "Would you check on Mr. McClure for me? See if he needs anything?"

She spun around and left the small room, not giving him a chance to respond to her question.

He'd never been so tied up in knots he couldn't think straight, but Eden had done it to him, hadn't she? Sullivan considered, for a few long, painful moments, crossing the street, climbing the stairs, and finding a woman, any woman, to ease his pain.

But he didn't want *any* woman. He wanted Eden Rourke.

Cash was right; Jed would kill him. Eden was right; they couldn't lie together. She wasn't a woman who'd give herself to a man without loving him, without expecting a lifetime commitment, and that was something he didn't have to give.

For the first time in his life he wanted a woman to distraction, wanted a woman so hard he couldn't think of anything else, and damned if it didn't have to be a nice girl like Eden Rourke.

He would die before he forced her, before he

hurt her. Damn it, he would not be like the Comanche renegade who'd raped his mother and hung for it before Fiona Sullivan had known she carried a child.

He wondered, as he watched Eden working diligently over the stove, if his mother had ever been as happy as Eden, if she'd ever smiled and laughed and played at falling in love. If she had, that part of her had died the night three bandits broke into her home to rob and rape her. Her father and brother had been out hunting. If they hadn't returned the next morning, she might've died there on the kitchen floor. Hadn't he heard his grandfather say a thousand times, that she, and he, would've been better off if she had died that night?

Better off if there had never been a baby; that's what his grandfather had meant. Better off if his only daughter's only child hadn't been born out of wedlock. Better off if the boy hadn't looked so much like the man who'd fathered him. Sullivan had often wondered if the hate in his grandfather's heart would have been less if the rapist who'd fathered him had been one of the other two, the Smith or the Roberts.

Hellfire, Eden had stirred all these memories up with talk about his hair. Why did he wear it long? To make damn sure everyone knew who and what he was. To make damn sure everyone kept their distance. Especially women. Especially *nice girls*. Eden said she knew who she was. Well, so did he.

"I think I should head on out to Webberville in the morning," he said softly.

Even though Eden didn't speak right away, he knew she'd heard him because she stopped stirring her chicken stew. "Why?" she finally asked.

"You know damn well why."

She kept a stiff back to him, as she resumed stirring her stew, more vigorously this time. "I don't suppose there's anything I can say or do to make you change your mind."

"No," he said, even though he knew it was a lie.

"I just ... can't ...", she said haltingly. "It's just that ..." In frustration, she banged her long-handled wooden spoon on the edge of the tall pot. "If you come back here bleeding, cut, and swollen like you were when I first saw you, I think I'll cry like a baby." She sounded dangerously close to tears already. "I hate to cry," she said angrily. "It gives me a headache, and when it's over I always feel worse instead of better."

"I can take care of myself," he said, touched that she would cry for him, amused that she was worried he couldn't handle himself. "I'll be careful this time."

She spun around and wagged the spoon in his direction. "You'd better be," she said, and then she smiled wanly. "Look at me. I'm being silly. I know you can take care of yourself. I guess I just have a tendency to worry excessively about the people I care for. Goodness knows I worry about Jedidiah all the time."

"I'm not your brother," Sullivan said lowly.

"I know," Eden whispered. "I just want you to come back unhurt. Is that too much to ask?"

Grady had it right. Eden Rourke was an angel. Good and beautiful and innocent. He had no business touching her, kissing her, pushing them both to the edge of something best left unexplored. He knew in that moment what he had to do. For her. For himself. "I'm not coming back."

Her eyes widened and her cheeks paled. "What do you mean you're not coming back?"

"What I said doesn't need any explanation. I'm not coming back to Rock Creek, not until you're gone."

Her fingers gripped the spoon tightly, and for a moment he thought she was going to rush forward and hit him with it. "Have I done something wrong? Have I made you angry?"

Sullivan shook his head. "You haven't done anything wrong. I just can't do this anymore. If Cash hadn't interrupted us this morning we'd still be in the tub."

She lowered her eyes. "I know."

"It's best if I leave. I should've done it this morning, but when you kissed me I forgot all the reasons why I can't stay."

She lifted her eyes. "If I kiss you again, will you change your mind again?"

"Probably," he admitted with a small grin. "So you'd better keep your distance."

She returned to her stew. "I know you're right," she said softly, "but I don't want you to go."

While she had her back to him, Sullivan left the kitchen.

"We could get married," Eden said softly. When she got no response, she looked over her shoulder to see that Sin was gone.

"Just as well," she said to herself as she looked down into the stew. "After all, I've barely known you a week."

A week was plenty long enough, apparently, for her to fall madly in love. It was wonderful; it was terrible; she didn't know what to do.

"Besides," she muttered, "I can't ask you. *You* have to ask me. That's the way it's done."

And that in itself was a problem, since Sin had shown no desire to have a wife and family. In fact, he seemed to hold those hallowed institutions in very low regard. Perhaps with time she could change his mind, but if he left tomorrow she'd never have the chance.

Romantic love was not exactly what she'd expected. She always imagined that when she fell in love her feelings would be similar to what she felt for Jedidiah and her late stepfather. She loved those men dearly, with a protective affection that warmed her heart and soul.

But what she felt for Sin went so much deeper it scared her. It cut to the heart like a sweet, sharp knife. It filled her, in a way that made her sure she must've been somehow empty inside before she met him. Love was so much more complicated than she'd ever suspected.

Apparently Sin didn't share her feelings. If he did, he certainly wouldn't talk about leaving so calmly.

Come tomorrow, she was going to lose him. A single tear fell into the stew.

Chapter 8

Sullivan pushed through the bat-wing doors of Rock Creek's sole saloon, looking for a few minutes of peace and quiet. The place wasn't quiet, not even at this time of the afternoon. At the moment he felt like he'd never know peace again.

Cash gave him a condemning, sarcastic grin. "Well, well, if it isn't the horny man with a death wish."

Sullivan saw no reason to argue. "I'm leaving in the morning," he said, trying to convince himself as much as Cash. Could he really do it? Ride away and not look back? Hell, he had no choice.

"I'll believe it when I see you go," Cash drawled, lighting a cigar and leaning back in his chair. "Tell me where you'll be, and I'll wire you when Miss Rourke leaves town and it's safe for your return."

Sullivan sat at Cash's table, ignoring the gnawing in his gut. He didn't like the idea of never returning to Rock Creek. He had friends here, and the people pretty much accepted him for who he was. But . . .

"She might not leave," he said. "She intends to settle here, and I don't think Eden changes her mind often or easily."

The change that came over Cash was so subtle, any other man might've missed it. His eyes darkened. The muscles in his neck tensed. The fingers of his free hand flexed unconsciously. "It isn't right that you leave Rock Creek *permanently* because of her," he said lowly. He narrowed his eyes and took a long drag on his cigar, obviously thinking hard. "She won't stay," he said with a long puff of smoke. "This place is too rough for her kind, too hard."

"She's tougher than she looks."

"Not tough enough," Cash murmured.

Nate wandered in, stopped a moment to let his eyes adjust to the dimmer light, and then headed for the table. He wasn't falling-down drunk yet, but he would be before the day was over. He sat down beside Sullivan and ordered a bottle.

When there was a battle to be fought and won they were different men, all three of them. Without a cause they were lost—Cash in his cards and women, Nate in his whiskey. And Sullivan . . . Hell, he went looking for fights that weren't his, hiring out his gun and his talent for scouting because he didn't know how to do anything else. And all the time he stayed as distant as possible from the people he worked for and with. Eden was right when she said he liked being alone. He didn't want anyone to depend on him for anything other than his gun. He could almost wish for war again.

"Sullivan here's headed out of town in the morning," Cash said, nodding to Nate.

Nate settled tired eyes on Sullivan. "You just got back."

Cash, cigar in hand, leaned slightly over the table. "He has the poor sense to lust after Jed's sister. Of all the women in Texas, why her?"

"Leave it alone, Cash," Sullivan said softly.

"I will not leave it alone," he said crisply. "It distresses me to no end to see you dangling in the wind over a *woman*. Don't you think she knows exactly what she's doing to you? She knows, and she's loving every minute of it, let me tell you."

"Jed's sister?" Nate said belatedly.

"The blond virgin who's been hanging around the hotel the last couple of days," Cash snapped.

The confusion fled from Nate's face. "Oh, her. She's attractive. Makes good soup, too. Talks too much. Jed's sister?"

Cash shook his head in dismay. "Yes, Jed's baby sister. And Sullivan has been trifling with her."

Nate lifted not-quite-drunk eyes to Sullivan. "That's not terribly smart."

"Even a man who has been pickled for the better part of the past eight years knows better than to . . ." Cash began.

Sullivan rose. He wasn't going to find peace and quiet here, not today.

"Ethel!" Cash shouted, raising his hand in the air. The girl made her way quickly to the table, a smile on her face.

" 'Afternoon, sugar," she said, laying a hand on Cash's shoulder. "What can I do for you?"

Cash grinned, his eyes on Sullivan. "Let's go upstairs and clean the tub, darlin'." He gave the suggestion a decidedly lewd flair.

"Whatever you say," Ethel responded.

The bat-wing doors swung open, and Sullivan

turned his head to see Teddy and Millie standing there, holding hands and setting wide eyes on him.

"Papa," Millie said, her voice high with excitement, "Mama says come quick." With that she turned and ran.

Cash shook his head in dismay. "Jesus, Papa, you allow the younguns in this godforsaken place? What kind of a daddy are you?"

Nate lifted his eyes to Sullivan and grimaced. "Okay, now I'm really confused. I think I need a drink."

Sullivan didn't respond to either of them as he headed for the door.

She wouldn't cry. She absolutely, positively *would not* cry. A single tear trailed down Eden's cheek as she stared at the man on the bed. The afternoon sun streaked through the window and illuminated his pale face. His chest rose and fell as he took shallow breaths. His skin looked like brittle, white, wrinkled paper.

"What's wrong?"

She lifted her head, so glad to see Sin standing in the open doorway her heart skipped a beat. "It's Mr. McClure," she whispered. "He's doing worse this afternoon, much worse, and I don't know what to do."

He shooed the children to their room and stepped inside to stand beside her and look down at the old man. "There's nothing you can do."

Without thinking, she reached out and took Sin's hand, holding on tight. "I thought I could make him better," she whispered, "with tea and soup and clean sheets. I'm such an idiot."

"No, you're not," Sin said softly.

Rico, passing in the hallway, did a double take and then stepped into the room. "What is this?"

Mr. McClure coughed weakly and opened his eyes. "I'm dying; that's what this is."

"Don't say that," Eden insisted. "You're just having a bad day, that's all."

Rico stood at the foot of the bed and looked down. "Is there anything I can get for you, *viejo?*" he asked, a tinge of true kindness in his voice.

Mr. McClure nodded. "You can get me the box that's under the bed."

Rico dropped down and reached beneath the bed, coming up with a small wooden box, no more than a foot long and half again as wide and high. He offered it to Mr. McClure. "This is what you are looking for?"

McClure waved a weak hand. "Open it for me."

Rico did as he was asked, and then he placed the open box on the bed beside the ill old man.

"Miss Rourke," Mr. McClure said, and then he met her eyes and she knew that he was telling the truth; he was dying. "Can I call you Eden?"

"Of course you can," she whispered.

"Such a pretty name," he said. "Paradise. A fitting name for the woman who made my last days good ones."

Sin squeezed her hand, perhaps knowing that she needed comfort at the moment.

"It has been my pleasure to know you, Mr. McClure."

"Grady," he said with a weak smile. "Call me Grady."

She tried to return his smile, but feared it was as weak and watery as his own. "Of course, Grady."

He reached into the box and came up with a

sloppily folded piece of paper. "I want you to have this," he said, offering it to her.

"I don't need . . ."

"Take it," he demanded. "You've made my last days on this earth the best ones I can remember in a very long time. You fed me good food, and made me mind my manners, and smiled at me like the angel you are."

Sin released her hand, and she took the paper Grady offered, unfolding it carefully to reveal that he had given her the deed to the hotel.

"This hotel and everything in it is yours, Eden," Grady said. "Everything . . ."

"Oh, I can't possibly . . ."

Sin rested his hand on her shoulder as the old man insisted, again, that she take what he offered.

"Raise those kiddies here; fix up the place; feed these boys well," Grady whispered, unable to speak any louder. "Make this hotel a home. Please."

She could not refuse him, not now, not like this. "It would be my honor, Grady."

"I'll rest better in heaven if I know you're here." With that, he closed his eyes and resumed his uneven breathing.

She looked at the paper in her hands, the deed. A hotel! She'd planned to open some kind of business to support herself, but as she had enough cash from the sale of her stepfather's business and home to support herself for a while, she had not planned to make those arrangements anytime soon.

"I've only known him two days," she whispered. "How can I accept this?"

"How can you refuse?" Rico asked, his voice as low as hers. "It is what the old man wants."

She looked up at Sin, silently questioning him. "Rico's right," he said. "Grady wants you to have this place. It's all he has to give, and he wants it to be yours."

"I don't deserve it."

"Grady thinks you do, and that's all that matters."

Make it a home, he'd said. For her. For the children. And maybe for Sinclair Sullivan.

Grady died peacefully in the night, and arrangements were made for his funeral. Sullivan knew he couldn't leave now, not today, not while Eden was grieving for the man she barely knew.

She really thought she should've been able to save him, and felt as if she had failed.

He found her in the kitchen, baking pies as if her very life depended on it. A delicious odor filled the air, the aroma of sugar and cinnamon wafting through the hotel. Here, in this room, the smell was intense.

When she saw him standing in the doorway, she lifted her head and pinned her eyes on him. "You're still here," she said softly. "I didn't know . . ."

"I thought I'd stay for the funeral," he explained.

She nodded and returned her attention to the pies she was fashioning, latticing crust across the top of what looked to be a dried apple pie. "What am I going to do with a hotel?" she asked softly. "Didn't Grady have any family? Any relations who are entitled to his property?"

"You don't want it?" Hell, maybe she'd already decided not to stay in Rock Creek. Owning the hotel would tie her here, make it impossible for her to leave.

"It's not that," she said softly. "I think the old place has quite a lot of potential."

Potential? It was a hulking, ugly monster of a building, and if Grady had ever made a profit off the place he hadn't shown it. "Well, Grady never married, that I know of, and if he had any family he didn't keep up with them. I think he was all alone."

Eden sniffled. "That's so sad."

"It was what he wanted," Sullivan said softly.

She turned her back on him, and with a folded towel removed two pies from the oven before setting the new pies in their place.

"I should hate to live my life alone," she said when she turned to face him.

"I'm sure you won't."

No, Eden wouldn't live alone, not ever. Some smart man would snap her up, make her his wife, and they'd have a dozen kids. If she ever did find herself momentarily alone, she'd pick up a couple of strays, like Millie and Teddy.

And him, Sullivan realized with a sudden bout of painful clarity.

Damn, he was one of Eden Rourke's strays.

"I'm glad you're staying for the funeral," she said, stepping toward him. "Grady would appreciate it, I'm sure."

"Webberville can wait a day or two." A knot formed in his throat as Eden drew near. She was going to kiss him, or lay those delicate fingers on his arm, or look at him with those big blue eyes, and he would be a goner. A *stray!*

He trained his gaze over her head. Hell, she'd rescued him as surely as she had those kids. She'd sucked him in neat and easy as you please, with

dimples and blue eyes and a kiss that shook him
to his soul and made him do very stupid things.

He should've seen it before this. He should've
seen it from the beginning.

When Eden was so close he could feel and smell
her in the air around him, he turned on his heel
and bit out a quick good-bye.

The funeral was well attended. It looked as if
everyone in town came out to say good-bye to Grady
McClure.

Eden and the children stood together, but Sin
seemed to make a point of standing as far away
from her as possible. She would've liked to have
him nearby, even if he didn't speak, even if he
didn't comfort her. The way he looked at her, or
more often didn't look at her, it was as if he'd
already left.

The Reverend Clancy, a middle-aged man with
lots of gray hair and a belly that attested to many
good meals, delivered a graveside sermon that was
full of hellfire and damnation. His words comforted her not at all. After the service was finished
he made a point of telling her it wasn't proper for
her to be living in the hotel with *those men,* and
then he consoled her since she was so obviously
distressed—managing to rake his hand across her
bottom in the process. She had just about convinced herself it was a simple mistake when he
reached past her to pat Teddy on the head and
brushed the side of her breast in the process. And
his wife stood just a few feet away!

Most of the mourners went home after the graveside service, but several of Grady's closest friends
and the residents of the hotel returned to the hotel

dining room for the big meal Eden had prepared: pot roast and vegetables, cornbread with sweet butter, and dried apple pie. Lydia was not in attendance. On hearing that Grady had left the hotel to Eden, she'd shaken her head in disgust and walked out. No one had seen her since.

The schoolmaster, Mr. Reese, was in attendance with his wife, Mary, and their baby daughter. The Reeses were a lovely couple, handsome and happy even at this somber time. The way the teacher spoke to Sin and his friends, it was clear they knew one another well, which made her wonder if he also knew Jedidiah. Somehow she could not imagine her brother and the refined schoolmaster as friends, but then, she was learning that not everyone in Rock Creek was exactly who they appeared to be.

Mary Reese smiled sweetly as she bounced the baby and cooed and tried to eat a bite or two. Eden offered to take the baby for a moment and let the woman eat, since Mr. Reese and Sin had their heads together. Mary was reluctant at first, and then handed the child to Eden.

Eden sat in a vacant chair and bounced the baby on her knee. The baby said goo and smiled and reached for Eden's nose, and suddenly everything was a little bit better. Not perfect, perhaps, not even wonderful. But better.

"I've been meaning to stop by," Mary said after taking a couple of bites. "I'm afraid between Georgia and James I barely have a free minute to socialize."

"James is Mr. Reese?"

Mary smiled, a happy smile full of secrets. "Just Reese, most of the time."

Eden bounced Georgia on her knee. "I hope

you'll find an opportunity to come by one afternoon and get acquainted. I really haven't met anyone but the residents of the hotel, though I did briefly meet the shopkeeper's wife, Rose Sutton." The harried woman had been trying to keep her twin boys in line and help three customers at once. "Bless her heart," she added softly.

"Poor Rose; she has her hands full," Mary said. Mary looked Eden square in the eye, unflinching and honest. This was a woman she could like, Eden decided. She had a good face, open and real, without artifice. "I wish Jo was still here," she said softly. "I miss her."

"Jo?"

"Josephine Clancy," Mary said in a lowered voice.

Eden unconsciously wrinkled her nose.

"Yes, the Reverend Clancy's daughter, though I have to point out that Jo is nothing like her father. Thank goodness," she added softly. "A few months ago the good reverend sent Jo to live with her aunt in Houston. That was right about the time he was married. For the third time," she said with a lift of her eyebrows. "I miss Jo terribly," she said, "but she's surely better off with her aunt than she was here, living with that odious father of hers."

They were dancing very close to gossip, and Eden felt almost uplifted. She really could make a home here, if she could have friends and confidants like Mary Reese.

But before the conversation could turn truly juicy, the baby began to fidget. Georgia Reese wanted her mother.

Too soon the Reeses left for home, and only rowdy men filled the dining room. They ate and drank and talked in low voices that grew louder as time passed. Eden was now the only female in attendance, and since she had no appetite she didn't sit and try to eat. She walked around the dining room restlessly and made sure no one's plate was ever empty.

Again Sin was close by, but he kept his distance. Of course he kept his distance. He was ready to leave, would probably ride away in the morning without so much as a glance back in her direction. She tried not to look at him, unless she had no choice.

The men told colorful stories about Grady and the hotel, and the somber mood turned almost jovial. Glasses of whiskey were raised in the deceased's name, and by the time Eden carried the pies into the dining room, the gathering had the atmosphere of a party, not a funeral.

Cash told a story about his brief stay in the hotel and a run-in he'd had with Grady once, an unpleasant experience that was now humorous and touching. The shopkeeper Baxter Sutton, Rose's husband who owned and operated Rock Creek's general store, talked about how Grady had always tried to bargain down everything he bought. He seemed to remember their sometimes unpleasant encounters with great affection.

Eden sliced the pie and began to serve, setting a piece before each man. Keeping busy kept her from crying. Whether she felt like crying because of Sin or Grady, she wasn't sure.

The men continued to talk, and a few of them picked at their pie. When she placed a plate before Baxter Sutton, he looked at it and grimaced.

"Is this dried apple pie? No, thanks," he said, waving a dismissive hand at the dessert. "I've had enough dried apple pie to last any two men a life-time. Swore the last time I'd never eat it again."

He surely didn't mean it as a personal insult, but Eden took it as such. It was all too much, and it hit her at once. She hadn't been able to save Grady, she wasn't going to be able to keep Sin, and what was she going to do with this big old hotel?

She turned quickly away from Sutton, and tears sprung to her eyes.

The laughter in the room stopped with a sudden-ness that startled Eden. Rico, who sat at the table next to Sutton, rose smoothly and quickly, slipping a very large knife from a sheath at his waist and flipping it in his hand with incredible ease. He stepped around Eden and placed the blade at Sut-ton's throat.

"Eat the pie," he said softly.

Sutton's eyes got big as saucers. "Sure, sure," he muttered, careful not to move against the knife that was held casually and expertly at this throat.

"Rico, don't," Eden said softly. "It doesn't mat-ter."

Rico raised dark eyes to her. He was deadly seri-ous. "You made the pie; he is going to eat it."

Moving blindly, since he was unable to move his head without risking injury, Sutton picked up his fork and took a stab at the pie. He raised a small piece to his mouth and took a bite.

"It's good," he said shakily. "Great."

In a lightning-fast move, Rico removed the knife from Sutton's throat. With a satisfied smile on his face he reclaimed his seat to eat his own piece of pie. Eden only had to glance around to see that every man in the room was diligently eating their dessert. Every man but Cash, who stared at her with soulless dark eyes, and Sin, who looked at her with a half smile on his handsome face.

"It is quite good," Sutton said, sounding as if he meant it.

A few other compliments filled the air, some sounding sincere, others prompted, she was sure, by Rico's unnecessary defense.

Going into the kitchen felt like escape. She closed the window against a sudden rush of cool air and began to clean up the mess she'd made fixing supper for all these men.

She was wiping down her worktable when she found the note, a single sheet of paper pinned to the cutting board with a long, thin-bladed knife. Chills danced down her spine as she read the large, crudely fashioned letters.

Get out of town while you still can.

With a great effort, she drew the knife from the cutting board and lifted the note to read it again. Was it a threat of some kind? A warning? She looked toward the window she had just closed and an unpleasant chill danced down her spine. Had someone climbed through that window and left this note for her?

She carried the note to the dining room, rereading it as she walked slowly. The mood of the men was jovial once again, the dried apple pie incident quickly forgotten. Eden didn't hear the laughter or the loud words, and in the crowded dining room she saw only one man.

"Sin?" she said softly, holding aloft the note.

Chapter 9

Sullivan's heart nearly stopped as he read the short note again, running his finger over the tear in the paper where the knife had pierced it. Leaving the others behind, he took Eden's arm and led her into the deserted hotel lobby. A single lantern burned on the front desk.

"You found it on the cutting board," he said calmly, repeating what she'd already told him. "And the kitchen window was open?"

Eden nodded. "Is this a threat of some kind?" she asked in a small voice. "Have I offended someone so much that they want to . . . to run me out of town?" It was clear by the tone of her voice that this was a foreign experience for her, *not* being liked.

"Looks that way. Unless the note was meant for someone else."

"Who?"

"Lydia, maybe." There was no one else who would've been in the kitchen.

"Lydia left here last night and I haven't seen her since. I don't think . . . I think this note was meant for me." She lifted frightened eyes, and the look she cast at him cut to the bone. "Who would want me to leave town so badly that they'd threaten me?"

A surge of anger rushed through Sullivan's tense body. *Cash.* "Don't worry," he said. "I'll take care of it."

The day had taken its toll on Eden. Her eyes were tired, and the smile she gave him was not her best effort. "Somehow I knew you would," she whispered. "You won't leave now, will you? I mean, you don't have to leave tomorrow morning. You can stay until this predicament is resolved, can't you?"

What choice did he have? The idea of leaving Eden here to face Cash alone was inconceivable. It would be like watching a kitten do battle with a panther. "I won't leave until I know you're safe."

She smiled, the corners of her mouth lifting slightly, and her whole face brightened with relief and . . . what was that? Contentment?

"Walk me to my room?" she said softly. "There's nothing left to do in the kitchen that can't wait until morning. Besides, I have this strange urge to check on the children."

He walked beside her. They were halfway up the stairs when she slipped her arm easily through his. He didn't fight it. How could he without giving away too much?

Eden stopped outside her door and looked up at him. The light from the single lamp in the second-story hallway hit her just so, illuminating her softly but completely. "Don't go away," she whispered. "I want to peek in on the children."

She opened the door and slipped inside, and Sullivan watched as she looked down first at Millie, straightening the quilt over the little girl, and then did the same for Teddy, smiling as she pulled the quilt over his shoulder. Sullivan looked around himself, to make sure there was no one lurking in the shadows. Surely Cash would not go that far!

Ah, Daniel Cash was capable of just about anything. He'd be smart to remember that.

Eden closed the door behind her as she returned to the hallway. "They had a hard day, too, and they're both sleeping like babies."

She placed her hand on his forearm, and her fingers, barely touching him, set off a riot of sensations throughout his entire body. Why her? The question Cash had asked whispered in his brain. Why, of all the women in Texas, did he have to lust after Eden Rourke?

He reminded himself of why she was here, why she came to him so easily, why she looked at him this way. He was just one of her strays, a convenient body to keep her from being alone until a better, more suitable man came along.

And he'd made it easy for her, playing along, trying so hard not to offend or distress the perfect Miss Rourke. Maybe he should put a little scare into her himself, show her what she was playing with.

He scooped Eden into his arms and kissed her hard, without warning, without asking, without tenderness. He forced her lips apart and plunged his tongue deep into her mouth, speared his fingers through the hair at the back of her head and held her tight against him. He pressed his arousal against her, letting her know just exactly what she was playing with.

The sudden move shocked her into stillness, but her inertia didn't last long. Her first response was a softening, a subtle yielding, and then she kissed him back hungrily and wrapped her arms around his waist, holding on tight and tasting him deep.

A kiss, no matter how fervent, would not be enough to scare Eden Rourke. He should've known. He pressed her back against the wall and crushed their bodies together, placing a hand on her hip, tracing her curves with his palm, digging his fingers into her flesh and caressing her boldly through layers of brown linen and petticoats. She was so small, so delicate. So passionate in her response.

She wasn't at all afraid. He raised his hand to her breast and stroked her with insistent fingers. A sharp intake of breath revealed her surprise, but she did not move away or protest. He tweaked her nipple and she gasped, but it was a gasp that came from somewhere deep inside, and it spoke not of shock but of pleasant surprise.

He forgot why he'd begun this, as Eden threaded her fingers through his hair and kissed him hard. He wanted to lay her on the floor right there and bury himself inside her, to hell with all the reasons he shouldn't.

She pulled her mouth from his and laid her head against his shoulder. Breathing deeply and erratically, she whispered, "This is happening so fast."

"Not fast enough to suit me," he muttered.

She laughed, breathless and light. "I should get to bed."

"Yes, you should," Sullivan whispered, kissing her again.

She didn't miss his meaning. "I'm sorry. You know I can't. . . ."

"I know. I know," he said as he released her. He'd tried to terrify Eden into letting go of this impossible relationship, and he'd ended up confusing himself. "You're a *nice* girl."

"You make that sound like something bad," she said, a trace of humor in her voice.

"Right now, it is," he muttered.

"Good night, Sin," she whispered.

Sin. The way she said his name sent chills down his spine. It made him want more, in the same way her response to his touch made him want more.

She closed the door in his face.

Sullivan waited until the others had left and only Cash, Rico, and Nate remained in the dining room. He dropped the note so that it fluttered onto the table, landing directly in front of Cash.

"You want to explain this?"

Cash gave the note a quick glance. "The penmanship is atrocious," he said casually.

Sullivan snatched up the note and waved it in Cash's face. "Tell me you didn't send this to scare Eden into leaving Rock Creek," he seethed. "Damn it, Cash . . ."

"I didn't send that ridiculous note," Cash said, glancing up. He was irritated, but not angry. "If I ever decide to take matters into my own hands and rid the town of Miss Rourke, I will do it with some style, you can be assured. This," he said, flicking his fingers at the note, "is an amateurish attempt at harassment."

Rico snatched the paper from Sullivan's hand. "Someone has threatened Eden?"

Cash *tsk*ed and leaned back in his chair. "Take note, Sullivan, and beware. It seems you have competition for Miss Rourke's affections in the form of our own knife-wielding Romeo. When the kid threatened poor Sutton in order to make the man eat a slice of pie, I knew there would be trouble."

Sullivan ignored Cash and tried to think of someone who might want Eden out of town, but came up with nothing. Rico started muttering in quietly spoken Spanish. Nate comforted himself with another drink. It was Cash who came up with an answer.

"I think our lovely Miss Rourke wrote the note, herself," he said calmly.

"What? That's ridiculous." Sullivan towered over a seated Cash with clenched fists.

"Is it really?" Cash asked calmly. "You want to leave town; she doesn't want you to go. What better way to keep you here than to give you a . . . a task, if you will. A mission, perhaps. You and I both know you will not leave town while Miss Rourke is in danger, and that, my dear Sullivan, is why you should know without question that I did not write that ludicrous note."

Cash made sense, so much so that Sullivan sat down, deflated. If not Cash, then who?

With the children off for school, Eden's only decision was which chore to attack first. The hotel was such a wreck, she felt it would be a very long time before she was able to rest.

Since the lobby was the first thing people saw when they entered the building, that would be the first room to be thoroughly cleaned and remodeled.

The long front desk was made of a fine wood. With a little polish and a lot of elbow work it would suffice. The brass bell needed a polishing, too, and the leather-bound guest book was dusty, but it had many blank pages and would serve for some time.

The upholstered furniture in the middle of the large room, a dark green sofa and matching chairs, was faded, but would do for the moment, with a good cleaning, though she could imagine someday replacing the grouping with something truly elegant. She was planning ahead and sweeping the bare wood floor when Sin came down the stairs.

"Good morning," she said with a smile, remembering last night's kiss. Well, it had been much more than a kiss. Goodness, she'd almost told Sin she loved him, right there in the hallway while he had his hands on her in a most improper way. "Did you sleep well?"

"No," he grumbled. "Did you?"

She nodded her head, thinking of the warmth that had rushed through her as she'd huddled beneath her quilt. The dreams that had followed remained with her still. "I slept very well, thank you."

He mumbled something obscene and headed for the dining room.

Eden leaned her broom against the front desk and followed him. "I'll make you some eggs," she said. "And bacon and grits. There are biscuits left from the children's breakfast. I'll warm them for you. . . ."

"Just a biscuit," he said. "And coffee."

"Oh, you need a bigger breakfast than that. . . ."

"I don't want a bigger breakfast," he said with a surly glance over his shoulder. "A biscuit. Coffee."

Eden lifted her eyebrows. "Well, someone certainly got up on the wrong side of the bed this morning.''

Sin sat in a chair at a small round table for two, stretching his long legs out and leaning back slightly to look at her. ''Forget the biscuit and coffee and come here,'' he ordered in a low voice.

With a smile, she went to him. When he indicated that she was to sit in the chair beside him, she did so, perching on the edge of the seat, waiting for what was to come next. Another kiss, perhaps?

But Sin didn't look like he intended to kiss her. He was obviously tense. A muscle high in his cheek jerked, and his hands were placed too casually on his legs as he sat there and glared at her.

''Tell me, Eden, are you most like your mother or your father?''

It was an unexpected question, but one she was glad to answer. Perhaps he simply wanted to know more about her and was shy about asking such personal questions.

''Jedidiah and I both have our father's coloring, but he got mother's curly hair and I didn't. In temperament, I am very much like my mother. Jedidiah is more like our father, everyone says. He died when I was five, and I really don't remember him well, so I can't say for certain.''

''Exactly how are you like your mother?'' he asked softly.

''She had no tolerance for injustice, and neither do I. Blue was her favorite color, and it's also mine, and strawberries make me break out in hives. She couldn't eat them, either.'' She cocked her head and stared at him quizzically. ''Is that the sort of thing you want to know?''

''It'll do,'' he said, setting his eyes on hers. His face hardened, his eyes narrowed, and a muscle in his jaw twitched. She still had no idea why Sin was asking these questions, but it was obviously not a pleasant moment for him.

"Now I'm going to tell you something I've never told anyone else."

Her heart skipped a beat. He must love her, if he was going to share his deepest secrets. She scooted her chair a little bit closer.

"My father was Comanche," he said quietly.

Eden nodded her head once.

"I guess you know, from everything I've said, that I have mixed blood. Comanche and Irish."

"I know," she whispered, ready to tell him that she didn't care. "A lot of people are of mixed blood. Teddy and Rico each had a Mexican parent." Oh, she wanted to make this easy for him, to tell him he had no reason to ever fear telling her anything. "If you think it matters to me . . ."

"You've probably manufactured an idyllic story in the back of your mind, something . . . pleasant and romantic," he interrupted. "A woman who leaves her family behind for love, a man who breaks tradition to be with the woman who's stolen his heart." His eyes grew dark and hard to read. "But the truth is, my father was a Comanche renegade, a thief and a rapist. He and two white men banded together and terrorized three counties for months. Drunk and laughing, they robbed, burned, and murdered. One night they raided my grandfather's farm and found my mother there alone. They beat and raped her, and then they left her for dead."

Tears welled up in Eden's eyes. She reached out to touch Sin, but he waved her back with an impatient hand.

"She was fifteen at the time."

Eden stifled a cry, biting her lower lip and grasping her hands in her lap.

"My father and the other two were hanged for their crimes before I was born, before my mother even knew I existed. Fiona Sullivan, who from all accounts was a lovely young woman before the attack, was never quite right after that night. She was, for lack of a better word, crazy. When I was fourteen she went down to the river and didn't come back. She drowned herself," he said without emotion.

He looked her in the eye, made certain she was paying attention to every detail. There were no tears in those eyes, no hint of the pain she knew he had to feel. "My grandfather assured me she killed herself because I looked more like my father every day."

She felt the pain for him, wanted so badly to take his heartache away. "I'm so sorry," she whispered. "But you have to know that it doesn't matter to me. . . ."

"Don't tell me it doesn't matter," he said. "All my life I've watched families walk down the street, the kids looking and walking and talking like their parents, sometimes looking like little miniatures of their mother or father. And I always ask myself— Who will I be like? My father, the violent, drunken thief, or my mother, the crazy woman who killed herself when she couldn't stand to look at me anymore." He offered his arm to her, wrist up, pushing up the white cotton sleeve to bare his flesh for her. "See this blood?" he asked softly. "That's the blood that runs in these veins. I thought you should know."

Eden didn't even try to stop the silent tears as she rose from her seat and sat on Sin's knee, surprising him. She placed her arms around his neck and laid her head on his shoulder, took a deep breath, and burrowed her nose against his warm neck. "I'm so sorry."

He remained stiff and unyielding. "I've told you where I come from, who I am. You should run like hell," he whispered, "not crawl into my lap."

She took a deep breath, inhaling his scent. There was such unexpected comfort in being this close. She could only hope that somehow she gave him the same comfort, when he needed it most. "Sinclair Sullivan, how could I possibly run from you when I love you so much that whatever hurts you hurts me more?"

He didn't move or respond at all, so she lifted her head to look into his eyes, so she could see his hard and beautiful face. "I love you, Sin."

"Don't say that," he said softly. "You're supposed to walk away when you hear the truth. Hell, woman, you're supposed to run away."

She smiled and leaned forward to give him a gentle kiss, a brief peck on the lips. "In case you haven't figured it out yet, I don't always do what I'm supposed to."

"No kidding," he muttered.

She made herself comfortable in his lap and placed her head on his shoulder again, and this time he wrapped his arms around her. At that moment, she knew she belonged right here. In Rock Creek, in this hotel, with Sin.

"I know, with all my heart, that you're a good man, Sinclair Sullivan. In spite of your parents and your past, you've become strong and decent and kind, and you should put those needless worries from your mind." She lifted his hand to her lips and laid her mouth against his wrist, there where the blood flowed. She traced the veins with her fingertip. "This is your blood and no one else's," she whispered. "And I love you," she added softly.

"Don't."

She lowered his hand but continued to hold it, as she settled herself more comfortably in his lap. "Too late." She sighed. "I'm much too far gone to change my feelings now. Why, I believe I fell in love with you the first time I looked into your . . . eye."

For a few moments all was silent, the room, the town, the world. If she tried, Eden could hear her heartbeat and Sin's, beating in a kind of soothing rhythm.

"Do you know how much I want you right now?" Sin finally asked softly, breaking the silence.

She adjusted herself just a little in his lap and smiled widely. "Why, yes, sir, I believe I do."

Chapter 10

"When the hotel is in good shape, I want to work in the garden out back," Eden said as she polished the front desk. "Just think how lovely it will be to sit out there in the spring, with flowers blooming and birds singing, and benches that don't wobble back and forth when you sit on them." She smiled widely at Sin, who sat casually on the green sofa, his fine, denim-clad legs extended to their full length as he watched her intently. "We can sit out there at night, after a long day, and"—*and you can kiss me again*—"and relax."

"I may not even be here in the spring," Sin said softly. "You know that."

She was not ready to accept the notion that Sin would leave her, no matter how often he mentioned doing just that. "I know no such thing," she said primly.

If only he would let go of the pain of the past, of his fears of becoming like his father or his mother. The morning's revelation told her so much about Sin and why he was the way he was. No wonder he mistakenly thought he wanted to be alone.

She left her polishing rag on the front desk and joined Sin on the sofa, sitting beside him and laying her hand possessively on his forearm. "I truly hope you will be here in the spring," she said sincerely. "I cannot imagine what my days here would be like without you."

Sin hesitated just a moment before putting his arm around her. It was all the invitation she needed to snuggle against his side, settling herself there comfortably. "Besides, Rock Creek is your home. You belong here. I would feel terrible if you left on my account. You don't want to make me feel guilty, do you?"

"I have no home and I don't belong anywhere," he said crisply. "There's no need for you to feel guilty."

She turned her head, raised herself a little, and kissed Sin soundly on the lips, answering an irresistible urge; how could she be this close to Sin and *not* kiss him? Impossible.

He held her tight and kissed her back, his arms around her, his thumb lightly brushing against the side of her breast.

She leaned back slightly, tipping her head to deepen the kiss, and Sin came along with her. Bodies aligned, lips locked. They seemed to magically dissolve together, melting and then melding into each other, growing closer and closer with every passing heartbeat. She wondered if he felt the same strange compulsion to continue the kiss, as if to end it was unthinkable.

"I love you," she whispered when he took his

mouth from hers to kiss her throat. She threaded her fingers through his hair and pushed the long strands back so she could see his face as he lifted his head slowly. She didn't mean to cause pain with her confession, but it looked as if that was what flickered in Sin's eyes, the pain he had been too strong and stubborn to reveal that morning when he'd told her about his mother and father.

"No, you don't," he protested.

"Don't tell me I can't love you," she insisted. "I know my own heart."

"Honey, trust me." He ran his hand along her side and cradled her hip. She shivered in response. "This is not your heart talking. It's not *love* that makes you quiver and shake and moan."

She smiled widely, even though he did not.

"Excuse me."

They both turned their heads to see a relatively sober Nate standing over the couch. He stood taller than usual, even though his fine suit was rumpled. After a moment, he swayed just slightly.

"Jed's here." He gave them a wink. "I thought you might like to know."

Sin and Eden both jumped, moving up and apart, and Eden tried to straighten her hair. "Jedidiah's here? Already? Really?"

Nate grinned and turned to walk away. "No, not really. I just thought it was my duty to remind you two that you're headed for serious trouble, smooching in the lobby like that. Hell, Sullivan, this is a hotel. And you already have a room."

"Well," Eden said indignantly, her heartbeat slowly returning to normal. "That was rather rude."

"But he's right," Sin said. "Damn it, Eden, why can't I keep my hands off of you?"

She stood, smiled, and offered him her hand. "There's no need to curse."

Sin took her hand and stood. "There's every reason in the world to curse, damn it."

She leaned into him. "Nate was, perhaps, right about one thing. The lobby is not the place to kiss. Why, anyone might walk in at any time."

"Yep." He took her in his arms and pulled her close. "So, how about we . . . clean the tub for a few minutes?" He glanced toward the wall near the foot of the stairs and the small room beyond that wall. Her heart leaped.

"Excellent idea."

Twenty-nine years old, and no one had ever told him they loved him before today. Sullivan didn't believe the words Eden said so easily, couldn't make himself believe that she felt that deeply. She simply didn't know how to express her newly discovered desire in any other way; she didn't know another way to explain away the heat they generated.

Any other possibility was too frightening to consider.

He'd stayed with her all day, moving furniture and opening windows that had been shut too long, and constantly keeping an eye out for any threat, kissing her, holding and touching her in the tub behind closed doors. Reminding himself, when he wanted to reach for more, that this was all he could have.

The day had been a quiet one, and there had been no more mysterious notes. He had to consider the possibility that Cash was right, that Eden had written the note herself to keep him from leaving town. He didn't think she had a devious bone in her gorgeous body, but he also knew she would do anything, *anything,* to keep the people she considered *hers* safe. The woman would do anything if she thought it would benefit one of her damned strays.

Eden was in the kitchen starting a pot of chicken stew for supper, and Sullivan stood alone in the center of the newly cleaned lobby. The front door was open to let in fresh air, and bright afternoon sunlight fell across a newly burnished floor. Eden had scrubbed and beaten and swept and polished until the room gleamed. The woman transformed everything she touched.

Teddy and Millie appeared in the doorway, holding hands as they often did these days. Eden had transformed the children as surely as she had this room, making their lives bright, giving them hope, offering them a future they had not had before meeting her. It would be easy to dismiss Eden Rourke as an interfering sanctimonious do-gooder but for one small detail: everything she did came from the heart.

Teddy's long hair fell across his face, and when he lifted it Sullivan's moment of peaceful reflection ended. Tear tracks were clear on the boy's face.

"What happened?" he asked gruffly.

Teddy shrugged his shoulders, dismissing the question, but Millie was quick to answer. "Frank and Jack Sutton made fun of Teddy's hair after school. They said he looked like a girl, and one mean boy, Billy Newton, said he was a freak because he can't talk." She lifted her chin haughtily. "I threw a rock at Billy, but I missed."

He'd never had the desire to go after a child before, but Billy Newton, the bully, deserved a good scare of his own. And those Sutton kids had never been anything but trouble. Words hurt as much as fists, as the tear tracks on Teddy's face proved.

Sullivan kept his voice calm. "I'm sure Eden will tell you it's not nice to throw rocks, but . . . I'm just sorry you missed."

Millie smiled widely, but Teddy remained visibly distressed. Hadn't the kid had enough problems in his short life without having to deal with the fact that he was different?

"Millie, Eden's in the kitchen. You go tell her you're home and that Teddy and I have an errand to run this afternoon."

"Okay," she said, skipping off to the dining room, winding past the tables toward the kitchen.

Sullivan joined Teddy in the doorway. "Come on," he said, placing a hand on the boy's thin shoulder and leading him onto the boardwalk.

He had pretended to be this boy's father, when it was necessary, but there was no real bond between them. No relation, no obligation. Still, he and Teddy had a lot in common, and he felt he owed the kid . . . something. A few words of advice, maybe. Words of wisdom from Sinclair Sullivan? What a joke.

"One thing you have to learn early on is that there are people out there who are just mean," he said, a hand on Teddy's shoulder and his eyes on the boardwalk ahead. Hell, he had to try. He had to do something. "Some are just born that way. They come into the world mean and stay that way until the day they die. There's not much we can do but put up with them, most of the time."

Teddy nodded, but kept his dejected head down.

"It would be easier if everyone were like Eden, don't you think?" Sullivan said softly.

Teddy looked up as he nodded in agreement.

"She's been good to you."

Teddy nodded again.

"She's a good woman," Sullivan said, meaning it.

He came to a halt and looked down at the kid. Teddy was small for his age, if Eden was right about him being nine. The kid had an almost delicate look, with his thin shoulders and arms and legs, and those big brown eyes in a narrow face. He looked like he would break, so easily. Black hair fell past his shoulders, as Sullivan's did, and he peeked warily past a strand that fell across his face.

"It's up to you," Sullivan said, nodding to the business behind them. "What do you say?"

Teddy looked through a dirty window, and then he nodded his head slowly. He reached up to nervously take Sullivan's hand as they entered the barber shop.

Eden stirred the cornbread fixings as she talked with Millie. The child was anxious to tell all about school, the good and the bad, and had already shared the day's excitement. Oh, she wanted so badly to give Teddy a hug! Where on earth had Sin taken him?

Millie was, with the exception of the rock incident, fitting in well at school already. She'd made friends, with Carrie Brown quickly claimed as her *most bestest* friend. While Mr. Reese might not look like your everyday average schoolmaster, he must've had some gift for his chosen profession. Millie adored him, and she was always excited to share with Eden what she'd learned that day.

Rock Creek was a good place to live, Eden had decided, a good place to raise a family.

"Millie, do you like it here?"

"Oh yes, Ma . . . Aunt Eden," she said. "I like it very much. It isn't as green as home, but the people are nice to me and I have new friends. Carrie and I played together at recess again today, and she's helping me with my letters." She leaned in close as if to share a secret. "She says my *Ms* are much improved."

Eden's smile faded at the way Millie stumbled over *Ma . . . Aunt Eden.* Things had happened so quickly; momentous changes had taken place in a matter of weeks. More changes were sure to come.

"Millie, I know you loved your mother very much," Eden said softly, putting aside the cornbread to join Millie, to sit on the lone chair in the kitchen and pull the child onto her lap.

Millie nodded and placed her head on Eden's shoulder.

"And I know your mother loved you, too, and would want you to be happy and have a good home."

Another nod was her answer.

"Would you like for me to be your mama for real?" she asked. "Not a game this time, not pretend. I could be your . . . your new mother."

Millie lifted her head to look at Eden. "Not pretend this time?"

"Not pretend."

"Can Mr. Sullivan be my papa?"

Eden smiled. "Maybe. We'll have to see about that."

Millie draped her arms around Eden's neck. "I think it's a very good idea. Can Teddy be family, too?'' she asked. "I always wanted a brother, and he needs a new mama just like me.''

"Absolutely," Eden said.

Eden took a moment to enjoy the warmth she felt, the indisputable realization that all was right with the world. How strange to feel this rightness now. The hotel she'd been given was a run-down disaster, someone was trying to scare her out of town, and there was still no sign of Jedidiah. Sin wanted her body. He liked to touch and kiss her, but he was being stubborn where love was concerned. He was so determined to protect his heart, even as his body reached for hers.

But she loved Sinclair Sullivan with all her heart, and she loved these children. She was even beginning to like this old hotel. Nothing would stop her from making herself a family in the midst of turmoil. Nothing and no one.

After Teddy was finished he held his head higher, his spine straighter. There were no more tears in his eyes, no more fear on his face.

And it was just a haircut. Sullivan ruffled the short, silky strands as they walked back to the hotel. "Looks good, kid," he said. No one would give Teddy any grief about his hair, though it was likely that as long as he remained small for his age and silent, he would have trouble with narrow-minded people, bullies like Billy Newton and the Sutton twins. Maybe what Teddy really needed was a lesson in fighting dirty.

Teddy stepped into the hotel, and Sullivan saw the hairs on the kid's back, hairs the barber had missed with his brush. Normally he'd take the shirt off here and now and shake it out, but since Eden had spent all day cleaning this lobby, he didn't think that was a good idea.

"Let's head out back," he said, giving Teddy a gentle shove in the direction of the rear door. "You've got hair on the back of your shirt, and you want to look good for Eden, right?"

Teddy nodded and headed for the door. They stepped into the neglected enclosed garden, and Sullivan closed the door behind them. The kid turned his back and waited, perhaps for Sullivan to brush off the hairs, but there were so many of the long, dark hairs a good shaking out was in order. Sullivan reached down and took the shirt in his hands, and pulled it swiftly over Teddy's head.

And then he stopped, the shirt hanging in his hand, forgotten. "Who did this to you?" he whispered.

Teddy's narrow back was badly marked with long, thin scars that spoke of unquestionable abuse with a weapon like a whip or a quirt. The scars were months old, some maybe years old, and while they would fade with time they would never completely disappear. They were too deep.

Teddy turned and reached for his shirt, obviously anxious to cover up his scarred back. Sullivan shook out the shirt, as he'd originally intended, and helped the kid slip it back on. All the time his blood roared. He'd never been so angry.

"Let's sit over here a minute," he said, heading for the bench against the hotel wall. Teddy followed, sitting obediently beside him. He didn't know what to say, and yet it seemed like he should say something.

Teddy reached up and tugged at Sullivan's long hair, a question in his eyes.

"You think I should cut my hair, too?" he asked, and Teddy nodded once. "Not today," he said. Maybe not ever. Teddy needed to fit in, to blend, to be one of the average children at school. Sullivan knew he would never blend in anywhere. He had no desire to try.

More advice. Hellfire, he was *not* good at this!

"You don't have to talk if you don't want to," he said. "I know Eden would love it if you did, and it would make your life easier. But if you don't feel like talking"—he shrugged his shoulders—"then don't. I reckon if you've ever got something important to say, you'll speak up."

Teddy relaxed and leaned his head against Sullivan's arm, trusting and warm in spite of what he'd been through.

Sullivan got angry all over again. "A man who would hurt a child the way you were hurt is no kind of man at all," he said, unmistakable rage in his voice. "My grandfather and my uncle used to backhand me at the drop of a hat, and any excuse for a whipping would do. But even they never . . . Damn it, Teddy, I wish you would tell me who did that to you. I swear, I'd hunt the man down and kill him with my bare hands."

Teddy came up on his knees and faced Sullivan. There was pain in his eyes, a fragility that made the kid look as if he could shatter at the slightest touch. His eyes looked suddenly ancient, old and deep and full of secrets. Those eyes were at odds with a face gone pale, a narrow nose, a quivering lip.

The boy leaned close, placing his mouth near Sullivan's ear. He made a small sound, a catch from deep in his throat, emitted a soundless breath of air, and then he whispered hoarsely, "It was my Uncle John."

Sullivan slipped an arm around the kid and pulled him close, and Teddy continued in an even lower voice. "I already killed him."

Chapter 11

Sullivan gathered Teddy onto his lap and made the boy look him in the eye. "What do you mean, you already killed him?"

Teddy remained silent, but he began to shake slightly, as if he'd caught a sudden chill.

"Please tell me."

It was a struggle, he could see that, but Teddy finally spoke again, his voice as soft as before. "Uncle John called me bad names, and he called my mother bad names. She was dead, and still he called her bad names, all the time." There was anger in his soft voice, and confusion. "He hit me with his lash and put me to bed with no supper, just because I yelled at him and told him not to call my mother a whore." His large dark eyes filled with tears. "When I went to bed I wished for Uncle John to die. I wished as hard as I could. I laid awake most of the night, just wishing for him to die. I wished out loud, whispering into the pillow while my back stung and my stomach growled. The next morning, my uncle's mule kicked him in the head and he died, just like I wished. So you see," he said, his voice growing raspy, "I killed him."

"Teddy," Sullivan said as he took the kid's face in his hands, horrified and relieved. "You cannot wish someone dead."

"But I did." The tentative voice was almost gone again. "Don't tell anyone." The last word was nothing more than a whisper of air.

"I won't," Sullivan promised. "But you have to believe me. You did not kill your uncle. What happened to him was just an accident."

Teddy, silent once again, looked as if he wanted to believe that was true. He didn't, though, not quite.

Hellfire, Eden's interfering ways were rubbing off on him. He wanted to fix this kid's life. He wanted to make everything right for Teddy.

"I've never lied to you, have I?"

Teddy shook his head.

"I'm not lying to you now. You are not responsible, in any way, for your uncle's death."

Teddy bit his lip.

"I'm not sorry the son of a bitch is dead, and I imagine you're not sorry, either."

A soft shake of the head and lowered eyes was his answer.

"But not feeling sorry isn't the same as being guilty."

Teddy moved closer. "Did you ever wish your grandfather and uncle dead when they hit you?" he asked, his voice a raspy murmur no louder than a soft gust of autumn wind.

"Yes," Sullivan admitted. "Many times."

"Did they die?"

Sullivan shook his head. "No."

Teddy looked relieved as he climbed down off of Sullivan's lap.

"Let's go show Eden your haircut," Sullivan said as he stood and ruffled the newly shortened strands.

Teddy nodded and whispered, "I'm thirsty, and my throat hurts a little. Do you think Aunt Eden has lemonade?"

Sullivan let the kid take his hand as they walked into the lobby. "I think if you ask her for lemonade she'll be more than happy to make it for you."

Rock Creek was turning out to be a lovely, lovely town. The next five days passed in a magical way, perfection from sunup to sunset. Teddy spoke. Not loudly or often, but he did make his presence and his wishes known, on occasion. Something had happened on the afternoon he had his hair cut, something between Teddy and Sin. They were closer than ever, two almost silent males who had somehow become the best of friends.

On Sunday she and the children had gone to church, in spite of the fact that it would mean listening to Reverend Clancy. Mary Reese was there, with her baby and her husband, and Eden was able to speak to the woman for a few minutes after a depressing service that somehow ended up being about Jezebel and harlots in general. Their conversation didn't last nearly long enough, as Mary's baby and her husband were both hungry. Eden felt confident that one day she and Mary would be friends. The thought warmed her heart and made Rock Creek an even more inviting place.

The hotel looked better already, and Eden had

begun to see the true potential of the establishment. There had been no more threatening notes, so she dismissed the first one as a bad joke or a warning meant for someone else—Lydia, perhaps.

Millie was adjusting to Rock Creek more easily than anyone. She called Eden Mama and had Teddy doing the same. Millie was very protective of her brother, and he followed her everywhere as if it were his duty to watch over her.

Eden and Sin cleaned the tub on occasion, retreating to the small room in the middle of the day while the children were at school or late at night while they were asleep. All they did was kiss, and touch, and laugh, even though Sin made it clear he wanted more. That was one reason the tub was a perfect place for their inappropriate but dazzling rendezvous. Once they settled in, there wasn't much room to maneuver. It was a relatively safe place to test the dangerous boundaries they occasionally threatened to cross.

Sin hadn't mentioned Webberville in days.

The children were asleep, and the other residents of the Rock Creek Hotel were across the street at the saloon, entertaining and being entertained. Eden sat on the first flight of steps, looking down into the lobby. Sin stood at the foot of the stairs, cast in an odd half-light. His long hair shadowed his face so she could not see it as clearly as she would've liked. Still, she knew that face so well, she needed no light at all.

"Cash is trying to put together some big poker game tonight," Sin said softly. "He said if I don't show up he's going to call me out."

Eden smiled. "Would he do that?"

Sin shook his head. "No."

"Are you going to play?" she asked. "It's all right. I don't mind staying here by myself."

"No," he said, taking the first step. "I'm not going to play poker tonight."

She smiled as he climbed the stairs and sat next to her, wrapping an arm around her waist.

"One dangerous game at a time is enough for me."

"Is this dangerous?"

"Deadly." He kissed her then, as she had known he would.

She knew him so well by now, the marvelous feel and scent of him, the way he tilted his head when he kissed her, the manner in which he encompassed her with his arms, his whole body, within seconds of a simple meeting of their mouths.

She laid back against the stairs, the hard ridge of a step against her back, Sin above her. Her arms encircled his neck, his hair fell across their faces, sheltering them from the light as they kissed.

"You taste so good," he said as he moved his mouth to her throat and lightly sucked at a particularly sensitive spot. "And I swear, I dream about the way you smell."

She smiled and relaxed, her legs spreading so that Sin rested between them. It just seemed more comfortable this way. "I dream about this," she whispered. "About the way your body feels over mine."

He rose to look down at her. "And you're asking me if this is dangerous?"

"You're right. Someone might catch us here," she whispered.

"The tub." Sin took her hands and pulled her to her feet, and together they walked to the tiny room off the lobby. He lit the single candle in the room and closed the door, climbed into the dry tub, and pulled her in after him. She fell on top of him, a soft peal of laughter erupting from her lips.

She couldn't get enough of kissing Sin. She wanted more. Deeper, longer, more complete. Here, behind the closed door, he touched her, stroking her breasts, caressing her hip. And she touched him, her hand on his chest and his neck, her fingers dancing down to his slim hips.

Feeling bold tonight, she flicked open the first few buttons of his shirt and peeled the fabric apart to kiss the base of his throat. She felt his pulse with her mouth, tasted his skin with her tongue. When he moaned, she felt the vibration with her lips and kissed him harder, sucking against his flesh. It seemed like she couldn't ever get enough.

When she raised her lips, he flicked open a couple of her own buttons and kissed her just as she had him. She leaned her head back and sighed, unable to decide which was better, kissing or being kissed. He moved his head lower, trailing his lips over the beginning swell of her breasts.

Every time they came to the tub, they went a little further. She knew this, accepted it, even anticipated it. When Sin flicked open a few more buttons and slipped his hand inside her blouse, she didn't protest, but held her breath as he placed his hand beneath her chemise and over her bare breast. She felt his touch all over, deep inside, between her legs.

She kissed him deeply while he very tenderly caressed her breast. What she wanted more than anything was to take his shirt off, take her blouse off, and press their bare flesh together. The insistent pulsating inside her increased, became unrelenting.

"Sin," she whispered as he trailed his fingers over her nipple, "if we were married, what would happen next?"

He stopped, became very still beneath her. "What do you mean?"

"I want something, and I don't know exactly what it is," she said breathlessly. "You're going to think I'm hopeless, I know, but until I met you I'd never even kissed a man. Well, not properly, anyway. I know, sort of, what happens. But not really. I don't really, really know. I have so many questions, but I don't even know enough to know what to ask. Tell me. Tell me what comes next."

"You're trying to kill me, aren't you?" he whispered hoarsely.

"No." She squirmed a little, trying to bring herself closer to Sin, if that was possible. She touched his neck with one finger, there where a bead of sweat had popped up. It was no surprise that he was perspiring. It had gotten awfully hot in this small room.

He took a deep breath. "First of all, we'd take off all our clothes."

"All of them?"

"Every stitch."

"Oh," she said, deciding right away that she wanted, very much, to see Sin without a stitch of clothing on. She trailed her finger down his throat. "Then what?"

"We'd lie down in the bed together, and kiss some more. Hard, long, deep kisses that would last as long as we wanted them to. I'd kiss you here"—he tweaked her nipple and she shivered—"and here." Using his other hand, he ran the tip of a finger on the inside of her elbow. "And here again," he said, brushing his palm over her breast. "And maybe here." He trailed his finger from her elbow, raked it slowly down her arm, and then laid his hand over her navel. "I'd kiss you until your body throbbed."

"It already does," she whispered.

"Don't tell me that." He sounded as if the idea pained him, more than a little.

She settled herself more comfortably against Sin and slipped her hand inside his shirt to caress his chest. "Then what?"

He sighed deeply. "You really don't know?"

"Really."

"You truly are trying to kill me," he muttered, shifting his body beneath hers and hiking her skirt to her knees. He pushed up her wide-legged drawers and settled his hand comfortably on her thigh, just above her knee.

"No, I'm just curious. What comes next?"

"I'd lie on top of you."

"Like on the stairs?" she asked.

"Like on the stairs. You'd spread your legs wide, and I'd touch you, to make sure you were ready."

"Ready?"

"Wet," he said, his voice raspy.

"Oh."

His hand rocked on her thigh. "Then I would . . . we would . . . we'd fit together. I'd push myself inside you."

Her heart skipped a beat. "And that's it?"

He laughed lightly. "Honey, that's just the beginning."

She sighed deeply. "So you would . . . stay inside me for a while?"

He shivered from head to toe. "Eden, please."

"Well, I shouldn't be ignorant forever," she insisted. "If anyone's going to tell me about such things, I want it to be you."

He groaned. "You ask a lot of a man."

She kissed him briefly and urged him to continue.

"We . . . move," he whispered. "All the way in and back out again. Slow at first, and then . . . faster."

"For how long?"

"Not very damn long at this rate," he muttered. "But long enough."

"Long enough for what?"

"For . . . we . . . It's hard to explain, but it feels better than anything you can imagine."

"Better than this?" she whispered as she kissed him again.

"Better than this."

She moaned against his mouth. Oh, she wanted more. She wanted to know what *better than this* felt like.

Sin's hand moved slowly up her leg, until he was almost touching her where she throbbed for him. His fingers danced across her inner thigh while his hand moved, ever so gently, over her bare breast.

He buried his face against her neck and mumbled something unintelligible.

"What?"

He lifted his head and looked at her. "Marry me. Tonight. Right now."

She smiled widely. "You shouldn't joke about such matters."

"I'm not joking. I'm deadly serious. I want you so bad I don't think I'll make it through the night without you."

"That's not a good enough reason to get married," she whispered. "Is it?"

He gave her question serious thought, and while he thought, his hands raked almost mindlessly over her body. "No, it's not," he admitted.

Her heart sank, but then he continued. "But I've never felt this way about any woman. I didn't think I ever would. It's more than wanting you, more than lust." He kissed her, sweet and much too short. "Like it or not, you're mine, Eden Rourke, and I want to do this right. For once in my life, I want something good and proper and honorable. I want you to be my wife. Now. Say yes."

She grinned and held him tight. "Yes."

Moving slowly, they untangled their limbs and stood to climb out of the tub. "Are you sure?" Sin asked as he took the candle from the shelf and opened the door. "No doubts?"

"No doubts," she said.

He snuffed out the candle and led her to the stairway. At the foot of the stairs, he stopped. His head was bent, so she could not see his face. When he lifted his head he gave her a look that made her heart stop. Maybe Sin didn't know it yet, but he loved her. She saw it in his eyes, felt it in the way he touched her.

"Wait right here," he said.

She sat on the bottom step and waited, certain that her wobbly legs would not hold her up long enough for Sin to fetch the preacher. A few seconds later she thought to refasten the buttons of her blouse.

Nate was pretty far gone already, but he remembered most of the words to a wedding ceremony.

He leaned against the front desk and did his best, having terrible trouble with words containing the letter *L*. *Sullivan* and *lawfully* gave him fits. Before the ritual was over, he hoisted himself up to sit on the front desk, his long legs dangling over the sides as he told them they were both crazy, and then he pronounced them man and wife.

As Sullivan kissed his bride, Nate laid down on the front desk for what he said would be a short nap.

Sullivan scooped Eden into his arms and carried her up the stairs, flying up the first flight, kissing her as he carried her down the hallway, and then racing up the stairs to the third floor. By the time he reached the doorway to his room, Eden was laughing. Completely relaxed in his arms, her head fell back and she laughed with a joy such as he had never known or seen before.

After placing Eden on her feet near the foot of the bed, he lit a lamp. He'd waited too long for this; he was not going to fumble around in the dark. He wanted to see Eden, to see her body revealed as she took off her clothing, to see her eyes when he sank into her.

She wasn't laughing anymore, but her smile was full of joy, the expression on her face seductive, and shy, and inviting. "What now?" she whispered.

He went to her, towered above her and laid his hands on her shoulders. "I'm not going to tell you this time," he whispered. "I'm going to show you."

She shivered as he ran his hands down her arms, lifted her face to ask for a kiss he gladly gave her.

As much as he wanted to have her, as much as he ached, he wanted to make this last. There would only be one first time, only one.

He took the pins from her hair and let it down,

running his fingers through silky strands that fell halfway down her back. The fair strands were shiny and thick and only slightly wavy. When they'd been traveling he'd watched Eden brush her hair and then twist it back up again, but he had never seen her like this, with those golden strands down around her shoulders and falling down her back, loose, soft, as she stared up at him and waited.

The buttons of her blouse slipped through his fingers, and the simple cotton parted for him, revealing inch after inch of perfect flesh. When he'd gone as far as he could, he lifted the blouse from the waistband of her skirt and pulled it over her head. Beneath it she wore a low-cut chemise, lace and a pink silk ribbon decorating the valley between her breasts. Her body was as beautiful as he'd imagined, soft and creamy pale, perfect in every curve. The tempting swell of her breasts rose with every breath she took. He trailed his fingers over the rising flesh before untying the pink ribbon and unbuttoning more buttons to bare her torso.

He laid his mouth over her coral pink nipple, tasting her gently, barely sucking her flesh into his mouth. Holding her tight, he savored the scent and feel of her, the way she touched his hair and sighed. He suckled her harder, drawing the nipple deep into his mouth, and she shuddered and held on tight, her breath coming fast and hard.

Her calico skirt followed the chemise, pooling on the floor. Her petticoat dropped next. He rolled her stockings down, resting on his haunches while he took his time with the chore, kissing her bare knees and slipping her shoes off, then tossing them aside.

All that was left was a pair of loose, flimsy drawers, as lacy and fancy as the chemise. He untied the

Introducing Ballad,
A LINE OF HISTORICAL ROMANCES

*A*s a lover of historical romance, you'll adore Ballad Romances. Written by today's most popular romance authors, every book in the Ballad line is not only an individual story, but part of a two to six book series as well. You can look forward to 4 new titles each month – each taking place at a different time and place in history.

But don't take our word for how wonderful these stories are! Accept our introductory shipment of 4 Ballad Romance novels – a $23.96 value – ABSOLUTELY FREE – and see for yourself!

*O*nce you've experienced your first 4 Ballad Romances, we're sure you'll want to continue receiving these wonderful historical romance novels each month – without ever having to leave your home – using our convenient and inexpensive home subscription service. Here's what you get for joining:

- *4 BRAND NEW Ballad Romances delivered to your door each month*
- *30% off the cover price with your home subscription.*
- *A FREE monthly newsletter filled with author interviews, book previews, special offers, and more!*
- *No risk or obligation…you're free to cancel whenever you wish… no questions asked.*

Passion-
Adventure-
Excitement-
Romance-
Ballad!

*T*o start your membership, simply complete and return the card provided. You'll receive your Introductory Shipment of 4 FREE Ballad Romances. Then, each month, as long as your account is in good standing, you will receive the 4 newest Ballad Romances. Each shipment will be yours to examine for 10 days. If you decide to keep the books, you'll pay the preferred home subscriber's price – a savings of 30% off the cover price! (plus shipping & handling) If you want us to stop sending books, just say the word…it's that simple.

A $23.96 value – **FREE** No obligation to buy anything – ever.
4 FREE BOOKS are waiting for you! Just mail in the certificate below!

BOOK CERTIFICATE

Yes! Please send me 4 Ballad Romances ABSOLUTELY FREE! After my introductory shipment, I will receive 4 new Ballad Romances each month to preview FREE for 10 days (as long as my account is in good standing). If I decide to keep the books, I will pay the money-saving preferred publisher's price plus shipping and handling. That's 30% off the cover price. I may return the shipment within 10 days and owe nothing, and I may cancel my subscription at any time. The 4 FREE books will be mine to keep in any case.

Name_____

Address_____ Apt._____

City_____ State_____ Zip_____

Telephone (____)_____

Signature_____

(If under 18, parent or guardian must sign)

All orders subject to approval by Zebra Home Subscription Service.
Terms and prices subject to change. Offer valid only in the U.S.

DN101A

If the certificate is missing below, write to:

Ballad Romances,
c/o Zebra Home
Subscription Service Inc.

P.O. Box 5214,
Clifton, New Jersey
07015-5214

OR call TOLL FREE
1-888-345-BOOK (2665)

Passion...

Adventure...

Excitement...

Romance...

Get 4
Ballad
Historical
Romance
Novels
FREE!

ցllուlll.ո.llll.ll.l.lll.ll.lll.ll.lll

BALLAD ROMANCES
Zebra Home Subscription Service, Inc.
P.O. Box 5214
Clifton NJ 07015-5214

tapes and let the last remaining garment fall to the floor.

He had dreamed of seeing Eden this way since the moment he'd met her. Naked, vulnerable, perfection. His. Her body curved softly, and he reached out to trail his fingers over every curve. To cup her breasts and run his hands over her hips. To trail his fingers up her thighs to her mound.

She jumped, startled, when he touched her there. "You're so beautiful," he whispered as he parted her thighs and touched her intimately, stroking her wet flesh.

She did not wait for him to take his own clothes off; she impatiently started for him. She unbuttoned his shirt and untucked it, forcing it higher, her hands on his skin, until he grabbed the shirt and shucked it over his head. He kicked off his boots as Eden unbuckled his belt and unfastened his jeans, one button at a time passing slowly through her fingers. She wrapped her arms around him and slipped her fingers into the waistband of his trousers. Those hands boldly moved lower to cup his buttocks and force down the trousers.

When he'd kicked the denims aside, Eden moved back, a single step, to look him over. "You're beautiful, too," she whispered. Her eyes landed and lingered on his arousal, and a new expression was added to the face he knew so well—skepticism. "But really, Sin, are you sure this is going to work? I mean . . . It's bigger than I thought."

"Trust me," he said, taking her into his arms and lowering her to the bed.

She placed her arms around his neck. "I do. Trust you, that is. And love you," she added with a smile. "And I want you," she whispered, laying her mouth over his and kissing him with soft, slightly parted lips.

It pained him to wait, but he wanted to give Eden all he had promised in the tub. He kissed her breasts, taking a nipple into his mouth and suckling until she moaned, then moving his attention to the other breast. He kissed the tender flesh of her inner elbow, flicking his tongue there when she sighed deeply and buried the fingers of her other hand in his hair. He kissed her flat belly and felt her quiver.

When he parted her legs and touched her intimately, she tensed, and then almost immediately she relaxed, her eyes drifting peacefully shut. She truly did trust him, with her body and her heart. She literally placed herself in his hands and trusted him to take care of her. He stroked her wetness gently, slipped a finger inside her, and felt her quiver.

He hovered above her, and her legs spread wider for him. The tip of his arousal touched her, and she rocked gently up. Against him, into him.

With slow deliberation, he entered her. She was so tight, so small, he was afraid he might hurt her if he moved any faster. But she didn't seem to be in pain as he gradually stretched her, rocking gently back and forth until he met and broke through her maidenhead.

Her only response was a small uttered "oh" and a mild twitch. She opened her eyes and looked at him, licked her lips and clasped her hands behind his neck. She lifted her hips again, rocking against him, urging him deeper. She cocked one leg and rested it over his.

With a moan and a push he filled her completely. Without hesitation she met his thrust, lifting her other leg over his, holding him tight. She kissed him deeply, her tongue mimicking the pace and motion of his length within her as they fell into a rhythmic, intimate dance.

She gasped, and still she did not take her mouth from his. Her body shuddered, and he felt the milking caress of her inner muscles around his shaft as she quickly climaxed.

He drove deep within her one more time, finding his own completion as her body tightened around him. Losing control, well beyond *all* control, he pumped his seed into her and groaned against her hungry mouth.

And then he collapsed against her, cradled her, spent and breathless.

"Oh, my," Eden breathed a few minutes later.

Sullivan could only murmur a response. He was drained.

He rolled onto his back and she came with him, resting her arms against his chest and gazing down at him with a satisfied smile on her face. "I was right to trust you," she whispered. "I was right to marry you."

Married. He had almost forgotten about the wedding. God, she'd had him half out of his mind in that damn tub! He would have done anything to get her into his bed, would have done anything at all to make her his at last. *Married.*

But now that it was done, he couldn't be sorry. He could think of worse ways to spend his nights than in bed with Eden Rourke.

Eden *Sullivan.*

Chapter 12

Eden rose and dressed and hurried downstairs to wake the children for school. She got them fed and out the door just in time. She didn't tell Millie and Teddy about the marriage, deciding that Sin should be with her when she shared the happy news. Sin was going to be their papa, just as they wanted him to be.

Apparently the rest of the hotel's residents had been out late last night. No one was roaming about, looking for breakfast or wondering where she was. She very quietly returned to Sin's room, closed the door behind her, and began to unbutton her blouse. She wasn't ready to give up this time in bed with her husband. Not yet.

She stripped, tossed her clothes on the floor, and slipped beneath the covers. Smiling, happy beyond words, she scooted close to Sin, loving the feel of his skin, his heat, so much, that she couldn't bear to stay on her side of the bed.

"Where have you been?" he asked softly, rolling over to face her.

She grinned widely. "I had to get the children off to school," she said, pushing back a long strand of dark hair that fell across his cheek.

"How are you this morning?" he asked, his fingers in her hair and settling comfortably on her waist. "Are you all right?"

"I'm much more than all right," she confessed. "I feel wonderful. A little sore, perhaps, but . . . not very." She'd never forget her wedding night, not as long as she lived. What extraordinary feelings Sin had introduced her to, what amazingly unexpected pleasures.

He kissed her good morning, a gentle kiss that didn't remain gentle long. His arms wrapped possessively around her, so that he cradled her gently and completely. There was something so right about being here, in this place, with this man, that she was as swept away by the rightness of the moment as she was by her physical response. She pressed herself to him, crushing her breasts against his hard chest, lifting one leg over his hip to bring them closer together. No matter how she moved, she could not get close enough.

Deep sensations of longing rushed through her, and her body began to throb. Everything she was, from her head to her toes, pulsated and yearned.

Sin rolled her onto her back and spread her thighs, and moving slowly, he entered her. He stretched her, stroked her, pushed so deep inside he stole her very breath away. She held on tight and rocked her hips against him, as he made love to her. She ceased to think, to breathe, as he loved her.

She shattered in his arms, lost in an intense pleasure that washed over her. At the same time, she felt Sin's own pleasure, his release deep in her body, the shudder that ripped through him. She cried out softly, unable to remain silent as the culmination of the act vibrated through her.

Sin toppled, descending gently over her body, cradling her in his arms.

"I love you so much," she whispered in his ear. "I never thought I could love anyone this way."

Sin had not yet told her that he loved her, too, but she was not concerned. She'd seen love in his eyes, felt it in the way he touched her. One day he'd tell her how he felt. Until then, she'd be perfectly happy to let him show her. Every day.

Sullivan was strangely content. Serenity was an entirely new feeling for him, and he didn't expect the strange contentment to last. Still, while it did last he was going to enjoy it.

It was midmorning before he and Eden left the bed. They dressed each other, taking their time and laughing and kissing. If he didn't think it would be too much for her he'd take her again, slow and easy this time.

Tonight would be soon enough.

They walked down the stairs, his arm over her shoulder, her arm around his waist. Eden thought she loved him; she thought the rush in her blood was love, not lust. Sullivan knew better, but he didn't waste time telling her. If she wanted to call it love that was fine with him. Right now he figured lust was as good a reason as any for getting married, and as long as they were both content . . . what difference did it make?

At the foot of the stairs he took her in his arms

for a long kiss. No one was around, and he couldn't seem to get rid of the urge to touch her, not even after last night and this morning. He knew, with a sudden twinge of uneasiness, that he wouldn't ever get enough of her. Eden Rourke—Eden Sullivan—was his one weakness, a chink in his armor, his Achilles' heel. At the moment he didn't care.

"You were right," she whispered, wrapping her arms around his neck. "Last night was better than anything."

"Tonight will be better," he promised.

She gave him a fleeting kiss. "Better? My goodness, is that possible?"

"I don't know, but I think we should try." He pulled Eden against him, cupping his hands on her buttocks and holding her tight as he kissed her properly. She responded by immediately parting her soft lips and flicking her tongue inside his mouth. He couldn't stop the groan that rose from his throat. "I want you again, right now," he said. "Right here."

"Hell, Sullivan," a familiar gruff and friendly voice rumbled from much too near, "looks like you and your lady friend came downstairs too soon. If I was you I'd . . ."

Eden's head snapped up and she looked toward the door just as Sullivan did.

Jedidiah Rourke, covered with trail dust and carrying his saddlebags and his rifle, quickly lost his friendly smile. "Eden? What the hell are you . . ." His eyes landed on Sullivan. "You bastard."

There was no telling how much Jed had heard. Enough apparently, as he dropped his saddlebags but not his rifle. "Get your goddamned filthy hands off of my sister."

"Jedidiah," Eden said primly, "watch your language."

Jed shook a finger in her direction. "I'll see to you next, young lady. First I've got to take care of this no-good backstabbing lily-livered mongrel."

Eden tried to place herself between them, but neither man would allow it. She was gently shoved aside.

Jedidiah Rourke was a good six-foot-three and built like a tree trunk. Dark blond untamed curls hung almost to his shoulders, and a few weeks' beard growth covered the lower half of his face. Sullivan figured he could take the bigger man in a fist fight, if he had to, but he didn't think a brawl in the lobby of Eden's hotel was the way to start this marriage.

"Listen to me, Jed," Sullivan said calmly as he and the big man danced around each other. "There's a lot going on here you don't know about."

"Tell me about it," Jed seethed. He leaned his rifle against the green sofa and flexed his fists.

Sullivan relaxed. At least he didn't have to worry about getting shot. Yet. "Last night Eden and I . . ."

Jed, not wanting to hear any more, roared and lunged forward, swinging wildly. "Damn it, I *don't* want to hear about it!" he bellowed as he let his fist fly.

Sullivan stepped aside safely under the wild swing. "Don't make me hit you."

Jed spun to face Sullivan and poised for another swing. "I come in here and find you with your hands on my little sister's ass and your tongue down her throat, and you want to explain to me what happened last night? I don't want to hear it, you bastard. I've heard enough already." Jed prepared to lash out again, and Sullivan got ready to move out of his way or to fight back if he had to.

Eden bravely stepped between them. "Jedidiah Rourke," she said primly, "I will not have you threatening my husband this way. Do you hear me?"

Jed did not lower his fists, but he did become very still as he looked down at his sister and narrowed his eyes. "Husband?" he whispered in a gravelly voice.

"That's what Sin has been trying to tell you," she said with a smile. "We were married last night."

Jed's fists loosened; his fingers flexed. "Sin?" He cast a quick, suspicious glance at Sullivan as Eden stepped up and gave him a big hug.

"I'm so glad you're finally here," she said, going up on her toes to place her arms around his neck.

"Married?" Jed said again, his hard blue eyes on Sullivan as he gave his sister a hug.

"That's what I was trying to tell you," Sullivan said. The *mongrel* comment still stung, but he let it go. For now.

"Nate performed the ceremony right here in this lobby," Eden said with a smile as Jed set her aside.

Jed's eyebrows raised in amazement. "Nate? Hell, Nate can't marry anybody!" He was ready to fight again, and this time Sullivan wasn't going to back off. "What did you do, rig up some fake wedding ceremony to get my little sister into bed?"

Eden cast a suspicious glance of her own at Sullivan, a split second before Jed moved in and swung. Sullivan stepped aside and delivered a swing of his own. A solid punch landed on a hard and sizable midsection. He also put out his foot to trip Jed. The big man landed on the floor with a thud that shook the whole hotel.

"What is all the noise about?" an almost aristo-cratic, coarse voice called from the stairway. Nate stood there, wearing the clothes he'd worn last night, raking a hand over his head. "Can't a man *sleep* in this hotel anymore?"

Jed rose quickly from the floor. "Did you per-form some kind of half-ass fake wedding ceremony so Sullivan could ... could"—the man actually blushed—"so he could take advantage of my little sister?"

"Of course not," Nate assured Jed in a calm voice.

Jed grinned at Sullivan, a wicked grin that said *You're dead.*

Nate continued. "The ceremony was quite real, not half-assed or fake at all, I can assure you. I am still an ordained minister, after all."

"Were you drunk?" Jed asked.

Nate flashed a twisted smile. "Of course I was. But not so drunk I don't remember that Sullivan looked like he was about to explode, or that Eden had a wide grin on her face and clung to her bridegroom's arm like she would fall through the floor without him. I was not so drunk that I don't remember that they both very willingly said *I do* before I pronounced them man and wife."

Jed groaned and placed his head in his hands, muttering an obscene word that had Eden blushing and stammering.

Sullivan backed up a single step. Why the hell was he surprised by this development? He wasn't good enough for Jed's sister. He was good enough to fight with, to drink with, to trust with another man's life. But to marry his sister? Of course not. No mongrel would be good enough for Jedidiah Rourke's baby sister.

Jed lifted his head and glared at Eden. "I thought you were going to marry Seymour Mayfield," he said tiredly. "In your last letter you said . . ."

"I said he *asked*," she interrupted. "After giving his proposal some serious thought, I refused."

Jed shook his head. "You should be in Spring Hill, living in a nice house, married to a nice man, knitting or sewing or doing some kind of female thing. You don't belong here."

"I do now," Eden said calmly.

Jed shook a long finger at Eden. "You and Sullivan are not married," he insisted. "I declare this so-called marriage null and void, as of now."

"You can't do that," Eden insisted with a gentle, understanding smile.

"Oh, yes, I can," Jed said softly. "If you really want to marry this . . . this . . ."

"Mongrel," Sullivan supplied in a low voice.

Jed snapped his head around to glare in Sullivan's direction. "Mongrel," he seethed before turning his full attention to Eden again. "Fine," he said. "But by God you're going to do it right. You're going to get engaged first. You're going to wait a few weeks, at the very least, to make sure you're not making a mistake. Then there will be a real wedding, with a fancy dress and a ring. If you want Nate to perform the ceremony, that's fine, too, but he will, by God, be *sober* when he does it."

Eden reached up to lay a small hand on Jed's face, the gesture one of love and understanding. Sullivan had seen her comfort Teddy and Millie just this way. And him, he realized with a start.

"That's silly," she said. "And too late. Sin and I are already married. It's done, Jedidiah."

"Sin," he seethed. "That's so goddamn *precious*, if I'd had any breakfast I'd lose it here and now."

She smiled at her brother and then looked over her shoulder to where Sullivan stood.

His heart sank, heavy in his chest. Damn it, Jed was right. Eden didn't belong here, and she sure as hell didn't belong with him. He would've known that last night, if she hadn't had him half out of his mind from playing in the tub. He'd been drunk on Eden, intoxicated by what he wanted, carried away by a touch and a kiss and the promise they offered.

"Your brother's right," he said softly. "It happened so fast. . . ."

Her smile faded.

"Maybe you should take some time to think it over," he said without emotion. "Take some time and be sure we're not making a mistake."

"Do you think we made a mistake?" she whispered, heartbreak in her eyes.

No. "I don't know."

She looked utterly devastated.

Jed smiled widely. "Null and void," he said. "And Sullivan," he added, "if you want to marry my sister again, you'll damn well come to me and ask for her hand in marriage, properlike."

Eden stared at him like she expected him to *do* something, to save her, to tell Jed that she was his wife and there was no going back. She looked at him as if she expected him to be someone he wasn't, her champion, her partner, the man who loved her.

And he knew then that Jed was right. He would never be the man Eden expected him to be. He left the hotel without saying a word.

* * *

Eden stared at the empty doorway, willing Sin to reappear. He didn't.

"Look what you've done," she whispered.

"You can't be married to Sullivan," Jedidiah said calmly, more in control now that Sin was gone.

She twirled around and stomped her foot at him. He actually flinched. "But we are already married." She looked to where an amused Nate lounged on the stairway. "Isn't that right?"

"Legally wed," he said with a crooked smile.

"So you can't just . . . just . . . make it go away," she said.

Jedidiah leaned close and spoke softly. "I think I just did."

She never lost her temper. Never. But right now she saw red and her blood boiled. "If I lose Sin because of this, I will never forgive you," she said, surprised to find that she meant it.

At the same time she was furious with her husband for not insisting that Jedidiah could not make their marriage null and void with the snap of his fingers. Deep inside she wondered if Jedidiah might be right about one thing, if Sin had only married her to get her into his bed. If there was nothing else but desire between them, he might never come back. He might be perfectly happy to have their marriage invalidated. He might even be relieved.

"We'll talk about it later," Jedidiah said confidently and with a condescending tone of voice. He gathered his saddlebags and rifle and headed for the stairs.

Eden placed herself at the foot of the stairs and blocked his path.

"After you've had a chance to calm down," Jedidiah added in a condescending tone.

"Where do you think you're going?" she asked.

"To my room. I live here."

"Not anymore you don't," she said, her chin and her nose high, her spine rigid. "You see, I'm in the process of remodeling my hotel, and I'm afraid there are no rooms available."

"Your hotel?" Jedidiah asked softly. He looked past her to Nate. *"Her* hotel?"

Eden glanced over her shoulder to see Nate nod his head once.

"I leave town for less than two months," Jedidiah said, his voice no longer so calm, "and come home wanting nothing more than a bath and a couple days' sleep and some of Lydia's hard-ass cathead biscuits. I expect to find things pretty much the way I left them, but I walk in here and find you messing around with *your* goddamn husband in *your* goddamn hotel. How the hell long have you been here?" he thundered, leaning forward as if he could intimidate her.

Eden smiled. It was an effort. "Oh, I've been in Rock Creek a little more than a week. And Jedidiah," she added primly, "don't swear."

He shifted uncomfortably on his big feet. "So, when do you think a room might become available?"

She moved her face forward to look her brother right in the eye. He had always been bigger and older and meaner, so she'd had to learn early on to hold her ground. She held her ground now as she poked him in the chest. "When I get my husband back."

Chapter 13

The saloon was all but deserted, but then it wasn't yet noon. Cash was up and drinking his breakfast at the bar, and Sullivan had claimed a seat at a table in the corner. Yvonne was busy cleaning up some of last night's clutter and watering down certain bottles of whiskey. The calico girls were still asleep, all but Kate, who stood by Cash at the bar and joined him for a silent breakfast.

Sullivan had come down to earth hard, after a night and a long morning of pretending to be someone he was not. How long had he expected it would last? Eden wanted something he couldn't give; she wanted a life he couldn't ever be a part of. She'd been right all along. She'd rather live with people she loved in hell than live alone in paradise, and he . . . Hell, he'd rather be alone in hell. Life was simpler that way, safer.

If she hadn't looked at him with those big blue eyes and asked what they would do next if they were married, he never would've asked her; he never would've thought that maybe ... just maybe ...

Jed slammed his way through the bat-wing doors and flung his saddlebags to the floor. Jedidiah Rourke was never what one would call a calm man, but he was also rarely frustrated. He was frustrated now.

"She tossed me out. Can you believe it? My own sister, and she tossed me out on my ear."

Cash lifted his head and stared sleepily at Jed. "You're back. Have I missed all the fun?"

Jed headed for the table in the corner, where Sullivan sat, and Cash patted Kate on the bottom and told her to get back to bed.

"I can't believe you'd stoop so low as to marry my little sister." Fortunately, Jed's hands were not balled into fists.

"Marry?" Cash asked, leaving the bar to join them. "Sullivan," he said tersely, "when I suggested that you do whatever was necessary I didn't mean ..." He stared down at Jed and amended his words. "What I mean to say is, you actually *married* her?" He lowered himself to a chair, seemingly deflated.

The three of them sat at the small round table, leaning in.

"Nate performed the ceremony," Jed muttered.

A light of understanding and relief lit Cash's eyes. "Oh, so it wasn't a *real* wedding." He looked from Jed to Sullivan and back again. "A clever plan, I must admit, but, well, that is a little low."

"A *little* low," Jed barked.

"The wedding was legal," Sullivan said.

"You are not married to my sister," Jed seethed. "I won't allow it."

Why had he ever expected anything different? The best thing he could do would be to ride out of town today, now, and not look back.

"God forbid that your sister should be married to a *mongrel*," he said calmly. "Your nieces and nephews would have Comanche blood, Jed. Your sister would be mother to little Sullivan mongrels who'd call you Uncle Jedidiah."

Jed lifted his eyes slowly. "Is that what you think? You think I declared the marriage null and void because you're a half-breed?"

"Isn't it?"

Jed almost smiled. "No. Hell, no. The truth of the matter is, none of us is good enough for Eden. We're all mongrels of a sort. Drifters. Hell-raisers. And the idea that you'd light on her like a fly on honey the minute she gets to town is . . . is . . . It just ain't right."

"This is not entirely Sullivan's fault," Cash intervened. "The girl has been leading him around by his pecker from the moment she set her eyes on him."

Sullivan and Jed both glared at Cash.

"Well, it's the truth," he added in his own defense. "He tried to do the noble thing and leave town, but she wrote a threatening note to herself to keep him around. Face it, she tied him up in knots and led him around by his nether regions until she got what she wanted. Married." He rolled his eyes. "For God's sake Sullivan, have I taught you nothing about women?"

"Shut up, runt," Jed said in a low, warning voice.

Cash bristled at the insult, as he always did. At five-foot-eleven he wasn't exactly a small man, but when the six of them stood together, the gunslinger was the shortest by at least an inch or so. His narrow build didn't help the matter any, especially when he stood next to the mountainous Jed Rourke.

"I see no reason for this to get personal," he said.

When Sullivan and Jed continued to glare at him, their faces growing stonier by the moment, Cash took his leave and headed upstairs.

Sullivan set his eyes on Jed. "You're right. I never should've married her."

Jed nodded in agreement. "It's nothing personal, I swear. It's just that Eden deserves better than . . . better than anything we can give her. She should lead a sheltered life, be safe, be taken care of. She can't get that here." He locked his eyes on Sullivan. "You can't give it to her."

"I know."

Jed ran an impatient hand through his hair. "Somehow we have to get her back to Spring Hill and married to Mayfield or Cooper. I don't know why she didn't get married years ago. It ain't because no one asked, and Seymour Mayfield was perfect for her, absolutely perfect. He's just a shopkeeper, but his business does real well so he could take good care of her. Eden's a gentle girl, she needs a . . . a dandy like Seymour," he added, almost as if he were apologizing for her. "The first time she sees a critter she doesn't recognize she'll probably faint dead away. The first time there's a dust storm she'll probably beg to leave for Georgia on the next stage."

Sullivan didn't believe Eden was as fragile as Jed seemed to think, but what did he know? He knew very little about the woman he'd called his wife last night. He knew she was beautiful and sweet and tender, and she had a tendency to want to take care of everyone she met. He knew she had a passion that made her heart beat fast and her body open for him. He knew she thought what she felt was love.

"What if there's a baby?" Sullivan asked softly. He'd been a bastard himself, knew how hard it was to live that way. Even though these circumstances were not the same, he did not want his child to be born without his name. He would not allow it. It was the reason he would not ride out of town today.

Jed closed one eye as if he could not bear to think of the possibility. "Then I'll have to kill you."

They stared at each other for a long while, until Cash came down the stairs with a woman on each arm.

Jed absentmindedly patted Ethel's nicely rounded butt as she lowered herself to his knee. He was still in shock over finding Eden in Rock Creek. She was supposed to be in Georgia, safe and sound, not trying to remodel that shit hole of a hotel and marrying—he laid his eyes on Sullivan—a man who could never take proper care of her.

Sullivan's feet were as itchy as his were, the life he lived just as dangerous. There was nothing good and beautiful in Jed's life, nothing but Eden. He needed to be able to think of her at home, safe and happy. Married to Sullivan? No.

Jed had been thinking about leaving Rock Creek for good, not coming back at all. If Eden stayed here he'd have to come back now and again, like it or not, and Jed wasn't sure he wanted to keep calling this place home.

Since Sylvia had married that damn good-for-nothing preacher, the place hadn't been the same. Sylvia had been a great lover, a widow who didn't

ask too much, at least for a while. Once she'd
caught the marrying bug, she'd set her sights on
Jed. When he'd made it clear he was not the marrying kind, she'd moved her attentions to Clancy,
who she said was stable and honorable and attentive.

Jed hadn't thought she'd really go through with
it. He'd been so sure Sylvia was trying to trick him
into marrying her by pretending to be serious
about the preacher. He didn't miss her, though.
Not much. There were lots of other pretty women
in the world. Sylvia had made her choice: she'd
made her bed. . . .

Hell, he did not want his thoughts to head in
that direction, so he returned his attentions to a
morose Sullivan.

Sullivan was a good man. Honest, quiet, a great
scout, and a fair shot. He was an outstanding soldier, but he was no more the marrying kind than
Jed himself was.

And the half-breed was not going to ruin Eden's
life. Jed would not allow it.

The children were at school, and Rico and Nate
had left the hotel together a while back. Something
to do with their horses, Rico had told her. She'd
been so angry, still, that she hadn't paid as much
attention as she should have to what he'd said.

She was alone in the hotel, brooding and preparing lunch, when she found the note. Again it was
pinned to the cutting board.

*This is your last warning. Get out of town while
you still can.*

If she hadn't already been upset about Sin and Jedidiah, she might have panicked. But the truth of the matter was, nothing at all had happened after the last note of warning. Perhaps in Texas this sort of thing was considered a joke, just as in Texas a marriage could apparently be set aside on a whim.

Last night and this morning she'd felt so completely and irrevocably married, a part of an unbreakable union, and now . . . Now she was alone again. Sin had been hers for a short time, and now, impossibly, she felt as if everything she'd known to be true was over.

She snatched up the note and headed out the door and across the street. If she knew Jedidiah and Sin, they were in the saloon at this moment, fighting over her. They each had their own plans for her future, and neither of them had any regard for her own desires. Without her there to intervene, they might have come to blows again. It made her heart lurch to think of the two men she loved most in the world fighting with each other, literally pounding each other with their sizable fists. They were family now. They were like brothers and should treat each other with love and respect. Men! She would never understand them.

Perhaps, if either of them cared for her at all, they could put their differences aside long enough to figure out who was sending these notes.

Laughter rang out as she pushed through the bat-wing doors and entered the saloon.

She was not prepared for the sight that met her eyes. Jedidiah and Sin were not fighting; they were sitting together at a table in the corner. Jedidiah was laughing, and so was the blonde on his knee. The brunette on Sin's knee laughed, too, and wrapped her arms around his neck. Cash stood nearby, surveying the scene with a smug smile on his demonic face.

Her heart sank. A scantily clad woman sat on Sin's lap, and she looked quite comfortable there. Her husband did not look inclined to push the hussy off his lap, though he did, at least, have the decency not to be laughing at the moment.

Sin saw her first, laid his eyes on her in a way so intense she felt it. The expression on his face didn't change one iota.

With her head high, she walked to the table. "I hate to interrupt," she said icily, "but it seems I have received another note of warning." She slapped the note on the table. "If there were a sheriff in Rock Creek I would take it to him, but since there is no lawman in office at the moment, you two will have to do."

"Eden," Jedidiah muttered, "you don't belong in here. This is a *saloon.*"

"I'm not staying," she said, giving Sin a quick glance. "I just wanted to hand this message over to . . . to someone."

They looked over the note quickly. Cash didn't glance at it at all, but Sin gently assisted the brunette off his lap and stood. "I'll walk you back to the hotel and take a look around."

"Yeah," Jedidiah said, patting his own companion on the rear end as she left his lap. "I'll go with you."

"No, thank you," Eden said icily. "I didn't mean to interrupt your fun. Besides," she added, "I don't want either of you in my hotel."

"Eden," Sin began in a low voice.

"I'm sure there's a room for you here," she said

calmly, furious for allowing herself to believe that there was something special between her and this man. He might just as well have spent last night with one of the saloon girls. What they'd shared in bed was all he wanted from her, all he'd ever wanted. She'd been a fool to imagine more.

"You're going to have a big old hotel and no people living in it!" Jedidiah thundered.

"Nate and Rico will be there," she said calmly. "And Millie and Teddy. Once I have the place fixed up, I hope to attract a better class of clientele."

"Who are Millie and Teddy?" Jedidiah asked, obviously confused.

"My children," she said simply, offering no other information. Let him figure it out for himself!

"Your . . . children."

"I'll explain later," Sin said as he stepped around the table.

It was embarrassing to have this personal exchange take place in front of Cash and Jedidiah and those horrid women, but she didn't want to face Sin alone, not ever again. And she had to know.

"You don't love me," she said, "do you?"

"I never said I did."

An unpleasant flutter jumped in her chest, and she felt momentarily light-headed. "No, you didn't. You have always been very honest with me, haven't you?"

She pulled her eyes away from Sin and looked at Jedidiah. "All right," she said. "Null and void. I hope you're satisfied." She walked away with as much dignity as she could muster. "But you still can't move back into my hotel," she added as she reached the swinging saloon doors.

* * *

He'd never seen anyone look so hurt, but what choice did he have? If he told Eden he loved her, she'd never let him go. She'd be determined to make their marriage work. She would never give up. And Jed was right; she deserved better. Eden deserved better than to hear a man tell her what she wanted to hear just to make her happy for the time being. She deserved better than a lie.

"There's a problem, you leave the hotel," Cash said, "and another warning mysteriously appears."

"She kicked me out," Sin said, waving Laurel aside when she made an attempt to sit on his knee again. "Why would she write a threatening note to keep me around when she just booted me out of the hotel?"

"Because she's a woman, and they rarely make sense." Ethel protested that statement, and Cash added a polite, "Present company excepted, of course."

And the truth was, Sullivan had to admit, Eden hadn't kicked him out until she'd come in here and found him with a woman on his knee. Now that he'd all but told her he didn't love her, she'd never forgive him. She was so sure what they had was love. He was just as sure it was purely physical and it wouldn't last.

"It's not like Eden to lie," Jed said, shaking his head slowly. "She wouldn't make up something like that."

"Is it like Eden to do whatever she has to do to get what she wants?" Cash asked dryly.

Jed shook his head. "No. Eden's always thinking about other people, not what she wants for herself. She's always been that way. You should've seen her as a little girl.'' A wry smile crept across the big man's face, a smile that spoke of his loving protectiveness of his sister. "Even then she was pretty as all get out and sweet as sugar. She was always taking in animals. She'd take in any old stray that crossed her path, wounded, disfigured, sick animals no one else wanted.''

"I don't think she's outgrown that trait,'' Cash muttered.

Jed apparently didn't hear. "One time we had a three-legged cat, a blind hound dog, a bird that couldn't fly, and a half-dozen scrawny kittens she'd found down by the lake.''

Sullivan's gut tightened. Damn it, he did not want to be one of Eden Rourke's wounded strays. He did not want her to feel obligated to take him in and heal him. "Teddy and Millie,'' he said.

Jed looked pained. "Her children. Is that what happened? Has she graduated to taking in people now?''

"I'm afraid so,'' Sullivan answered softly.

They both agreed that Eden didn't belong in Rock Creek, that she deserved better, but they couldn't decide on how to make her leave.

Cash looked thoroughly disgusted. "You're both considerably bigger than she is. Why don't you just toss her in that wagon of hers and take her home?''

Jed shook his head in dismay. "She'd just turn around and come straight back. She has to want to leave. She has to be ready to go.''

"So,'' Cash said, being unusually helpful today, "how do we get rid of her?'' When Sullivan and Jed both glared at him, he said, "I mean, how do we convince Eden that it's in her best interest to return to Georgia?''

In the still air that followed his question, in that

moment of complete silence, a far-off scream split the air. Sullivan jumped up and ran toward the door; Jed was right behind him.

"That was Eden," the big man said as they ran across the street.

"I know."

Chapter 14

Eden slammed the cast-iron skillet against the floor and then stepped quickly away to observe the results from a distance. She shivered, but she did not scream again.

Mere seconds later Sin ran into the kitchen, a six-shooter in his right hand. Jedidiah, armed with his rifle, was directly behind him.

They stopped abruptly when they saw her standing there with the skillet in her hand.

She knew good and well why they were here; the scream had been quite loud. "Sorry," she said. "I've never seen one of those things before." She pointed to what remained of the creature on the floor.

"Scorpion," Sin said in a lowered voice.

Eden wrinkled her nose. "Are they poisonous?"

"Yes," Sin and Jedidiah answered at the same time.

"I suppose one just wandered into the kitchen,"

she said with a weak smile. "I looked down and . . . there it was."

"And you killed it with a skillet," Jedidiah said proudly, casting a grin in her direction.

"You should've gone across the street to get me," Sin said, censure in his voice and in his eyes. "You had no idea what you were dealing with."

She was too annoyed with him to acknowledge his concern. "I knew it was considerably smaller than me," she snapped. "And there was just the one."

"Two," Jedidiah said, his smile fading as he stepped past Sin and stomped on a scorpion that skittered out from under her worktable.

"Three," Sin muttered as he caught sight of yet another scorpion boldly making an appearance from near the base of the sink. After he squashed the creature with his boot, he lifted Eden off her feet and tossed her over his shoulder. She landed with a sudden expelled whoosh of air and a gentle bounce, and she dangled there while Sin and Jedidiah checked the corners and crevices of the kitchen for more scorpions.

From her undignified position, Eden gathered her breath and said haughtily, "This is not necessary, Mr. Sullivan. Please put me down. Jedidiah," she said when Sin did not comply, "would you please tell him to put me down?"

"Later," Jedidiah said as he found and killed a fourth scorpion. "We don't want one of these scorpions running up under that skirt of yours."

The idea made her shiver, and then she sighed, trying to maintain her self-respect as she hung from Sin's shoulder like a sack of meal. When she spotted something slithering near the rear door that led to what had once been a vegetable garden, she pointed and squealed. So much for dignity, she thought as Sin spun around and did away with the small but dangerous creature.

All in all they killed seven scorpions before Sin carried her from the kitchen and set her on her feet in the dining room.

"How do you suppose they got in the kitchen?" she asked as she did her best to straighten her hair. Hanging upside down from Sin's shoulder had ruined her once-neat hairstyle.

Jedidiah and Sin exchanged a look that excluded her.

"You don't suppose someone purposely *put* them there, do you?"

If the two most important men in her life were worried, and they clearly were, she certainly should be. A note was one thing, but this . . . This was more than she'd bargained for.

"You stay with Eden," Jedidiah said, wagging his rifle in Sin's direction. "I'll check the hotel from top to bottom." He took a couple of long strides toward the lobby before stopping and turning around. He frowned and narrowed his eyes. "On second thought, I'll stay with Eden and you check the hotel."

Sin didn't argue, but left without so much as glancing in her direction.

"Where are Rico and Nate?" Jedidiah asked when they were alone.

"I'm not sure," she said. "They left about an hour ago. Before I found the note."

It was the first chance she'd had to be alone with Jedidiah since his return, her first chance to be alone with her brother in years. She looked him over thoroughly. He hadn't changed too much in the past five years. There were, perhaps, a few lines around his eyes that hadn't been there before, and his hair was a little bit longer than she remembered. Apparently, he still didn't think to shave often, and his clothes were chosen with comfort in mind. He favored soft buckskins and leather and always had. But, oh, he was a sight for sore eyes . . . even when she was angry with him.

He took a long stride toward her. "What the hell are you doing here?" he asked in a kind voice.

"You're here," she said softly. "I don't have anyone left but you, Jedidiah. We're family. We belong together."

He shook his head. "If you'd married Mayfield or Cooper or any one of the dozen other suitable gentlemen in Spring Hill, you'd have your own family by now."

"I didn't love them," she said softly.

Jedidiah stopped in his tracks. "But you came to Rock Creek and within what—a few days? maybe a week?—you thought yourself in love with Sullivan?" He shook his head. "Just like a woman. That just doesn't make any sense at all."

"You're right," she whispered, not bothering to tell him that it hadn't taken any time at all to fall in love with Sin. "It doesn't make a lot of sense. But that doesn't make what I feel any less real."

"He's not good enough for you," Jedidiah said without anger. "Sullivan's . . . Well, he's too much like me. We stay on the move; we live by our guns; we're beholden to no one. We're too rough around the edges for the likes of you, Eden."

"Maybe I like a man who's rough around the edges," she said, trying to remain calm.

Jedidiah shook his head almost viciously. "No, you don't. You're a woman. You don't know what you want."

"So, would you like to choose my husband for me, Jedidiah?" Eden asked, her anger and frustration rising. "Goodness, how silly of me to think that I have the right to choose my own!"

"Now, Eden," he began.

"How foolish of me to listen to my heart, instead of asking you who I should love."

Jedidiah shook his finger at her. "You can't tell me it wouldn't be just as easy to fall in love with a shopkeeper or a gentleman farmer back in Georgia, as it was to fall in what you *think* is love with Sullivan. You're just ... fascinated with him because he's different. That's all there is to it." He nodded with finality.

She shook her head in wonder at his skewed reasoning. "You don't know anything about love."

"I know all I need to know," he said in a wise voice that made Eden roll her eyes. "Come on, Shorty, you know I only want what's best for you."

"Yes, I know," she conceded. "Misguided as your actions are, I know your intentions are good."

He gave her a big bear hug, lifting her off her feet and spinning her around. "It is good to see you," he admitted, "even if you shouldn't be here."

"It's good to see you, too," she whispered. "I've been so worried about you lately. I started to have those dreams again, like I had during the war, where people I can't see are shooting at you."

"I told you not to worry about me," Jedidiah said, his anger fading as he set her on her feet again.

"Easier said than done," she replied. "Were the dreams true? Have people been shooting at you?"

"Now and again," he said, trying to appear unconcerned. "This last job I was on did get a little risky at times. There were lots of bad guys," he added casually. "A few of them we thought for a while were on *our* side. But we rooted them out." He winked at her. "As you can see, they were all lousy shots."

"How can you make light of danger when I worry so? You know I adore you."

Jedidiah leaned down, placing his rough and hairy face close to hers. "So, can I move back into the hotel?"

"No."

His friendly grin disappeared.

"I adore you, but I'm also very angry with you," she said calmly. "With you and Sin both. What do you expect? You chased my husband of less than a full day away, and then I find him sitting in a saloon with a floozy on his lap. I love Sin with all my heart, but he doesn't mind telling me and everyone else who's present that he doesn't love me. I thought he did. I made myself believe I could see it . . . and now I'm just disappointed and confused. And to top it all off, someone is apparently trying to scare me into leaving town."

"You really should leave town," Jedidiah said softly. "This place is too rough for you."

She lifted her chin. "Maybe I'm tougher than you think."

That got an annoying grin out of him, just as Sin appeared in the doorway.

"Nothing," Sin said. "The place is empty, and no one's lurking around outside, either."

"What next?" Jedidiah asked, turning his back on Eden and walking to Sin.

Sin spared a quick glance for Eden, then returned his attention to Jedidiah. "We don't leave her alone, not for a minute. Rico and Nate will help keep an eye on her.''

''Excuse me,'' Eden said, stepping toward the big men to join the conversation. ''Don't you two think you're overreacting over a few ugly bugs?''

They ignored her.

''I need to check with the sheriff in Ranburne,'' Sin said. ''We ran across some rough characters on the way to Rock Creek. I want to make sure they're still in jail.''

''The Merriweathers?'' Eden asked in a lowered voice.

Sin cast her a quick glance and nodded once. ''Then there's Lydia to consider. She disappeared as soon as she found out Grady had left the hotel to Eden. Maybe she thought the old man was going to leave the place to her and this is her way of getting even.''

Eden decided she'd much rather face Lydia than the two remaining Merriweather brothers. The memory of that morning on the trail gave her chills.

''There's a third possibility,'' Sin said softly. ''I'm heading over to the saloon to check it out.''

''What possibility is that?'' Eden asked, but again Sin ignored her.

While it was true that Eden needed to get out of Rock Creek, he'd be damned if he'd sit back and allow someone to frighten her, or worse, *hurt* her. Scorpions!

Cash was sitting at the table in the corner, cleaning one of his fancy six-shooters.

''I want you to tell me right now,'' Sullivan demanded. ''Did you do it?''

Cash lifted tired, bored eyes. ''Did I do what?''

"Did you plant scorpions in Eden's kitchen?"

To Sullivan's dismay, Cash grinned. "No, but at least her adversary is showing some imagination this go-round."

"Runt," Sullivan muttered. "You think this is funny?"

Cash sighed. "Of course not, but I assume all's well with our nice girl Eden. Otherwise you wouldn't be here harassing me."

Sullivan didn't always like Cash, but the gambler had a way of reasoning things out, of making sense of a situation that didn't make sense to anyone else. It was like he could see around corners. His judgment was never clouded by emotion.

He took a seat and leaned slightly over the table. "Okay, if it's not you, then who? You can't believe that Eden would release seven scorpions in her kitchen just to make me think someone was after her."

Cash set dark eyes on Sullivan's face. "Seven?"

He nodded. "And we can't be sure who put them there. Could be what's left of the Merriweather brothers. We ran across a threesome of bandits on the way to town and they tried to ambush us at sunup. One of them ended up dead, and Eden shot one in the gun hand."

Cash grinned. "She did? Well, maybe there's hope for your girl. That's not *nice*, not at all."

Sullivan ignored the comment. "Sheriff Tilton was supposed to collect them, but I want to make absolutely certain they're behind bars. This doesn't feel right, not for those two, but until I know for sure . . ."

"I'll ride to Ranburne this afternoon and check on the Merriweathers' situation, myself," Cash said, taking the threat seriously at last. "Any other ideas?"

"Lydia," Sullivan said softly. "She disappeared after Grady died and left the hotel to Eden. Maybe this is her way of getting revenge."

"Notes and scorpions," Cash said thoughtfully. "Sounds like a woman to me. There is, however, one other possibility." He set his six-shooter aside. "What if the stories are true?" he said softly.

"What stories?"

Cash grinned. "Did you never hear a drunken Grady ramble on about his days as an outlaw?"

"Sure, but . . ."

"Did you never hear the story about the last big haul he and his partner made? The gold he supposedly hid away?"

"I never believed it. Did anyone?"

"Maybe someone did," Cash supposed. "Maybe someone wants Eden out of that hotel so they can tear it apart to look for the gold. Think about it. They waited and waited for Grady to die. Hell, he's been dying for months, an inch at a time. They figure he dies, the old place gets closed up, and they'll have all the time in the world to search for the gold. But then Eden comes along, and Grady leaves her the hotel, and she acts as if she has every intention of staying. Maybe this someone doesn't want to wait anymore. Maybe they figure they've waited long enough."

"Who could it be?" Sullivan asked softly, an unpleasant gnawing in his gut.

"Could be anyone," Cash said with an air of indifference. "Anyone at all."

* * *

Eden was already tired of her contingent of guards, and it was just now suppertime. Good heavens, she couldn't turn around without running into an armed man!

All four of her guards, as well as Millie and Teddy, were presently eating steak and potatoes and green beans in the hotel dining room. Even Nate was eating a little bit. She hadn't seen him take a drink all afternoon.

She had instructed them all that Teddy and Millie were not to be told about the problem. There was no reason to worry the children unnecessarily. Still, she felt better knowing that someone would keep an eye on the little ones, as well as watching over her. Sin had already spoken to the schoolteacher, Mr. Reese, about the situation. No one would bother them while Reese was around, he assured her.

Uncle Jedidiah sat with Millie and Teddy, in order that they all get better acquainted. Teddy had been his usual quiet self at the beginning of the meal, but already he'd begun to open up a little. Millie had charmed the big man from the moment she'd opened her mouth.

When everyone was fed, Eden gathered up as many dirty dishes as she could handle and carried them to the kitchen. Eventually she would have to hire someone to help her. If only Lydia had stayed! Maybe the girl couldn't cook, but she might've learned. She could certainly wash dishes and help with the cleaning.

She turned around to make another trip to the dining room and was startled to see Sin standing right behind her. He hadn't made a sound as he'd followed her into the kitchen.

"We need to talk," he said softly.

"We don't have anything to talk about," she said primly. Sin had told her he didn't love her. She'd seen him with a floozy sitting on his lap, and still her heart did funny things when he was near. She didn't know if she wanted more to slap him or to cry or to kiss him. Instead, she did nothing at all.

"Last night was a mistake."

"The wedding or making love with me?" She lifted her head to look him in the eye, showing no fear.

"Both," he whispered.

It hurt, worse than she'd imagined, to hear him actually say the words, to hear him admit that what had happened between them was a *mistake*. She didn't want to believe him.

"What are you more afraid of?" She looked him squarely in the eye. "That I truly love you or that you might love me?"

"I'm not afraid of anything."

She reached up and pushed back a long strand of dark hair that fell across his cheek. He didn't flinch, but she could see him almost turn to stone, steeling himself against her touch. It would be easier if she could fall out of love as quickly as she'd fallen in, if she could convince herself that Jedediah was right and she only thought she was in love because she'd never known anyone like Sin before.

"You don't believe in love. You don't believe in fate. You don't believe in anything," she whispered. "I think you don't want to believe in love because if you did then you might have to consider that what's happened between us is good and real and true."

"Eden . . ."

"It's easier for you to dismiss what's happened

between us as something physical and temporary," she said, thinking this out as she spoke, "because you're scared of what might still be to come if it's more than simple passion. You're afraid this might be something you can't ride away from at the drop of a hat," she whispered. "You're afraid a mere woman will change your life."

"No woman, not even you, is going to change my life."

She smiled softly. "Maybe not, but I surely did want the chance to try."

He placed a gentle hand on her shoulder, and then almost immediately moved that hand to the back of her neck. The way he touched her, even now, made her think—no, made her *certain*—that he did love her.

"If I was going to allow any woman to change my life," he said with a touch of bitter humor, "it would be you."

That reluctant admission was enough, for now, to make her forgive Sin everything. Eden raised up on her tiptoes and laid her mouth, lips slightly parted, over his. He met her for a simple, deep, searching kiss that didn't last nearly long enough.

When they drifted apart Eden whispered, "No matter what Jedidiah says, we *are* married. You can set me aside; you can pretend last night never happened; you can tell yourself that the wedding and what came after was just a foolish mistake. . . . But that won't make it go away. It certainly won't make *me* go away."

"I know," he whispered.

"But until you can tell me you love me, what we have won't be complete. You have my heart and my body. I've given you everything I have to offer a man. But what do I have of you, Sin? All I have is the little piece that you're willing to share. It's enough, for now, but it won't be enough forever."

"We don't have forever," Sin said. "You need to go back to Georgia and forget this marriage ever happened. You have to forget you ever met me." He laid his hand on her shoulder again. "I'd prefer that you go willingly, but once we're sure there's no baby I'll tie you up and carry you to Spring Hill myself, if I have to."

Baby. Her heart skipped a beat.

She was about to argue with him when a familiar voice bellowed from the dining room, "Where the hell is Sullivan?"

Chapter 15

Sullivan had been banned from the hotel by Jed, after being caught in the kitchen with Eden. Just as well. He couldn't look at her and not want her, and no matter what she thought, he knew no good would come of this so-called marriage.

Since he'd retreated to the saloon, the girls, all three of them, had tried to cheer him up. Ethel had been persistent and Kate had been bold in her suggestions. Laurel had set herself down on his lap again and called him Sully in her most seductive voice. He'd waved them off, one at a time. He didn't want to be cheered up, damn it, and he sure as hell didn't want to try to forget Eden with another woman. Right now he was content to wallow in his misery.

Another lively evening at the saloon was well underway when Cash pushed his way through the doors. His black attire was dusty. His usual calm had forsaken him for an intensity that seeped through his pores. The mood in the saloon dimmed. Even the girls steered clear as Cash strode to Sullivan's table.

"I have bad news," he said, choosing to stand over the table instead of sitting down. "The Merriweather brothers escaped while en route to San Antonio for trial. Killed a deputy and wounded a U.S. marshal. Tilton said he was just about to ride over here and warn you, since the brothers have been cursing your name and your lovely *wife* since the day he arrested them."

"I was afraid of that," Sullivan muttered as he stood. He would have to take this news to Jed and the others. Bad as this was, it was almost a relief knowing exactly who they were up against. An unseen enemy was the most dangerous; they all knew that too well.

"Not so fast," Cash said with a raised hand. "I have more bad news."

Sullivan sank into his chair, and Cash sat down, placing his forearms on the table and leaning forward. "They escaped three days ago, well after the first warning note was left for Eden. Now, if she will admit to writing that warning herself, we'll know we're only up against one enemy. If she doesn't . . ."

"She didn't write the note," Sullivan said, never more sure than he was at that moment.

"It's possible the Merriweathers don't know where to look for you and your wife just yet. But they know your name, and if they ask the right questions in the right places, they'll be here soon enough; you can count on that. In addition to the Merriweathers seeking revenge, someone out there is trying to frighten Eden into leaving town. Once they discover she doesn't scare easily, the problem will only get worse." Cash brushed a spot of dust from his black sleeve. "How on earth did such a nice girl get herself into so much trouble?"

"We can't escort Eden out of town until we know where the Merriweathers are," Sullivan muttered. "Bushwhacking travelers is what they do, and she'd be too exposed on the trail, too vulnerable."

"So we sit tight, for the moment."

Sullivan laid his eyes on Cash, trying to read the gambler's face. As usual, it was damn near impossible. "You don't like her much."

"No."

"Why not?"

Cash gave the question some serious thought. "I don't like her because she brings trouble wherever she goes. Women like her always do. I don't like her because she's trying to wrap you around her little finger. She's doing a fine job of it, by the way."

He feared Cash was much too close to the truth. "If we have to go do battle, are you with us?" he asked.

Cash lifted surprised eyebrows and almost smiled. "I consider a woman to be the worst possible reason to go to war, but if you need me, I'll be right beside you. We are not the most remarkable of men, Sullivan. We are, at times, selfish and callous and shiftless. But we are notable soldiers, and when the time for battle comes, there are none better. If there's a fight, I will not miss it."

"Thank you," Sullivan muttered, wondering how he could have ever suspected Cash of being so underhanded as to try to scare Eden out of town.

Cash ordered two whiskeys and shooed an attentive Ethel aside. "One drink, and then we tell the others what we know." He lifted his glass, and with a twinkle in his eye said, "War I can handle. I even look forward to it. Dangers such as pretty, *nice* girls are more likely to do men like us in. Don't forget it."

Sullivan drained his glass, keeping to himself the sudden uneasy conviction that it was much too late for such advice.

Eden's annoyance at the constant presence of a guard dissolved when she heard that the Merriweathers had escaped. She and Sin had not told the brothers where they were headed, but as Cash so bluntly pointed out, anyone asking questions about Sinclair Sullivan would soon know where to look.

Rico checked her room before she put the children to bed, and Nate positioned himself in the hallway, just outside the door. Sin and Jedidiah took turns walking the perimeter of the hotel and climbing into the bell tower to scan the land surrounding Rock Creek, keeping their eyes open for anything or anyone suspicious. Cash had returned to the saloon.

Eden sat in the lobby with Rico and Jedidiah while Sin circled the hotel. She found herself perching stiffly on the edge of the sofa, her hands clasped in her lap. She couldn't possibly sleep, and if she tried she'd only disturb Millie with her tossing and turning.

Rico anxiously fingered the knife on his belt as he paced. "I cannot believe you and Sullivan are actually married." He grinned crookedly. *"Ah, matrimonio."*

"They're not married," Jedidiah declared with finality. "There were no witnesses, the preacher was drunk, the ceremony was held in a hotel lobby and not a church, and no one asked my permission. I didn't see it, I didn't give her away, and it doesn't count."

Rico's grin widened. "I heard about your brotherly position on the subject. I also heard that Senora Sullivan kicked both you and her *esposo* out of the hotel."

"That's Miss Rourke to you, Kid," Jedidiah snapped, and then he laid narrowed eyes on Eden. "Forcing me out of the hotel is not an option anymore. You know that, don't you?"

"I know." Eden sighed. "You can collect your things and move back in tonight."

Jedidiah grinned in victory. "I'll do that."

"Sin, too, I guess," she said softly. Oh, it was not a good idea to live under the same roof with her husband! How was she supposed to remain cool to him when she had to see him every day? When she knew he was sleeping just above her head?

"I don't think so," Jedidiah said. "He can stay in the saloon."

With a distaste that made her lips pucker, Eden remembered walking into the saloon and finding her husband with a hussy perched on his knee. She was not about to force him to live in that awful place, surrounded by those terrible women!

"No," she said calmly. "If I allow you to move back in, I have to let Sin return, too. It's only fair."

Jedidiah muttered something that was surely obscene. The only word she could decipher with any certainty was *fair*, the word spit out like a bite of something bitter.

When Sin returned from his reconnaissance, announcing that all was clear, Jedidiah left to collect his things from the saloon. He instructed Rico to stay put while he was gone. Goodness, her brother was not about to leave her alone with Sin, not even for a few minutes.

"You should get to bed," Sin said gruffly, without looking at her. "It's been a long day."

A long, terrible day following a long, wonderful night. Just twenty-four hours ago, she and Sin had stood in this lobby and promised to stay together forever. They'd laughed and quivered and kissed. They'd rushed up the stairs to lie in each other's arms and make love. How could it be over?

It wasn't, not if she wouldn't allow it to be over.

"I'm not tired," she whispered. "I'd rather stay here." *With you.*

She wanted everything of Sin, his affection and his love, his body and his heart. If she could only have that little piece of him he was willing to give, would it be enough? If he touched her, it would be impossible to refuse him. If he kissed her, she would do anything he asked. It was truly unfair that she found herself so terribly weak where her husband was concerned.

Rico turned on his heel and headed for the dining room. "I am going to swipe a piece of that custard pie from the kitchen. I will not be gone long, I promise," he added as he stepped through the doorway, leaving them alone.

"I guess he thinks we need to talk," Eden said, settling herself against the soft cushions of the lobby sofa.

"He's wrong." Sin didn't even look at her, but stared at the front door as if he expected Curtis Merriweather to appear there at any moment.

"No," Eden said softly. "He's right. Sin, what are we going to do?"

"We're going to wait."

"For what?"

"For the Merriweathers. For the man who's been trying to frighten you into leaving town." He turned and looked down at her. "We're going to wait until we know if last night resulted in a child. If it did we'll have to stay married, somehow. If not . . ."

Her heart did a quick, unpleasant flip. "You can't just undo what's already happened. You can't let Jedidiah's temper decide the rest of our lives." She gave the seat beside her a gentle pat. "Sit down."

"No . . ."

"Afraid?"

Sin took the seat beside her, but he didn't relax.

"We don't have to resolve anything tonight," she said. "But for one thing. We decide what happens to us. Not Jedidiah. Not anyone else. *We* decide."

"There's not much to decide." Sin finally looked at her. "What do you expect me to do? Give up my life to live in an old run-down hotel and raise other people's children? Settle down and spend my days being papa to every stray you bring in?"

"Is that all you think we have ahead of us?"

"I'm not the kind of man who wants to settle down into domestic misery."

Misery! How could he? "Didn't you think of that last night, when we got married?" Eden's heart sank. She should've known a man like Sinclair Sullivan would never be content to live the life she wanted.

"Last night I was thinking of one thing," Sin admitted. "Getting you into bed. I didn't even consider what might come after."

It was not what she wanted to hear, but at least

he was being honest with her. "If all you wanted was sex, you could've gone across the street."

"I didn't want to go across the street," he seethed. "I wanted you. No one else."

Eden smiled. It wasn't exactly a declaration of love, but it would do. For now.

She leaned just a little bit closer to him. "I hope I'm not going to have a baby," she whispered. "Not yet."

She could see the hurt in his eyes, the rejection. Ah, he didn't know what he wanted, and the indecision was tearing him apart.

"I want you to stay for me, not for a child." She laid her hand on his forearm. "I want us to stay married because you love me, not because you feel obligated."

"I already told you . . ."

"I know. You don't believe in fate. You don't believe in love. You don't believe we have a future together." She smiled and settled her head on his shoulder. "It all sounds very cynical, perhaps even hostile, but there's one small problem. I don't believe you." She closed her eyes and made herself comfortable against Sin's side. "In my heart I know you want the same things I do. You want love and family and a home."

"You're wrong," he said softly, not pushing her away but shifting until they were both more comfortable. "I like you, Eden, you know I do, but don't make more of this than that. Sooner or later you'll go back to Georgia, and I'll go back to being a hired gun."

"I don't think so," she whispered, and then she drifted off to sleep.

* * *

Eden fell asleep leaning against his shoulder, and a moment later repositioned herself so her head was in his lap with her legs curled up beneath her green calico skirt. Sullivan knew it would be best if he just eased off the couch, or maybe woke Eden and sent her to bed, but he didn't. Instead, he settled his hand lightly in her hair and leaned his head back. At least here she was safe.

"Well, that did not take long," Rico said as he stepped into the lobby from the dining room. "Senora Sullivan sleeps like only the truly innocent can."

"Yeah," Sullivan said softly. "She's exhausted." He cut a sharp gaze to the kid. "And cut the Senora Sullivan crap."

Rico sat in the chair nearest the sofa and stretched out his long legs. "For such a sweet *muchacha*, Senora . . . Eden, if you prefer . . . certainly has found herself a heap of trouble in a very short time. Those *banditos*, whoever wants her out of town." He grinned. "You."

"Where Eden goes, calamity follows." And it was all her fault. If she wasn't constantly sticking her nose into other people's business, she'd be safe in Georgia right now, married to some boring, reliable greenhorn who'd thank his lucky stars every day that such a good, beautiful woman had consented to be his wife. "As soon as this is over, she's going back to Georgia."

Rico shook his head. "Stupid."

"Stupid?"

Rico gestured toward a sleeping Eden with his knife. "She is yours. I can see it in the way she turns those big blue eyes on you, in the way you stare at her when you think no one is watching. I can see it in the way you two look together.''

"That doesn't make a damn bit of sense," Sullivan muttered quietly.

"Perhaps not, but that is what I see," Rico said impatiently. "I saw it the day Eden arrived in Rock Creek, when I stepped from the hotel and you were helping her from the wagon. Your eyes were pinned on her; her eyes were riveted on you." He cast out an impatient hand. "I am surprised either of you saw me at all. Eden is beautiful; she is kind; she has a smile that can make a man's heart stop. Why do you think I have not presented myself as a suitor? Because she is yours and I see it even if you do not. *Dios*, Sullivan, if a woman looked at me that way, if she trusted me enough to lay her head in my lap and sleep like a baby knowing danger is near, I would do whatever I had to do in order to keep her."

"I can't . . . keep her."

"Of course you can."

"I don't want to keep her." That was the truth of it, wasn't it? "If I do, one day she'll wake up and look at me and wonder what the hell she was thinking when she married me. One day she'll realize that she could've done better." And on that day, how would she look at him? With hate, disappointment, revulsion? He didn't plan to be around to see it. He'd seen that look in the faces of the only family he'd ever known, for the first fifteen years of his life. He wasn't about to put himself in a position to be confronted with the hate of someone he loved again.

He had loved his mother dearly, and there had been days, he was convinced, when he saw a mother's love in her eyes. But the older he got the less frequent those glimpses of affection were. The more he began to look like his father, the more his mother had hated him. He'd even tried to love his grandfather and uncle, but they'd made it impossible. There had never been any affection in their eyes or in their words.

He looked down at Eden and stroked her hair. And he loved her. Damn it, he didn't want to, he *did not* want to love her or anyone else. It wouldn't last and it wasn't real, but for now . . .

Jed came bursting through the door, his saddle-bags in hand. As soon as he saw Eden's position he frowned and dropped the bags. "Damn it, Sullivan."

"She's asleep," he said in a lowered voice. "Since she's exhausted, I think we should let her sleep as long as she wants."

Jed grumbled as he took the closest chair, his eyes on Eden the whole time. "She's my baby sister, the only truly good thing in my life. If anyone were to hurt her, I'd have to kill them. I wouldn't have any choice in the matter. It would be my duty as her brother."

"I know," Sullivan said softly. He felt the same anxiety, the same urge to protect her. "The Merri-weathers we can handle, once they show up, but this other . . ."

"Hellfire," Jed mumbled impatiently. "I wasn't talking about the Merriweathers or whoever's been writing those notes. I was talking about you."

Jed lit a cigar and stepped onto the boardwalk. The sun would be up in half an hour or so, and then maybe he'd go to bed. He didn't know if he could sleep or not, not with a bunch of bandits after Eden and Sullivan sniffing after her like a mangy dog after a bitch in heat. He took a long draw on the cigar and thought of all the reasons he *shouldn't* kill Sullivan.

They'd ridden together on too many bad days. They'd laughed together too much and gotten pickled when they just couldn't stand to think any more. Sullivan had saved his life more than once, and Jed had returned the favor.

But this was Eden they were talking about. All bets were off.

"Jed?"

He recognized the voice right away and showed no surprise as Sylvia came closer. He'd heard her a while back, as she'd approached cautiously, but he'd also recognized the step as that of a woman. There had been no threat in her stealthy advance.

"Sylvia," he said, turning toward her and taking another drag of his cigar, "a little early for you to be up and about, isn't it?"

She looked no different, hadn't changed at all. Her hair was black and silky, her eyes dark—even though he could not see them well in the near-dark. Her figure, in a dark dress that cinched her waist and emphasized her bosom, was breath-taking.

"I was hoping I could catch you alone, for a few minutes," she whispered.

"Not exactly proper for a preacher's wife to be out hunting down her old lovers, is it?" He hadn't known he still felt so hurt until he heard the bitterness in his voice.

Sylvia moved so close he could smell her. The smell was familiar, so he took a long drag on the cigar and blew smoke toward her. She ignored the smoke and lifted her head to look up at him.

"I made a terrible mistake," she whispered. There was just enough light for him to see the sheen of tears in her eyes. "A terrible mistake. I never should've married Maurice." She reached out and laid a trembling hand on his arm. "And I miss you. I never knew how I would miss you until it was too late." She took a step forward and laid her head on his chest.

Jed sighed. Hellfire, he didn't need this! "Isn't he good to you, Sylvia?" He wondered if she wanted him to take her away from Rock Creek, if she was looking for a way to escape her husband.

"He tries." She sighed against his chest. "But . . . But he's not you." She slipped her arms around him and held on tight. "Don't you miss me at all?" she whispered.

He couldn't say he'd ever loved Sylvia, but they'd had a helluva good time, for a while. Did he miss her? Sometimes, he did. "Do you want me to take you away from here? Do you want to leave Rock Creek?"

"No," she breathed. "I just want you to be my lover again."

"You want to leave Clancy?"

She shook her head. "I can't leave Maurice, but that doesn't mean I don't want you back in my life." She lifted her head and came up on her toes to lay her lips against his neck. "Make love to me, Jed."

He wasn't what anyone would call an upstanding man, but he did draw the line at sleeping with another man's wife. "No, thanks."

She stiffened and stepped back. "No, *thanks?*"

He took her chin in his hand and made her look up at him. What he saw in her face was anger, pure and simple. "If you hadn't married Clancy

I'd probably be in your bed right now. But you did, and I'm not, and that's that."

"Well, you're not interested in getting married," she snapped in a low voice. "All you wanted was sex. That's all I'm asking for now. It shouldn't make a bit of difference that I have a husband."

Jed shook his head. "Makes a difference to me."

"But he's not . . . very . . ." She sighed. "He's not like you, Jed."

He grinned and chucked her under the chin. "Nobody is, darlin'."

"You're going to punish me for marrying Maurice," she said incredulously.

"Nope. Looks to me like you've done a fine job of punishing yourself."

Sylvia pulled her shoulders back and stood tall. "I'll find another lover."

"I don't doubt it," Jed said softly.

"You'll miss me."

He shook his head softly and diligently studied what was left of his cigar. "I don't doubt that, either."

Sylvia left as quietly as she'd come, if a good bit quicker, leaving Jed to stand on the boardwalk and ponder the fairer sex.

By the time the sun came up he wasn't fit company for any man or woman in Rock Creek.

Chapter 16

After two days without any threatening activity, her contingent of guards seemed to relax. Still, they were always close at hand and armed. Eden tried to go about her normal business, cleaning and fixing up the hotel, trying to make it a home for Millie and Teddy.

She'd already set aside a couple of rooms on the third floor. The two bedrooms were in a quiet corner and had a connecting door. For now, she slept in one room and the children slept in the other, but eventually she wanted to expand the suite to four rooms, all with connecting doors for privacy. Yes, four rooms should suffice. One for each of the children, one for her and Sin, and a sitting room for reading or studying or simply sitting by the fire.

She did not tell Sin that one of the rooms would be theirs. He was still stubbornly insisting that

Jedidiah was right, that their marriage wasn't real and binding.

Jedidiah and Nate were eating breakfast, and Rico, who had been up all night, slept. Sin was her guard at the moment, but he stood silently on the stairway between the second and third floors. Jedidiah had backed off a little, actually allowing her to be alone with her husband for brief periods of time. Since he was not a man given to surrender, she assumed he thought he no longer had anything to worry about. Perhaps he was right. Sin barely looked at her anymore.

She opened the door to the room that was now solely hers, intending to air it out on this fine autumn day. The room was not much better than the one she'd moved into on the day she'd arrived in Rock Creek, even though she'd already given it a good cleaning. It was sorely lacking in the warmth that would one day make this place a home. Well, it would take time to make this room homey.

Who was she kidding? It wouldn't feel like home until Sin moved in, until she'd slept with him in that big bed.

She saw the stalk on the bed, resting on her pillow, but for a moment she didn't know what it was. Closer inspection revealed a dried and broken bouquet of weeds, all tied together with a red silk ribbon. Her first thought was that Millie had put together an arrangement, much as she'd done on their journey, but the blooms had died too quickly. When she saw the note, she knew she was wrong.

You think your guardians can keep you safe? Soon you'll be as dead as these flowers. They were once beautiful, too.

"Sin," she whispered, her voice so low he surely couldn't hear her.

And still, a moment later he was standing in the doorway, his Colt in one hand. "What's wrong?"

She turned her face to him and pointed at the note and dead bouquet on her bed. Tears filled her eyes, and without so much as a second's hesitation she walked into his arms. Once he decided there was no imminent danger, he sheathed his six-shooter in the holster he'd borrowed from Cash and wrapped his arms around her.

"It's all right," he said in a soothing voice as she buried her head against his chest.

"It's not all right," she whispered. "Someone wants me dead. And whoever it was walked into my room and left this . . . this *thing* for me. They were right *here* sometime in the past two hours, while I was in the kitchen or serving breakfast in the dining room or dusting in the lobby."

Sin tried to disengage himself. "We need to tell the others."

Eden held on to him tight. "Not yet," she whispered. "Please don't let me go just yet. Give me just a minute here. Please," she said again. Being in his arms comforted her, made her heart begin to slow to a normal pace, made her fears gradually fade.

Sin's arms tightened around her, and she closed her eyes to get lost in his embrace. How could he say he didn't love her? How could he deny this?

"I won't let anyone hurt you," he whispered in her ear.

"I know."

"Only a coward would do this," he said angrily. "Damn it, when I find out who it is . . ."

He let the sentence die without telling her what

he wanted to do to her tormentor. She knew, well enough, how angry and protective he was. He sheltered her. He only wanted what was best for her. She had never doubted that.

No longer afraid, she lifted her head and stared up at Sin. "I wish you could tell me you love me as easily as you show it," she whispered.

His body went tense, but he didn't release her.

"I am a selfish woman, I suppose. I want you," she whispered. "But I want all of you. Not a small piece, not a tiny fragment that you're willing to give away without granting your heart."

"I don't have what you want."

"Yes, you do." She lifted herself up on her toes and kissed him. Softly, tenderly. His whole body responded; she felt it. "You're everything I want, Sinclair Sullivan. Everything I will ever want."

"You don't know what you're saying. This is just . . . just . . ."

"Lust?" she finished for him. "Maybe that's part of it, but I know we have more than sheer physical attraction between us. What we have is extraordinary, and it's much more than physical, no matter how you fight accepting the truth.

"But the physical craving is a part of it." She boldly reached down and laid her hand over his arousal. "I won't deny that." She stroked him lightly. "I'm not so ignorant anymore. Not as innocent as I was a few days ago. I still dream about you, Sin, only now I know exactly what I'm dreaming about."

He kissed her hard and deep, thrusting his tongue into her mouth, catching her against his body and holding her there. Her body throbbed and so did his; it was a wondrous feeling.

Through her layers of clothing, Sin touched her.

He touched her breasts, he raked his hand over her mound, and forced his fingers between her legs. When she moaned, he caught the sound in his mouth and pushed harder. Her legs parted, and she raked her hands against his denim-clad buttocks, holding on for dear life.

She heard Jedidiah on the floor below. In a moment he'd be on the stairs to the third floor, then in the hall, then right outside her open door.

"I'd like to clean the tub," she whispered.

Sin moaned. "Jed will never leave us alone for more than a few minutes."

She heard a footfall on the stairs. "I know."

"Unless he thinks you're safe from me," Sin whispered in her ear. He made himself pull away from her. "So when he gets here, tell me you hate me. Tell me you're sorry you married me and you hope you never see my ugly face again as long as you live."

Eden smiled. "I love your face."

"Do you want to clean the tub?"

More than anything. "Of course, but . . ." In a flash, she knew what his plan was. When Jedidiah appeared in the doorway, her smile was gone. But could she lie to her own brother?

"Eden found another note," Sin said tersely. His eyes narrowed. "But I don't see how anyone could've gotten past us. Maybe Cash had it right. Maybe she wrote the notes herself."

She was truly shocked, for a moment. Then she realized what Sin was doing. "How dare you?" she said coldly. "I would never stoop to such treachery." The indignant words made her feel guilty. What she was doing right now was more than a little treacherous. Still, if it was the only way she and Sin could be alone . . .

Sin shook his head. "You're a woman, aren't you? A spoiled, pretty, empty-headed . . ."

That one hurt, in truth. "And you're an imbecile who knows nothing about women," she interrupted. "I don't know what I ever saw in you. It's a good thing Jedidiah came along and made me see the light."

Her brother smiled. They had almost forgotten about the note and dead bouquet on the bed.

"As soon as this mess is over," Sin said in a low, gruff voice, "you're going back to Georgia if I have to drag you there."

"I found my way here, I can find my way back," she said, her nose in the air. "And not a moment too soon!"

She turned her back on Sin and looked at Jedidiah. She hoped he thought her red face was due to anger, not complete embarrassment at her wickedly deceptive performance. "I'm going to clean in the bathing room for a while. You look over the note and decide how to proceed. I don't need or want a bodyguard while I . . . clean the tub."

She spun on her heel and walked into the hall. As she'd suspected, Jedidiah ordered Sin to follow, *at a safe distance,* he suggested in a wry voice.

Eden practically ran down the stairs. Sin was right behind her.

Sullivan leaned against the partition that separated the door to the bathing room from the lobby. He tried to look casual, unconcerned, a little pissed, as Jed came down the stairs.

"I'm going to run these over to the saloon and see what Cash and Nate think," Jed said, shaking the bouquet of dead flowers in Sullivan's direction.

"Then I'll run by the general store and see if Baxter remembers selling anyone this ribbon."

Sullivan nodded once.

"She in there?" Jed asked, nodding toward the room beyond the partition.

"Yep."

"I know it's rough, but I'm glad you two came to your senses." Jed tried a sympathetic smile that didn't quite work. "I gotta warn you, though. My little sister doesn't lose her temper often, but once she gets mad she *stays* mad for a while. She doesn't forgive easily."

"Neither do I," Sullivan said softly. He waited until Jed was well beyond the hotel entrance, and then he turned and walked to the door of the bathing room. With his fingers on the handle, he hesitated. This was a bad idea and he damn well knew it. He swung open the door and stepped inside, closing the door behind him. Sun pouring from the tiny window set above the tub lit the small room with yellow light.

Eden stood beside the tub, her hands clasped demurely before her. "I can't believe I lied to Jedidiah," she said softly. "Did I hear him leave?"

Sullivan nodded. "Are you having second thoughts?"

She smiled and shook her head. "Not a one."

He took her in his arms and kissed her, lifting her up so she had to balance on the tips of her toes, holding her so tight he could feel the beat of her heart and the quiver that shook her when he plunged his tongue into her mouth.

He caressed her breasts, fondled the sensitive peaks. She moaned into his mouth, parting her lips wide, pressing herself against him.

"I do love you, so much," she whispered

hoarsely. "I need to know that you love me back, Sin. I've seen it. I've felt it. But I need you to tell me."

"Isn't this enough?"

"No." She unbuttoned his shirt and slipped her hand inside. "I love the feel of your skin," she whispered.

"You fight dirty," he muttered.

"This isn't fighting."

Ah, but it was. This was the battle of a lifetime; a fight he couldn't win. A war he'd lost long ago. "I want you," he whispered.

She boldly laid her hand over his denims, over his erection. "I know you want me." She opened a button, stroked once, opened another button. "I also know that you love me."

His resolve deteriorated. "Even if I do, it doesn't matter."

"It matters to me."

He lifted her skirt and reached beneath to untie the tapes at her waist. Her drawers dropped to the floor and she kicked them away. When he touched her intimately she gasped. When he slipped a finger inside her, she closed her eyes and melted against him.

"Sin," she whispered, "what if someone comes in?"

"They won't." He stroked her until she gave over completely, until she forgot that there was no latch on the door to this small room. She pressed her body to his and held on with all her might, tender and strong.

She didn't ask him again to say that he loved her. She threaded her fingers through his hair and held on tight. She touched him, teased him, caressed and kissed him, and opened one button of his denims at a time. Her body rocked against his as he touched her, stroking her wet entrance.

The moment passed when she had no more words. He knew the exact moment, savored it the way he savored the feel of her. There was simply her body and his, raw pleasure, unbridled need. He lifted her into his arms and spun her around, placing her back against the wall. She was so light, so tiny, so beautiful. He didn't deserve her, and he certainly didn't deserve her love.

But he did love her.

She wrapped her legs around him, searching for the joining she craved as he did. He touched her, barely began to enter her, but he held her up and back.

"Look at me," he whispered.

She opened her eyes. No one had ever looked at him this way before—hungry, open, loving, wanting, and vulnerable.

"I want you so bad I ache with it. I need you like I've never needed anything else." With that he plunged inside her, stretching and filling, wrapping her body around his. She held on to his neck and lifted her body, then moved down and against him so that he filled her completely, so that he was buried deep inside her.

He wasn't gentle, and she didn't ask for gentleness from him. This coming together was built on need and lust and promise. It was a fierce mating, an uncontrollable force. When Eden climaxed she cried out, and as she milked him with her inner muscles Sullivan again pumped his seed, his soul, into her waiting body.

She melted, with her legs still around him and her head resting against his shoulder.

"We never made it to the tub," she said breathlessly.

"Not enough room."

They sank to the floor, still entwined.

"We really *must* put a latch on the door," Eden said, a touch of humor in her breathless voice as she reached out to brush her fingers against the door.

Sullivan mumbled his assent.

"You do need me, you know," she said sweetly. "And I need you. I don't want to go back to Georgia, no matter what the two of you have to say about the matter." With a deep, satisfied sigh she adjusted her position, cuddling against him. "So what do we do next?" she asked. "Do we tell Jedidiah that we're married and that's that, or do we pretend to hate each other until he's had time to get used to the idea of us together?"

"I don't know. We'll have to think about it."

As much as she wanted to hear it, he couldn't tell Eden that he loved her. Even though it was, unfortunately, true, he wasn't yet convinced that the love would last—or that it would be enough.

It was difficult to lie, especially to her brother, so Eden decided the best course of action was simply to ignore Sin when Jedidiah was present. The plan was amazingly successful. By nightfall everyone had noticed the change. Over supper in the hotel dining room Jedidiah was pleased with himself, Nate shook his head in disapproval, and Cash almost celebrated.

She had an idea that Rico wasn't fooled, but at least he had the decency to keep his suspicions to himself.

What she really wanted to do was go to Jedidiah and tell him the truth, that she loved Sin and he needed her and they were married. End of discussion. Unfortunately Jedidiah was not likely to take the defeat well, and with so much else going on, now was not the time for more turmoil.

Eden ate supper at a table with Millie and Teddy. Sin was all the way on the opposite side of the room, eating dinner with Rico and Nate. Jedidiah shared a table with Cash and his twittering, giggling dinner companion, a busty blonde in a low-cut red dress. Ethel.

After this afternoon, Eden had no doubts that Rock Creek was her home and always would be. She was going to have to make an effort to meet other women in town, women besides those who made their livings in the saloon across the street. She needed to invite Mary Reese and Rose Sutton to lunch, when she was settled and the hotel was in better shape. They could introduce her to the other women in town.

"Mama," Teddy said in a low voice, capturing her attention with little more than a whisper.

Eden smiled down at him. "Yes?"

"Why are you mad at . . . at Mr. Sullivan?" He turned those big brown eyes up, and Eden's heart melted.

Millie put her fork down and waited expectantly for a response. "Yeah. I thought he was going to be our papa. You said he might be, and now he's not even talking to us."

Oh dear. "Well," Eden said in a low voice, "it's a very complicated story. I'm not really mad at Mr. Sullivan."

"You looked mad at him when you put his plate

down so hard his chicken jumped," Millie said, lowering her own voice.

Eden looked around the room. While the men were close enough, no one was listening. Still, she whispered. "It's a kind of game, like the one we played on the way to Rock Creek. And like the other game, it's a secret."

"Okay," Millie whispered conspiratorially. "I won't tell. Do I have to be mad at him, too?"

"No."

Teddy frowned and pushed at his peas on his plate with his fork. "Why isn't he eating with us? Did I do something wrong? Did I make him mad?"

Eden placed her hand over his. "Of course not. Just a game, remember."

It was clear Teddy did not like this particular game. "How long is it going to last?"

Eden glanced across the room, just as Sin lifted his head and looked at her. Her heart leaped, and she had to work much too hard to contain her smile. "Not very long," she said. "I promise."

When she jumped up and began to gather the dirty dishes, Rico left his seat and headed for the kitchen. As had become the custom, the room would be thoroughly inspected before she entered it. Since two of the notes, and the scorpions, had been left there, it was clear someone was finding their way through the back door or the window.

A few minutes later Rico emerged from the kitchen and gave her a nod, acknowledging that all was clear, and Eden carried a stack of plates to the counter. When she turned around, she was surprised to see Ethel standing in the doorway with another stack of dirty dishes.

"You look like you could use a hand," the saloon girl said, almost shyly.

Eden prided herself on being fair, always. Had she been fair to Ethel and the other girls from the saloon? Of course not. She'd condemned them from the beginning without even attempting to get to know them. Like she wanted to get to know the woman who'd had the audacity to sit on Sin's lap!

"That's very nice of you," she said. "But you shouldn't have. Cash paid for your meal and his. I really shouldn't put paying customers to work."

Ethel answered with a wide smile. "I grew up in a house with six sisters. Sitting there and watching one woman do all the work while I sit just doesn't feel natural."

Taking the plates from Ethel's hands, Eden said, "I do have an awful lot of work on my hands. I need to find a replacement for Lydia. She left after Grady died, and I could use her right about now. I suppose I could advertise in the weekly paper for someone to help out around the place, but I have no idea what kind of response I might get to such an ad." She studied Ethel with a critical eye. Bless her heart, beneath all that face paint, the saloon girl was just a woman making her way in the world, much as Eden was trying to do.

She had a wonderful idea, a stroke of pure genius. "I can't afford to pay much at the moment, but free room and board would be part of the package, and as soon as I make this hotel into a profitable venture the salary would be raised."

Ethel's bright smile faded and she looked away. "That sounds very nice. I'm sure you'll find someone."

"Do you like your job?" Eden asked softly, wondering if she was going too far. "What I mean to say is, if you wanted to work here I'd be happy to have you." Ethel smiled and laughed a lot and looked as if her life was easy and carefree, but Eden couldn't imagine that making yourself available for any man with enough money was a pleasant way to make a living.

"You don't want me here," Ethel said in a low voice, as if someone might be listening. "People will talk. . . ."

"Goodness gracious, I don't care one whit about gossip," Eden said adamantly. "If you want the job, it's yours." She handed the dirty dishes back to Ethel. "Starting immediately, if you're willing."

Ethel took the dirty dishes with a smile and headed for the counter.

Chapter 17

"This time she's gone too far," Cash seethed. "Can you imagine Ethel cooking and changing sheets and doing laundry? What a waste!"

Sullivan tried not to smile, but he couldn't help himself. Taking in one of the saloon girls and effectively reforming her was so like Eden, he shouldn't be surprised.

Four of them sat in the hotel lobby—Rico, Jed, Cash, and himself. Nate was already in position on the third floor, outside Eden's room. Thank goodness Rico wasn't taking the evening watch. Sullivan knew he'd have no trouble sneaking past Nate, when the time came. Rico was another matter.

"That woman of yours . . ." Cash began, his finger shaking in Sullivan's direction.

"She's not *my* woman."

Rico muttered something in low Spanish. Since

Sullivan had an idea what was being said, he didn't ask the kid to speak up.

"Well, you brought her here," Cash accused.

Sullivan raised his hands in surrender. "Fine. Blame me if you want, but I can't see that Ethel's retirement is such a catastrophe. There are still two girls working in the saloon, and you can't tell me you won't be able to find a new woman to take Ethel's place."

The idea soothed Cash. "Someone new would be nice. Ethel was getting a little clingy. Maybe when this is all over I can make a trip to San Antonio to see about bringing someone else in. But I still say that woman of yours, that . . . that Eden, is nothing but trouble."

"That's my sister you're talking about," Jed snapped.

"Senora Sullivan . . ." Rico began. When Jed and Sullivan glared at him, he nodded in silent apology and began again. "Eden is a sweet girl," he said, flashing a wicked grin. "And she is also very pretty. We do not see enough of the beautiful senoritas in Rock Creek. Since Sullivan does not want her anymore and claims so convincingly that she is *not* his woman, maybe I will ask her to walk with me one evening, or if she will allow me to escort her to the next town social. . . ."

"Not you, too." Cash groaned in dismay.

"That's my *sister* you're talking about," Jed rumbled. "And she's too good for any one of us, I can tell you that. You keep your fancy ideas to yourself, Kid."

Rico gave Sullivan a quick glance. His dark eyes danced, and his mouth worked into a crooked grin. Hell, the kid knew everything.

Eventually everyone would know. Jed wouldn't

like it, but at the moment Sullivan didn't care what the surly man thought. He'd likely have to fight for Eden; he'd likely lose one of his closest friends. And since he didn't have many friends left, that would be a real sacrifice.

But right now all he could think about was Eden. She was upstairs in her bed, right this minute. Had she fallen asleep yet? Did she know he would go to her tonight?

"I'm going to take the early morning watch," he said, standing slowly, "so I'd better get to bed."

Rico grinned. "The man needs his rest."

Sullivan cut a sharp glance to the kid. No one else seemed to notice.

Eden burrowed into the pillow. She needed to sleep. She needed rest to prepare herself for the day to come.

But her mind was spinning with thoughts of the children, and Ethel, and plans for the hotel, and Sin. Mostly she thought of Sin.

She lay on her side and faced the window. Soft moonlight lit wafting clouds in the sky. They needed rain, and it looked like they might get it, soon. Maybe tomorrow, maybe the next day . . .

"Are you asleep?" The whisper startled her, made her jump, but a smile quickly crossed her face. She knew that voice.

"No." She rolled onto her back and looked up at the figure by the bed. "How on earth did you get in here without me hearing you?"

"It's what I do."

She smiled and scooted to the side, making room for him on the bed.

He sat down and reached out to touch her, his

hand on her neck and in her hair. "Are you sure about this? About us?"

"Very," she whispered. "Aren't you?"

He rocked his fingers gently and hesitated before answering. "No. Sometimes I think your brother's right. None of us is good enough for you."

The very notion irritated her. Not good enough? How could he think that? "So how should I fall in love. Tell me that? Perhaps I should ask Jedidiah to compile a list of suitable candidates, and then the three of us can decide together. We can draw up a list of pros and cons and debate the worthiness of each candidate as if we were choosing a horse."

"That's not what I meant," Sin said lowly. "I just want you to be safe and happy."

She sat up and moved closer to him. "I don't want to argue with you," she said, reaching out to touch his cheek. "I don't even like pretending to argue. Do you really think I could be happy in Georgia now? Do you think I could ever walk away from you? Lock me in the safest house in the world away from the ones I love, and I'll wither and die." She came to her knees and faced him, feeling his body heat mingle with hers. "I love you most of all."

Sin kissed her, hungry and deep, and slowly worked her nightgown up and over her head. He tossed the nightgown aside and laid his hands on her breasts, around her waist, on her bare bottom. He pulled her tight against him and held her closely as they kissed.

He had come to her room on bare feet, so all they had to do was remove his shirt and denims. Eden sighed as he held her, his bare chest against her breasts, his arms around her.

"I never knew I could feel like this," she said breathlessly.

"Me, either."

"Do you think it will always be so wonderful for us?"

Sin hesitated, pressing his lips to the side of her neck, kissing her there while he pondered the question. Eden held her breath.

"Yes," he finally answered. "I do."

There was no rush tonight, no urgency. They kissed and touched and whispered, first sitting on the bed, then lying side by side, face-to-face, and as close as humanly possible.

"I want to touch you," she whispered. Without waiting for his response, she wrapped her hand around his manhood. He moaned as she raked her exploring fingers along the hot, velvety length.

He rolled her onto her back and hovered above her, blocking out the moonlight as he lowered his mouth to hers. She spread her legs to bring him closer, arched her back to press herself to him.

Sin lowered his mouth to her breasts, suckling as he placed his hand between her legs. She quivered as he drew a taut nipple into his mouth and slipped a finger inside her. Ribbons of pleasure fluttered through her body.

She would be content to touch and kiss all night, to give up sleep completely and pass each night just this way.

Sin's head moved lower to kiss her belly, his tongue circling her navel. Everything Eden was and wanted were wrapped up in this man and the way he made her feel. It was everything they talked about, lust, love, need. His hands reached beneath her and grasped her hips. "I want to taste you," he whispered, and then he moved lower to lay his tongue on her in an intimate way that sent her soaring, her back lifting off the bed.

He held her hips and made love to her with his mouth, gently at first and then insistently. She grabbed the sheet and balled her hands into fists as she shattered, arching off the bed, crying out softly as the intense pleasure shot through her body like a bolt of lightning.

Sin worked his way back up her length slowly, kissing and touching as he worked his way up her body. Her heart beat so hard she was afraid it would come through her chest. She couldn't breathe, and her legs quivered.

Sin seemed not to be in a hurry. He took his time, beginning again as if he'd just come to her bed. She didn't think it was possible, but soon she felt the beginning waves of passion, of need, flitting through her body again. She reached for him with her hands and her mouth, her entire body. She craved this and more.

When Sin barely brushed his manhood against her, touching the flesh where she throbbed for him and then moving away, she rocked up slowly to bring him closer.

She wrapped her legs around him and lifted her hips, taking his head in her hands and looking him in the eye. "I want you inside me," she whispered, "now."

He plunged to enter her, to fill her completely. She moved against him and met his fierce thrust with one of her own. He rocked his hips, and again drove forward to be completely sheathed inside her. Again climax shattered her. She felt Sin's own response as he held himself deep inside her and shuddered in her arms. Their mouths met, their muffled cries lost in a long, ardent kiss.

Sin's body collapsed over hers; the kiss turned gentle, and Eden melted against the bed.

"I will never be able to move again," she whispered. "I have nothing left. No energy, no breath, no working muscles."

Sin laughed softly in her ear. "How am I supposed to pretend not to like you tomorrow? How am I supposed to look at you and pretend not to want you?"

"It won't be easy." She threaded her fingers through his hair. "I think we should just go ahead and tell Jedidiah the truth."

"He won't take it well." Sin rolled off of her, but kept her close in his arms.

Eden snuggled against his shoulder. "It doesn't matter. No one's ever going to take you away from me. Not even Jedidiah."

Sin speared his fingers through her hair. "I do need you," he whispered. "Scares the hell out of me sometimes, because I've never needed anyone before, but that doesn't make it any less true."

Eden smiled against Sin's shoulder. "I love you," she said, not caring at the moment that Sin wasn't ready to say the words himself.

His body tensed slightly.

"You shouldn't be afraid of love," she whispered. Knowing what his life had been like, she couldn't hold his reticence against him. It was up to her to show him that love wasn't frightening, that it was more wonderful than he'd ever imagined. She snuggled impossibly close. "I'm never going to let you go. What we have is too good."

"Right this minute," he said breathlessly, "I'll agree with you. As for tomorrow . . . We'll have to wait and see." He sounded almost solemn.

She placed her leg over his and drifted toward sleep. "Sin?" she whispered.

"Hmm?" He was almost asleep himself.

"I won't stop loving you tomorrow. Or the day after that, or the day after that, or ever. I'm not the kind of woman to give my heart or my body on a whim."

"I know that."

"We should tell Jedidiah tomorrow. I'll make a custard pie for lunch. That'll soften him up a little."

"I don't know that a custard pie will balance out having me for a brother-in-law," he said with wry humor. Still, she detected a note of real apprehension in his voice.

It was still dark when Sullivan rose from the bed, dressed, and left a sleeping Eden behind. It was harder to leave her than he'd imagined, and he gave her one last glance before cracking open the door to see where Nate was positioned. As he had been a few hours earlier, Nate stood at the top of the stairs.

Sullivan slipped through the door and down the hallway, remaining silent, staying in the shadows, becoming a shadow. Nate never moved.

In his room, he sat on the side of the bed to put on his boots. He'd fought battles, he'd faced death, and he'd faced hate. Why was he scared half to death of what a woman was doing to him?

He and his wife had nothing in common. Nothing but the sex. That was great, but would it really last? Sinclair Sullivan feared nothing, but he was truly afraid that one morning Eden would wake up, take one look at him, and be horrified by what she'd done. By then there would be a baby, maybe two. Hell, there might already be a baby. The thought of the blood he'd cursed every day of his life flowing in another body, the body of a child, gave him chills.

He relieved Nate and positioned himself outside Eden's door, where he sat for several hours. The sun came up, and he heard Eden stirring inside her room, heard the kids in their own room, opening drawers and talking about the day to come.

Hell, he was even beginning to think of those kids as *his*.

What would he and Eden be like ten years from now? Twenty years? She'd still be taking in strays of one kind or another, and he'd still be hiring his gun out on occasion, if he didn't get himself killed somewhere down the line. There would be other children, theirs and more strays, and women like Ethel. And men like himself.

If he'd been the one kicking ass in Webberville, instead of getting his ass whupped, would she have fallen in love with him? Or would she have thought herself in love with some other poor sap? How much of what she felt stemmed from her obvious need to heal and care for every wounded creature she ran across?

Jed came down the hallway, his rifle in his hand. Well, this would be as good a time as any to break the bad news.

"A quiet night?" Jed asked.

Hell, no. "Yep."

"I've got a raging headache," Jed said gruffly. "After you went to bed last night I let Cash talk me into a few drinks, and it was *not* a good idea. God, I just want to . . . to break something." He shook one big fist.

Eden opened the door and stepped into the hall, dressed for the day in a linen blouse and a red calico skirt. As Jed turned his back, she smiled widely at Sullivan and came toward him as if for a kiss.

He shook his head to warn her back. "Maybe Eden has a headache powder, or a special tea or something."

Eden's smile faded. "Jedidiah, you have a headache?"

He nodded and headed down the stairs.

"Oh," she said, following him, glancing over her shoulder. "I remember, even when you were young you were always a real bear when you had a headache."

"Well it *hurts,*" he bellowed.

"You are such a baby," she said sweetly.

In the dining room, Sullivan passed Eden and her brother to check out the kitchen before she prepared breakfast. Finding nothing, he waved her in.

"Not when he's like this," she said softly. "He might . . . hurt someone."

Sullivan looked through the doorway to see Jed sitting at a table with his head in his hands. "Coffee!" he bellowed. "How long can it take to make a pot of damned coffee!"

"I just got in here, Jedidiah," Eden said patiently. "Give me a few minutes."

Jed groaned and dropped his head to the table.

"Maybe we can tell him after lunch, if his headache is gone and the custard pie puts him in a good mood."

Sullivan nodded. "Or we can just tell him now and take our chances."

Eden smiled and stepped out of Jed's line of

vision to kiss him quickly. "I want the two most important men in my life to get along. I want you two to continue to be friends. We're family now, and more than anything I want us to get off to a good start this time. We can wait a few hours."

"Whatever you want."

"Coffee!"

Eden bustled to the stove and put a pot of water on to boil while she measured out the grounds.

Sullivan had a feeling coffee and pie weren't going to be enough to soften the blow.

It was a beautiful day to work outside. A few fluffy clouds dotted the blue sky, and there was no sign of the rain she'd sensed in last night's sky. A breeze cooled her as she yanked dead plants from the ground with her gloved hands. Sin helped, though he did grumble about being reduced to manual labor.

"I think the medicine I gave Jedidiah put him to sleep," she said, yanking viciously at a long dead plant and plucking it from the ground. "Maybe when he wakes up he'll feel better."

"I don't think custard pie and a clear head are going to make him like this any better," Sin grumbled. "Maybe we should just tell him while he's feeling lousy and get it over with."

Eden wrinkled her nose. "I don't know. Jedidiah has such a temper. Trust me, I know how to handle him."

Sin worked twice as fast as she did, clearing the land. In the spring, they'd plant new flowers and bushes and make this an oasis, a place to come to at the end of the day. A small piece of paradise.

"I want this to go well, though," Sin said. "It will make things much easier, later on."

Eden nodded. If Jedidiah would take her marriage to Sin well, everything would be easier! "I know what you mean."

"Jed doesn't like to stay put any more than I do, but if we can work our schedules so that one of us is here with you all the time, I'll rest easier."

Eden spun slowly to face him, a frown forming on her face. "What do you mean, *one* of you will be here all the time?"

"It means when I'm traveling Jed will be here, and when he's traveling . . ."

"Why would you travel?" Eden asked calmly.

Sin dropped a rather large, dead stalk. "It's what I do," he said. "I hire out, mostly to lawmen in trouble, sometimes to ranchers at war with rustlers, sometimes to towns in trouble. You know that."

She could not believe what she was hearing. "You *used* to hire out your gun," Eden said, to clarify. She shook her head vehemently. "You can't do that anymore," she insisted. "You're a married man, now. We have children to think of. You can't just go . . . go riding off for goodness knows how long."

Sin cocked his head and narrowed his eyes. "I can't?" he asked softly.

"No," she said, knowing as the word came out of her mouth that she'd made a mistake, but unable to back down. "You can't continue to fight other people's battles until you wind up dead. I . . . I won't have it."

The look on his face surprised her a little. He wasn't angry, but he was clearly disappointed. "So what do you have planned for me, Eden? Let's see, your other strays are all taken care of. Teddy and

Millie are in school. Ethel is presently making stew in the kitchen and will soon, no doubt, fall at your feet and thank you for saving her from a life of decadence." *Now* he was angry. "What do you have planned for me?" He kicked at a dead plant. "Am I to be the gardener? Maybe a porter or a bellman. I know, I can take in laundry!"

"I do not take in strays," she said indignantly.

He grinned wickedly. "Of course you do. I ought to know; I'm one of them. I forget that, sometimes, but you just reminded me. You won't *have* it," he muttered beneath his breath.

She could not understand why he was so upset. "Is it wrong of me not to want you to get hurt?"

Sin pinned his eyes on her, hard, unflinching. "Honey, you're great in bed, and in the tub, but no woman tells me what to do with my life. Not even you."

Now *she* was offended. "I'm not just some woman," she snapped. "I'm your wife. If you're going to ride off for goodness knows how long and place yourself in danger, don't you think I should have some say in the matter?"

"No," he said softly.

No? All of a sudden she could feel everything, the sun on her face, the gentle wind, the hard ground beneath her feet. She could see everything with a clarity that only came with a rush of fury. After everything that had happened, he was going to leave her here, again and again, and purposely place himself in dangerous situations. He had no regard for her feelings. Her love meant nothing to him.

"You are so . . . so uncivilized," she whispered.

His face hardened, and his eyes darkened. His

hands folded into fists at his sides. "Yes," he said, "I am. It's in my blood, remember?"

Her heart fell as her anger melted a little and she realized what she'd said. "I didn't mean . . ."

"Inside," he said stalking past her and throwing back the door that opened on to the lobby. "I've had enough gardening for one day. Besides," he said quietly as she passed, "you can make all the plans you want. You can whisper all the honeyed words you want to in the dark. You can tell yourself, and me, that what you feel is love, if it makes you feel better about what we do." He turned to face her and leaned slightly closer, pinning his cold eyes on hers. "But we both know you won't be here in the spring. Rock Creek and the people in it are much too *uncivilized* for you."

Sin spun around and stalked away from her. Rico sat on the green sofa, diligently sharpening his knife, and Sin passed without so much as looking down. "She's all yours," he said as he walked through the doors and across the street to the saloon.

Chapter 18

Sullivan sat in a hardback chair and leaned against the wall. Cash was in a similar position beside him.

"I shoulda seen it," he muttered, shaking his head. "Since the day I met Eden, she's been talking about how she can *handle* her brother. Now she thinks she can handle me."

"A lesser man would say I told you so."

"Thanks for not stooping so low." He didn't know what had made him more angry, the fact that Eden suddenly thought she had the right to tell him how to live his life, or that word that had fallen so easily from her mouth as she'd looked at him— *uncivilized*. All his life he'd been branded with the blood of his father. *Heathen. Renegade. Uncivilized.*

"But I did warn you," Cash added, unable to take the high road. "Women like that, they turn your insides upside down and twist your mind around until you can't think straight, and then they look at you with wide-eyed innocence as if nothing happened."

"That's Eden," Sullivan muttered. He cast a sideways glance at Cash. "How do you know so much about . . . about women like her? You saw from the beginning that there would be trouble. No one else did."

Cash took a long draw on his cigar and blew the smoke out slowly, almost thoughtfully. "I knew a girl just like her once, a long time ago. Damn it Sullivan. I tried to let you benefit from my misfortune, but you had to find out the hard way. You had to discover for yourself that women like Eden Rourke are more dangerous than any soldier or brigand you'll ever face."

He wanted to ask about this woman from the past, the woman who had soured the gunslinger against *nice girls*, but he knew Cash wouldn't share any details. Sullivan's heart sank. He didn't want to be as cynical as Cash. He didn't want to push Eden to the back of his mind, a bad memory and nothing else, just so he could bear to survive without her.

But what else was he supposed to do? She wanted to change him, to turn his life upside down. The way she'd said *no,* when he'd told her he would continue to travel . . . It was as if she simply expected him to obey, as if no one had ever told *her* no before.

She wanted safety and security, a peaceful life. She wasn't going to find it in Rock Creek.

"When this is over, when the Merriweather brothers are captured, she has to go home."

"Amen." Cash raised his glass in salute. "Of course, you don't actually *send* a woman like Eden home. You and Jed were right about that from the beginning. She has to want to go.''

"She won't go if she thinks there's any chance ... if she thinks we'll ever ...''

"So make sure she knows there's nothing left," Cash snapped. "Women like her, they're hopelessly romantic. Give her a nasty dose of reality, and in a matter of days she'll be begging to return to Georgia.''

"A nasty dose of reality?''

"Don't clean yourself up for her. Don't try to make everything pretty and nice." Cash waved a dismissive hand. "Put her in her place, once and for all.''

Eden was still angry as she served lunch. How could Sin possibly think he could continue to travel and chase outlaws and fight one battle after another? The very idea was inconceivable to her. Husbands stayed home. Fathers didn't just ride off whenever the mood struck them.

She sniffled as she slopped a pile of potatoes onto a plate, next to a piece of braised chicken. And besides, she didn't want to be left here alone!

As she and Ethel were serving lunch, Sin came in and sat at a table by the window. He barely glanced her way as he crossed the room and took his seat. Just looking at him made her angry all over again. How could you love someone so much one minute and then in a heartbeat become so furious with them that you shook all over?

She had Ethel serve Sin his lunch, not wanting to approach him until she'd calmed down a little. He was not an unreasonable man, she decided. He was just resistant to change, stubborn. Eventually she'd be able to convince him that she was right.

Jedidiah shuffled into the dining room, rubbing his head as he sat at the nearest table to the door. Since he refused to shave on a regular basis, he always looked a little rough. There was a handsome face beneath that pale stubble; he just wasn't interested in showing it to its best advantage. Too bad. He should be married and have a couple of kids by now.

"Do you feel better?" she asked as she placed his lunch before him.

"Yeah." He looked up at her and grinned. "Thanks for the medicine. It did the trick."

"I made custard pie for desert." She sat beside him and pulled her chair closer to the table.

His grin got wider. "You're a jewel."

"Jedidiah," she said, leaning closer as he began to eat, "why did you never get married?" She held her breath. He and Sin were alike in many ways; they wandered; they defied convention.

"What woman would have me?" he asked with a wink.

She was not going to be put off so easily. "I don't believe for a minute that there aren't lots of women out there who wouldn't love to have you for a husband. You're handsome and smart and funny. . . ."

"And you're my baby sister, so you're a little prejudiced about my better qualities."

Oh, she was not going to let him make light of this conversation! "Why don't you want to be married?"

His smile faded. "This isn't about me at all, is it?"

"Well, just a little," she said softly.

Jedidiah's sharp gaze crossed the room and landed on Sin. Sin ate his lunch and pretended he was all alone, in this room and in the world. "I don't want to be tied down. The idea of living the rest of my life in one place, with one woman, scares the hell out of me."

"But the *right* woman . . ."

"Doesn't exist," Jedidiah interrupted. "Not for someone like me. I might enjoy being married, for a while, but eventually I'd get itchy feet and want to move on. That's not fair to a good woman."

She knew he was no longer talking about himself. "But what about love?"

Jedidiah shook his head and dug into his lunch. "Like the concept of the right woman, it isn't real. It's just . . . attraction between a man and a woman prettied up a bit."

Eden's lower lip trembled. She wanted love more than anything. More than that, she needed it.

"Now, those greenhorn fellas, like Mayfield and Cooper, I reckon they think differently," Jedidiah added, no doubt realizing his mistake. "They likely want the same kind of things you do. Home and family and all that. When you get back to Georgia, you'll see what I mean."

For once, she didn't argue with him about returning to Georgia. For once, she considered that maybe he was right. "I really don't belong here," she whispered. "I've been such an idiot."

"No." Jedidiah shook his fork at her. "You are not an idiot. You just didn't know what you were getting into when you headed for Rock Creek."

"Sometimes I only see what I want to see."

"Sugar, that doesn't work out here," Jedidiah said kindly. "You've got to keep your eyes open at all times, else you'll run smack dab into a scorpion or a rattlesnake and that's your ass.''

Eden glanced toward Sin, who had quickly finished his lunch and headed for the lobby with long, impatient strides. "A rattlesnake," she muttered.

When she looked at Jedidiah again, he had a wide, satisfied grin on his face.

From the hotel lobby, Sullivan watched Eden saunter down the stairs. She had adapted, in many ways, to her new environment. Her hair was loosely piled on her head, the style not so severe as it had been when he'd first met her. Her blouse was loose and cool, her skirt a bright blue, color in an otherwise colorless picture. She carried a large basket of dirty clothes.

In the two days since their argument in the garden, they hadn't spoken a single word to each other. When it was his watch, he quietly kept an eye on her. When it wasn't his watch, he stayed across the street or in his room.

She was still irate, but on occasion he caught a glimpse of unbridled softness in her eyes. Softness and hope. If he was going to scare her off, if Eden was going to break down and ask to go home to Georgia, that hope had to go.

"I need to go to the river," she said crisply.

"That's not a good idea."

"The well is low, and I have laundry to do."

"Let Ethel do the laundry," Sullivan seethed.

"This is a personal chore, not hotel laundry," Eden snapped. "I will do my own laundry. If you don't want to go with me, fine. Stay here." She spun around and stalked toward the back door.

Sullivan cursed as he followed her. She knew damn well he couldn't let her go alone.

"Watch your language, Mr. Sullivan," she said. "This is a *family* hotel."

He opened the back door and Eden stepped through without looking at him. He almost offered to take the basket from her as they walked through what had once been a garden, but he thought better of it and kept his hands and his offers of help to himself as they headed toward the river.

The walk was long, but not arduous. On a pleasant autumn day it was nice to be outdoors, he had to admit. He'd been spending too much time indoors lately, in the hotel and the saloon. Something inside him wanted to be on the trail again, but he couldn't leave until this business with Eden was taken care of.

She walked ahead of him, her hips swinging beneath that blue skirt, strands of pale hair escaping the bun and falling to her shoulders and beyond. He wanted her still, damn it. He wanted her as much, maybe more, than he ever had.

The land was greener by the river than it was in town. A few tall oak trees shaded much of the bank, and the grass here was thick and soft. Wildflowers grew in abundance along the bank.

"I should bring Millie here one afternoon," Eden said as she set her basket on the ground. "She'd love these flowers."

"Yes, she would." He had a vivid memory of Eden with an orange flower in her hair, smiling at him. He fought to push that memory back. It was too pleasant. Too tempting.

Eden carried her basket closer to the river, over by a grouping of rocks, and kneeled by the flowing water. She went about her chore without another word, scrubbing at spots with vigor, washing and rinsing and wringing with all her might. He had a feeling she was taking her rage out on the linen and calico that passed through her hands.

He'd never imagined that a woman doing laundry in the river could be seductive, but with the sun on her pale hair and the gentle way she leaned toward the water, Eden was a tempting sight. Powerfully tempting. If he didn't care about her at all, he'd tell her he loved her, take what he could get, and ride out of town when the time came—when he got tired of her, when she got sick of him, when the road called to him stronger than she did.

But he did care about her. He didn't want to make her think they had something that would never work and then leave her. It wasn't fair.

Fair? Hell, he was even beginning to think like her!

He leaned against a tree and watched while she wrung out the last of her laundry and put it in the basket. When she turned to face him his heart sank. There it was again, that soft, hopeful, yearning expression that said too much.

She went to lift the basket and grunted. The wet clothes were much heavier than the dry ones had been.

"I'll carry it," he said, stepping into the sunlight and heading for the bank, trying like hell to ignore the expression on Eden's face. Maybe he shouldn't ignore it. What had Cash said? A good dose of reality.

Instead of reaching down to pick up the basket, he grabbed Eden, pulled her tight against him, and kissed her. Hard. There was no tenderness in the kiss, just want, and need, and demand. He grabbed her hair and tilted her head back to allow greater access to her mouth. He got lost in her smell and her taste. He couldn't kiss her deeply enough.

He held her tight so she could feel his erection, so she'd know what she'd done. When she started to respond—softening against him, kissing him back—he pulled away, breaking the contact with a sudden fierceness that left him light-headed.

"You don't look at a man like that unless you're willing to spread your legs for him."

Her eyes went wide, and her face lost its color. *A good dose of reality.* "You think that just because I don't love you, that just because I won't be your goddamned bellman, that I don't want you? Sex," he whispered, "and what you want, have nothing to do with each other. Men and women have sex every day, without love, without promises. That's what we have."

She swallowed hard. "I don't believe you."

He scooped the basket from the ground and turned from her. "Of course you don't," he snapped. "If it's not what Eden fancies, it must not be." He glanced over his shoulder to see that she followed. "Sorry, honey, but everything in this world doesn't fit into your orderly little plan. Sometimes a stray turns mean."

She increased her step. "That stray business again!" she snapped as she climbed the hill behind him. "I swear, Sin, you are the most impossible man. . . ."

He heard the shot just as the tree trunk not two feet from Eden's head exploded. His heart nearly stopped as he dropped the laundry basket and lunged to knock Eden to the ground and cover her body with his.

She couldn't breathe! She couldn't see anything,

either, until Sin slithered to the side, dragging her with him, shielding her body with his own as he pulled her behind the tree and drew his gun.

"Someone shot at us," she whispered breathlessly.

"Honey, someone shot at *you,*" he muttered as he peered around the tree to scan the horizon.

Holding her breath, she waited for another shot to be fired, for whoever had been tormenting her to come charging over the hill. Was it the person who'd written the notes? Curtis Merriweather? Someone else she'd annoyed since arriving in Rock Creek?

Sin crouched down beside her. "I didn't see anything," he said softly. "Whoever it was might've fired once just to scare you and then run off."

"Might've?" she whispered.

He looked her in the eye. "There are lots of places to hide out there. A boulder, a few hills, another tree."

She tried to melt into Sin, feeling safer with every shift that moved her closer to him. "So, what do we do?"

"We wait," he said grudgingly. "I would try to move forward and check those hiding places, but that would mean leaving you unprotected and I can't do that." He sounded almost as if this were her fault! "I don't suppose you're carrying that derringer with you today."

Eden shook her head in response. Since their violent run-in with the Merriweathers, she'd had any desire to arm herself. She was sure she couldn't possibly fire at another human being, no matter who it might be.

"Until I moved West, no one had ever tried to

shoot me. First the Merriweathers and now this."
She sighed.

"Once you get back to Georgia it's likely no one
will ever shoot at you again."

She glanced up into Sin's face. He wasn't looking
at her. He kept his eyes peeled for the enemy,
whoever that might be. Since his attention was elsewhere, she felt free to look her fill.

When she'd first seen him, he'd been such a
mess! One eye swollen shut, cuts and bruises and
knots marring the surface of his face. But he'd
healed with no physical reminder of the beating
but a small scar near his eye, the remnant of a cut
that still might fade completely, with time.

The face she saw now was valiant, and handsome,
and vital. Long hair was a symbol of his defiance.
His narrowed eyes were suspicious, wary of everyone. Cheekbones and a strong jaw were gifts from
his father, she supposed. Perhaps the hint of softness in his heart, the kindness he tried to hide,
was what he carried of his mother.

"Sin?" she whispered.

He stiffened. "What?"

"I'm sorry for what I said the other day in the
garden. I've been thinking about it. . . ."

"Don't," he snapped. "You made it pretty clear
what you wanted. So did I. There's no need to hash
it out all over again."

"I shouldn't have called you uncivilized," she
said. "I didn't mean it."

He glared down at her. "Yes, you did, and you
were right. You're a *lady* who wants a home and a
family. I'm an uncivilized half-breed bastard. . . ."

"Don't say that."

"It's the truth." He scanned the horizon again,
dismissing her.

Eden wasn't ready to be dismissed. "You think all we have is physical," she whispered. "Sex and nothing else. I don't agree, but . . . but . . ."

"But what?" Sin snapped.

"Maybe it's enough," she whispered.

He slowly turned his head to look down at her. She saw the surprise in his eyes. "What are you saying?"

"I think what I said is pretty clear," she said, blushing. "Maybe I'm wrong to expect you to change who you are just to be with me. Maybe I should take what we have and be happy with it. Surely there are worse reasons to be married than . . . than sex." She could feel herself blushing again. "It's powerful, almost otherworldly. I . . . I forget myself when you touch me. I want you until I hurt with it from the top of my head to the tips of my toes."

"Eden." He said her name through gritted teeth. "You don't know what you're saying."

She wrapped her arms around his waist and leaned into his chest. "I'm saying I love you and I'll take what I can get. I'm putting my pride aside for you, Sinclair Sullivan. I'm making a fool of myself because I'd rather live with a little bit of you than everything from any other man." She sighed.

"You're going back to Georgia as soon as this is over," he said, no room for argument in his stern voice. "And once you're there you'll know I'm right about this. You're not the first woman to confuse lust with love and you won't be the last."

"You're going to make me go back, even if I don't want to?"

"Yes."

"Even if I beg to stay here?"

"Yes."

Sin sounded like he'd made up his mind and there was no use in arguing with him now. "And until then?"

He turned his head to look at her, a hint of puzzlement in his eyes. "Until then?"

She smiled. "Come to me tonight. If it's just sex and nothing more, you have nothing to lose. If it's just physical, no one's heart is at stake. After I return to Georgia we'll never see each other again, and it seems a shame to waste whatever time we have left."

She had no intention of surrendering so easily, of giving up on Sin without a fight. She had no intention of leaving, but now was not the time to tell him so.

"Who knows?" she whispered. "Maybe by the time I leave we'll be so tired of each other we'll both be glad to part." She knew full well that she would never be tired of Sin, but she didn't want to fight with him right now. She wanted the healing to start.

"Tonight," he whispered.

She grinned. "And this afternoon, I'm thinking of cleaning the tub."

Chapter 19

Even with the heightened guard on Eden, since the shot had been fired that afternoon, Sullivan was able to slip past Nate and into her room. He tried to tell himself that she would be safer with him nearby. He even tried to convince himself that she'd been telling the truth when she'd said she would be satisfied with the sex, if that was all they had. The truth of the matter was, he wanted her so much he didn't care.

She waited for him, sitting on the bed in her simple white nightgown, her hair loose and falling over her shoulders. His heart constricted in his chest, and for a moment he could not breathe. God, she was beautiful, more beautiful than anything he'd ever seen.

"I didn't know if you'd come tonight or not," she whispered when the door was closed.

He didn't answer but began to undress, yanking his shirt over his head, unbuttoning his denims.

Eden smiled. "It's too bad we were interrupted this afternoon. Why, we probably hadn't been in the tub ten minutes before Jedidiah started looking for me."

"Five," he said as he shucked off his pants.

"You're quite the genius." She didn't wait for him to come to her, but lifted the nightgown over her head and discarded it. Pale moonlight cast through the window illuminated her body, bare and perfect and much too fascinating. "I actually liked the idea of putting a spout in that outer wall, so we can pour water almost directly from the well into the tub. It'll save carrying it through the lobby, like we've been doing."

"I'd been thinking about that anyway," he said. "Hell, I had to come up with some reason we were both in that small room."

She lifted her hand and touched his forearm as he reached the bed. "At least we got out of the tub before he found us."

Harsh reality, Sullivan reminded himself. No prettying up the picture for Eden, no pretending that there was more to this than physical need. "I've got to put a latch on that door."

Eden's hand moved to his hip, where it rested gently. "Yes, you do," she said absently. "You said there wasn't room in the tub to do, well, everything, but this afternoon I decided you were wrong. If we positioned ourselves just right . . ."

He placed a knee on the bed, tipped Eden over, and leaned slowly down until he hovered above her. "Maybe *after* I put a latch on the door."

"The lack of a latch didn't stop you last time," she whispered, grinning and reaching out to hold him, raking her fingers along his back and his hips.

No matter what she said about *this* being enough,

he knew it was a lie. He could see the tenderness in her eyes, could almost feel the hope in her heart. Somehow, he had to make her realize that he would never be the man she wanted him to be.

He placed his hands on her thighs and spread her legs wide, and then he touched her intimately, stroking her wet flesh, slipping a finger inside her heat. With no more preparation, he thrust to fill her. He made love to her hard, without tenderness, without the pretty words she liked to hear. He sheathed himself inside her, stroked her again and again. She had to know this wasn't love; it was mating, pure and simple.

Eden surprised him. She didn't shy away from this fierce encounter but embraced it. She lifted her hips to take all of him. She wrapped her legs around him and threw her head back with a deep-throated sigh that was so full of pleasure it made him ache.

She climaxed with another low moan, closing her eyes, clasping on to him as her body shuddered. His own release rocked him hard, as she milked him completely, as she depleted his body and his soul.

He collapsed atop her, sweaty skin to sweaty skin, pounding heart to pounding heart. His breath came as hard as hers did, and as they lay in a warm, entwined heap of flesh they said nothing. Nothing at all.

When he felt Eden's fingers in his hair, the strokes there tender and loving, he knew it was time to go. He rose slowly, disengaging himself from her with a reluctance he could not afford to show. She didn't say a word until he bent down to pick up his denims.

"You're not going to stay with me tonight?"

"No."

She was quiet for a few minutes, as he dressed. His back was to her, but he could feel her eyes on him. Wanting, hoping, loving eyes. Hell, this was a mistake. He wasn't ever going to get tired of her, and she was not going to surrender and decide to go home.

"All right," she whispered. "If that's what you want."

He turned and watched Eden collect her nightgown from the floor and pull it on, her movements slow and easy. She crawled into the bed and slipped under the covers with a soft sigh of contentment. He expected tears, pleading, a request for just one kiss before he left.

But instead, she smiled and wished him good night, and then she closed her eyes. Perfectly agreeable. Unmistakably satisfied.

Damn it, Eden had him right where she wanted him, didn't she?

"Uncle Jed! Uncle Jed!"

Jed turned just as Millie threw herself at him. He caught the little girl and lifted her from her feet. As always, a more sober Teddy was right behind her.

"What are you doing up so early?" he asked in a soft voice. After all, it was not yet light outside.

"We have school today," she said with a serious nod of her head, looking him directly in the eye as he held her. "And Mr. Reese said we're going to learn all about the Alamo today. I don't even know what an Alamo is!" She grinned widely.

"Well, then this is an important day for you," he said solemnly.

Reese, a teacher! He still had a hard time dealing

with that change. As excited as Millie always was about learning something new, Reese must be as good a teacher as he was a captain. God knows he'd never gotten excited about going to school!

"What about you?" he asked, looking down at Teddy. "Do you know what the Alamo is?"

Teddy nodded and gave him a look that said *moron* as clearly as if he'd spoken the word aloud.

It was so like Eden to take these kids in as her own. To make their lives better, to give them a home. They'd be better off in Georgia, too.

He twirled Millie around and then set her on her feet. "I've got an errand to run," he said, "so I'd better get going."

She waved him back down, wagging her fingers at him. Knowing what was coming, he leaned down so she could give him a kiss on his stubbled cheek.

"What about you?" he asked, winking at Teddy. "Don't you want to give your Uncle Jed a kiss, too?"

Teddy still didn't talk much, but he did manage to emit a disgusted grunt as he walked past—without the kiss.

"I like Uncle Jed," Millie said as the children walked toward the dining room. "I never had an uncle before. Don't you like Uncle Jed?" she asked, looking at Teddy.

Teddy glanced over his shoulder and looked directly at Jed. The kid was small, skinny even, but the look he gave Jed was audacious.

"No," he said, quite clearly.

She'd put off giving Grady's room a good cleaning, not anxious to reenter the room where the sweet old man had died. Still, she couldn't leave it closed off forever. Eventually she might need the space, if the hotel became successful.

All morning she'd been cleaning the guest rooms, Rico right behind her. He was more vigilant than ever since someone had taken a shot at her down by the river. Every now and then he'd look up and down the hall as if he expected to see an armed assassin waiting there, and the way he caressed his knife gave Eden a chill. He was definitely comfortable with the weapon.

Very early this morning they'd received word of Lydia's whereabouts. A cowboy from a ranch outside town had come to town for a visit to the saloon, and he'd mentioned to Kate that his boss had recently married Lydia. Kate had told Cash sometime before sunup. Jedidiah had left for the ranch shortly after that. The news only confused Eden. If Lydia had run off to marry a rancher, then who was trying to run her out of Rock Creek?

She took a deep breath and opened the door to Grady's room, expecting stale odors and bad memories. But the window was open to allow a breeze to circulate, and a familiar calico-covered derriere was hoisted in the air, as the intruder looked under the bed.

"Ethel?"

Ethel bumped her head on the bed as she quickly withdrew. She rubbed the spot gingerly as she came to her feet. "Eden, my goodness, you gave me a fright."

"What are you doing here?" Part of the room had been cleaned, but for the most part everything was simply topsy-turvy. The mattress was askew, the quilt had been tossed onto the floor, and the box containing Grady's personal belongings, what little there was, had been opened and obviously searched.

"I wanted to surprise you," Ethel said with a wide smile. "Since you and Grady were such close friends, I decided it might distress you to go through his things and clean his room."

"It's true, the thought has not been pleasant."

"The room was rather a mess." Ethel looked around her. "It still is, but I've barely gotten started."

"I can help," Eden stepped toward the trunk and the scattered clothes on the floor. "Working together, it shouldn't take us long to finish up."

Was that a sigh she heard behind her? Surely not.

Eden glanced over her shoulder to Rico, who stood in the open doorway. "Why don't you take a break and go get a cup of coffee."

Rico shook his head and fingered his knife.

"You're making me nervous," Eden said with a smile. "If you stay, I'll put you to work cleaning out the dust bunnies."

The threat worked. Rico stepped back and then disappeared from view. She heard his footsteps on the stairs.

"You must be terrified," Ethel said softly, picking the quilt up off the floor. "I know I would be if someone had been threatening me."

"It hasn't been pleasant."

"Why, I bet you can't wait to get back to Georgia." Ethel took the quilt to the open window and slipped it through the opening, then gave it a hearty shaking. She wrinkled her nose as dust particles filled the air, catching the sunlight.

Eden looked at Grady's clothes. He'd been buried in his best suit, and what remained wasn't much better than a pile of rags. "Oh, I'm not going back to Georgia." She held up a particularly disgusting shirt. With a good washing, it might make a decent dust cloth. "Jedidiah and Sin think I plan to go quietly, but when the time comes I'll tell them differently."

Ethel pulled in the quilt and folded it over the foot of the bed. "So you plan to stay?"

Eden smiled. "Yes. I like this old hotel. I think with a little work it can be . . ."

With a sigh much like the one Eden had heard earlier, Ethel crossed the room and closed the door. When she turned to face Eden, her smile was gone.

"Why couldn't you just leave?" she asked softly. "Most highfalutin ladies would've run out of town with their tails between their legs after finding that first note." She slipped a hand into her bodice and pulled out a pearl-handled derringer.

Ethel? Chattering, sometimes-sweet, always-smiling *Ethel* was her enemy? Eden saw something new in Ethel's usually empty eyes. Desperation.

"You can't shoot me," Eden whispered. "Rico knows you're here."

Ethel shrugged her shoulders, and with the weapon she gestured toward the window. "You're right. I guess you'd better just jump."

"I'm not going to jump," Eden said with a lift of her chin. It was difficult to be scared of Ethel. The woman was not much bigger than she was, and they'd done dishes together, for goodness' sake. And Ethel was a woman. Women simply didn't go around shooting one another.

"But I would like to know why you're doing this. Did I do something to offend you so much that you'd go to such lengths to run me out of town?"

Ethel shook her gun at Eden like it was a censuring finger. "You didn't do anything but show up at a bad time. A very bad time. My father and that old bastard Grady were partners, once. They made a big haul before the war. Gold. Grady made off with it. He's hidden it somewhere in this hotel. I know it. And it's mine! We ended up with nothing. My father died without a penny in his pockets, and I had two choices. I could marry a fat, greasy pig farmer or I could sell myself."

"What about your sisters?" Eden asked softly, hoping to appeal to Ethel's love of her family.

"There are no sisters!" she snapped. "I made them up. There was only me and Pop, for as long as I can remember. That gold is my legacy from him."

Now Eden felt a rush of fear. Ethel was growing frantic. "If there's gold here, you can have it," she said softly. "I have no claim to whatever your father and Grady . . . confiscated. But Ethel"—she held Grady's shirt aloft—"would a man who has a fortune in gold stashed away wear this shirt? Would he allow his hotel to practically fall down around his ears?"

"Grady was a crazy old man." Ethel stepped forward, the derringer aimed steadily and unforgivingly toward Eden's heart. "I don't know why he lived this way when he had the gold, but I know he had it. He hid it somewhere."

"You can have it."

Ethel smiled. "You say that now, when I have a gun pointed at you, but what will you say when I'm unarmed and you're surrounded by your guardians?"

"I don't go back on my word," Eden said softly.

With the derringer touching Eden's chest, Ethel propelled her toward the window. "You'll be gone.

There will be no one to run the hotel. The men will move out, and I'll have free run of the place to search it from top to bottom.''

"I told you . . ."

"You should have left when you had the chance," Ethel whispered, just as Eden reached the open window.

She was going to die. Ethel was going to push her from the open window, and she was going to fall into the garden she had such hopes for. With the derringer now against her throat, Eden's head actually went through the window.

And there, to her right, she saw a familiar boot precariously perched on a narrow ledge.

A brief knock on the door startled them both.

"Say a word and you and whoever that is at the door are both dead, you got it?" Ethel whispered.

Ethel spun around, the derringer concealed in the folds of her skirt. The door flung open, and Eden gratefully pulled her head into the room.

Cash gave Ethel a wide smile. "Ready to move back across the street where you belong, sweet thing?"

Ethel tilted her head slightly. "How on earth did you know where to find me?"

Cash nodded toward the hall. "Rico's sitting in the lobby, half asleep. He said you girls were up here, cleaning."

Eden felt movement behind her. If she hadn't already seen the boot on the ledge, she'd probably have screamed. A leg slipped silently through the window, snaking into view directly beside her. Another leg followed as Sin slithered, without making a sound, into the room by way of the window.

"Cleaning," Cash said, rolling his eyes. "Ethel,

darling, you were meant for better things." He took a long, casual step forward.

Ethel tensed. "I'll head over to the saloon in a little while," she said, her voice unnaturally high. "Let Eden and me finish up here. . . ."

Sin moved in front of Eden, shielding her. He drew his gun and Cash took another step toward Ethel.

The telling sign might've been the look in Cash's eyes or the soft sound of Sin's weapon being drawn from its holster. Ethel suddenly realized what was happening, and she spun around as she raised her derringer. Next to Sin's six-shooter, the weapon looked less threatening than it had before.

"Drop it," Sin said.

Ethel showed no signs of complying.

"Don't shoot her, Sin," Eden whispered. He ignored her.

But she realized, very quickly, that no one here wanted to see Ethel die. They simply wanted her to put down the derringer. With a hand on Sin's back, Eden peeked around him and watched as Cash reached out and touched Ethel's shoulder.

Ethel spun around and pointed the derringer at Cash. Surrounded, outnumbered, and outgunned, she panicked.

Cash reached out to take the pearl-handled derringer from Ethel, but she hung on tight. He forced her arm down, into a less threatening position, and the weapon discharged.

Cash cursed as he yanked the derringer away from Ethel. He uttered, quite clearly, the most vile words imaginable in bizarre combinations. He sprinkled in a few of Jedidiah's favorite words, the ones that made Eden blush. She didn't dare chastise him.

Sin grabbed a disarmed Ethel from behind and held her arms tight behind her back as Nate and Rico burst into the room.

"She shot me!" Cash shouted, his hand pressed firmly over a spot high on his left thigh. He had put all his weight on his right leg, and he stood there leaning unsteadily to one side. He limited himself to what was obviously his favorite curse word. "Shit!"

Nate offered Cash an arm of support and he took it, as Rico took custody of an unrepentant Ethel and led her from the room.

Eden stepped out from behind Sin, determined to do something useful. "Get him to bed. Not this one," she said quickly. "The room across the hall is cleaner. Let's have a look at that wound. Is there a real doctor in town?"

"Slow down, sweetheart," Cash said calmly. "I'll heal up across the street, in my own room. Nate can patch me up as well as any *real* doctor." *Or you.* The unspoken censure hung in the air between them.

"At least wrap the wound tightly to slow the bleeding before you try to walk." She bent over Grady's chest and came out with a clean shirt. "This will do." She turned to do the chore herself, but Cash lifted a hand to stop her, one finger demonstrative and insistent. Well, the wound *was* in a rather delicate place.

Nate took the shirt from her and dropped down to wrap it around Cash's thigh. "A couple inches to the left and a little higher," he said with a smile, "and you'd have to restrict your immoral activities to gamblin' and drinkin'."

"Just bind it up and let's get out of here." Cash glared at Sin. He did not show the pain he had to feel on his face. "You know, I haven't lived a sainted life. In the back of my mind I guess I always figured that one day I'd get myself shot over a woman. I did assume, however," he said crisply, "that it would be *my* woman."

"Thank you, Mr. Cash," Eden said softly, knowing her thanks were insufficient. "I do so hate it that you were injured helping me."

Cash cursed again as Nate led him from the room. He refused the offer of Sin's added assistance, saying he would not be *carried* to his room like an invalid.

When they were alone, Eden slipped her arm around Sin's waist and leaned into him. It was a wonderfully comforting feeling, warm and intimate. "How did you know?"

"Rico said the room looked like it had been searched, and he didn't buy Ethel's explanation. He said she looked shifty eyed."

"I'm glad Rico is so observant. Otherwise . . ." She shivered. "Sin, Ethel was actually trying to push me out the window! She thinks Grady hid a fortune in gold somewhere in this old hotel, and since her father helped to steal it, she said it was hers. Her legacy. I would've let her have it, if there really was any gold. Do you think there is?" She looked up at him.

Sin ignored her question. "She could've shot you," he said in an unaffected voice. There might not be any emotion in his voice, but he held her close and wrapped his arms completely around her. She could feel his relief and his fear. "At any moment while the two of you were alone. One afternoon while the two of you were cooking supper." A note of fury crept into his voice.

"I don't think she wanted to hurt me. She just

wanted me to . . . to leave." She took a deep breath and closed her eyes. "It's over," she whispered.

"We still have the Merriweathers to contend with," Sin said darkly.

"Maybe." She looked up at Sin and smiled. "If I were a Merriweather, and I knew what I was up against, I'd stay as far away from Rock Creek as possible."

Sin looked down at her. "Yeah, but I have a feeling you're a lot smarter than the Merriweather brothers." He touched her face. It was amazing to her that he could be so big, so hard, and still so gentle. "I just don't want you hurt."

"Because you love me?"

"Because I *like* you."

"That's something, I suppose." She dropped her arms, let Sin go, and headed for the door. She still shook, a deep quiver from head to toe, but she felt no real fear. The danger was over, and her mind turned to more immediate matters. "I really should make Cash some soup. Will he ever forgive me?"

"Probably not."

"I do make *very* good soup."

Chapter 20

Eden made a conscious effort not to look from side to side as she walked through the saloon. It was not yet dark, but the evening had begun. Rough men drank, painted women laughed, and gamblers caressed their cards the way a lover might caress a woman's flesh. She kept her eyes on the stairs at the rear of the room, even when she felt a growing number of eyes on her back.

Nate stayed close, and she could feel, too, the temptation this place held for him.

"Honey," one of the saloon girls hollered, "if you're going to visit Cash, you might as well save yourself the trip up the stairs. He's kicked us both out already. Twice. He's in a foul mood."

Eden glanced over her shoulder. "Being shot is bound to put anyone in a foul mood. Besides," she added, lifting her tray aloft, "I brought soup."

She didn't see any reason for laughter, but a few drunken men did just that. Turning her back on them all, Eden climbed the stairs. Nate stayed right behind her.

"They're right," he said softly. "Cash is not going to be glad to see you."

"He was injured helping me. The least I can do is bring him some chicken soup. He'll need nourishment to heal." She stopped at the top of the stairs. "Which room is his?"

Nate pointed, then stepped around Eden to knock curtly and swing open the door. Cash's room was smaller than those in the hotel, cramped but clean. It was also rather ... decadent. The bedspread that covered him to the waist was bright red and surely made of the finest silk, as were the sheets and the pillows. The single chair was covered in red velvet, a fabric similar to the thick curtains that covered the single window.

On his bedside table there was a deck of cards, two distinctive six-shooters, an almost full bottle of whiskey, and a cut-glass tumbler with just a drop of whiskey sitting in the bottom.

Cash opened his eyes as she stepped into the room. "What the hell are you doing here?"

She refused to be put off by his rude tone of voice or the blackness of his eyes. "I brought you soup." She lifted the tray slightly.

"I hate soup." He waved a dismissive hand. "Get out."

Eden ignored him, stepping into the small room and perching on the edge of the red velvet chair. "I can feed you or you can feed yourself. I won't have you wasting away."

Slowly, using the strength in his arms, Cash moved into a sitting position. Crimson silk pillows cushioned his back. A crimson silk coverlet covered his legs. His mouth, surrounded by a precisely trimmed mustache and goatee, pursed and twitched. Finally, he pinned his dark eyes on her, and not for the first time she thought of the devil.

"Let me assure you that I have no intention of wasting away, Miss Rourke," he said in a dangerous voice that positively dripped sarcasm. "Or is it Mrs. Sullivan? I'm often confused these days."

"Call me Eden," she said, taking the spoon in her hand and dipping it into the soup. "Open wide."

He looked horrified, his black eyebrows arching, his head rearing slightly back. "You are not going to spoon soup into my mouth as if I were a baby or a feeble old codger."

"All right," she said, standing with the tray in her hands. She very gingerly placed the tray on Cash's lap.

The gambler reached down with both hands and grasped the bowl. She knew, immediately, what he intended to do.

"Surely you wouldn't be so childish," she said softly.

He cut his eyes up and narrowed them. "You'd be surprised." But he didn't toss the bowl across the room.

"While you two argue about the soup," Nate muttered, "I'm going downstairs for a drink."

Eden spun around. "No, you really shouldn't." It broke her heart to see the man lose himself in whiskey, to drink until he was insensible. "You drink too much, Nate. It's not good for you." She kept her voice low.

"Not good for me?" he asked, amused by her concern.

"No," she said softly. "You really shouldn't . . ."

"If I need a drink it's none of your business."

"Well, yes, that may be true," she said, unable to let it go. "But you don't *need* a drink. You want it, and that's entirely different. I'm not one to say that whiskey is evil, but . . ."

"Lady, when you've seen what I've seen, you can preach to me," Nate said with a touch of bitter humor. "Until then, leave me the hell alone." With that he stalked out of the room, leaving the door open.

So far the day had been a complete disaster. First she'd been confronted by Ethel and her nefarious plans, then Cash and his stubbornness, and now Nate.

"Sullivan was right about you," Cash said softly.

Oh, she was in no mood to be on the receiving end of Cash's sarcasm, not now. "Right about me how?" she snapped, trying, and failing, to stop her eyes from filling with tears.

Cash smiled wickedly. "He said you were out to save the world, one person at a time. If that's the case, Rock Creek is as good a place as any to be. Lots of people here need saving."

Dejected, she sat again in the red velvet chair. "But I'm not doing a very good job of it. Grady died, Ethel tried to kill me, Sin only wants to send me back to Georgia, Nate put me in my place, and you"—she pinned her eyes on him—"you nearly get yourself killed on my account, and now I can't even get you to eat a bowl of soup." Her lower lip quivered.

"Save the histrionics," Cash drawled. "I'm too damn old to fall for that practiced con. The tremulous lip, the watery eyes. You're quite the actress, Miss . . . Eden."

"You hate me," she whispered, certain of the fact.

"Perhaps."

"Would you like to tell me why?" She didn't really care if this man liked her or not, but he was in Sin's closest circle and that meant something to her.

"I don't like to see my friends jerked around by their nuts."

Shocked, Eden tilted back and widened her eyes. "Well, you don't mince words, do you, Mr. Cash?"

"In the past I've found it a waste of time to do so," he snapped.

Amazingly, she found a tender spot in her heart for Cash at that moment. Tough as he was, he obviously cared about his friends.

"Let me put your mind at ease," she said softly. "I love Sin, very much. I would never jerk him around by . . . by anything." She could feel herself blushing, the heat rising to her cheeks. "If I've made mistakes since coming here, it's because I've never been in love before." She smiled. "I'm learning as I go."

Cynicism filled his black eyes. "Maybe you really think you love him. . . ."

Eden stood and glared down at Cash. "Don't tell me I don't know my own heart. Don't you dare. I am getting heartily tired of the men of Rock Creek trying to tell me I don't know what I want. Do you want to know a secret?" She leaned slightly forward and unabashedly met Cash's stony gaze. "Sin and Jedidiah think I'm going back to Georgia once the Merriweather brothers are caught, but they're wrong. I'm not leaving. Unless, of course, Sin leaves. I'll follow him if I have to. I'll become the kind of woman I need to be in order to be his wife."

"You would trail after a man who doesn't love you?" Cash asked coldly.

Eden was tempted to tell him that Sin *did* love her, but that wasn't really the question he'd asked, was it?

"Yes."

She turned on her heel so she didn't have to look any more into those dark, emotionless eyes. "I'm going to leave before Nate has too much to drink. Eat the soup or don't, Mr. Cash. And thank you, again."

After slamming the door behind her, she waited a moment, expecting the crash of a bowl against the door. But all was silent.

Sullivan sat back on the green lobby sofa while Jed paced and raged.

"She's in the Rock Creek jail?"

"Until we transport her to Ranburne, *si*," Rico said calmly. "We hired Sam Sanders to keep an eye on her and feed her until then. Until we get a sheriff of our own, there is not much else we can do."

It had been well after dark before Jed had returned, frustrated that his visit to the newly married Lydia had led him nowhere in his investigation. He'd been incensed to know that Ethel, who had been living under this roof, was Eden's tormentor. He'd been just as livid that he'd missed all the action.

"I should skin Eden's hide for coming here in the first place," he seethed. "The sooner we get this Merriweather mess over with and get her back to Georgia, the happier I'll be."

They all turned toward the door as it opened.

Cash limped in, his white ruffled shirt on but only halfway buttoned, his face unnaturally pale. He carried a tray in one hand and an empty bowl in the other. As he stepped into the light, Sullivan saw a spoon sticking out of his pocket.

Rico stepped forward and offered an arm of support, but Cash waved him off. "It's just a scratch," he said as he limped into the room. "I wanted to return these."

Eden came into the lobby from the dining room, Nate right behind her. "Would you please quit following me," she snapped. "Ethel is in jail, and I seriously doubt the Merriweather brothers are hiding in the pantry."

"Just doin' my job, ma'am," Nate said with a wry smile, weaving unsteadily as he came to a halt.

Eden stopped dead in her tracks when she saw Cash. "What on earth are you doing out of bed? Don't you have a lick of sense?"

"I'm fine," he said again. "It's just a . . ."

"Fine my foot," she said, walking to where Cash stood. "You should be resting."

"I came to return these," Cash said, barely lifting the tray and bowl. "And to . . . thank you for the soup. It was very good."

Sullivan sat up straight. He came here to *thank* her?

Eden took the bowl and tray and handed them to an unprepared Nate, who almost dropped both. "How can you boys just stand there?" she snapped. "Don't you realize that Mr. Cash has been shot?" She placed an arm around his waist. "Lean on me, Mr. Cash."

Cash grinned as he complied, leaning much too familiarly against Eden and placing a casual arm around her shoulder. "Why don't you call me Daniel."

Daniel?

Jed and Rico exchanged a surprised look.

"Daniel," Eden said with a smile. "What a lovely name." She led Cash to the sofa and brusquely ordered Sullivan to move aside. She didn't completely let go of her charge until he was settled comfortably on the sofa, his back resting against one arm, his legs stretched out.

"When did you take Cash *soup?*" Sullivan growled.

"This afternoon," Eden said sweetly, "while you were sleeping."

"I had to sleep a couple of hours in order to take the night watch. Can't you stay out of trouble for two hours, so I can sleep?"

She didn't seem at all offended. "I didn't get in trouble, Sin. I just took Daniel a bowl of chicken soup. Nate was with me."

Daniel. Sullivan glared at Nate, who shrugged his shoulders.

Jed shook a long finger at Sullivan. "Wait a minute. You've got the night watch? Why not . . ." Jed looked at the men around him, at a weaving Nate and a grinning Rico and a smug Cash. Apparently, at this point, there was not a man among them he trusted with his sister. "Maybe I should take the night watch myself."

"You were up before dawn to ride out and question Lydia," Eden said sensibly. "I would not sleep any better with you snoring outside my door. In fact, I don't think there's a need for this constant guard any longer."

"Not a *need?*" Jed roared. "What about the Merriweathers?"

"Really, Jedidiah"—Eden reached up to pat her brother on one rough cheek—"if you were a cowardly highwayman who made a business of killing and robbing defenseless families, would you ride into town to face"—she glanced around, her gaze moving from one man to another—"all of you? I seriously doubt they are so foolish. They're probably halfway to California by now."

Jed grinned. "Good. Then we can leave for Georgia tomorrow."

Eden wrinkled her nose. "I don't think so. I'm not ready to go." She spun around before Jed could argue, leaving her brother standing there with an open mouth and a wagging finger.

"Daniel," she said sweetly, "you look pale. Would you like a cup of hot tea? I think you need the sugar."

Sullivan held back an evil grin. Hot tea? That offer would wipe the contented smile off of Cash's face.

But Cash continued to look quite pleased with himself. "That would be wonderful, Eden. Hot tea. Now, why didn't I think of that?" While Jed and Rico watched Eden and Nate return to the kitchen, Sullivan glared down at Cash. He got a friendly wink in return.

Eden woke as the bed dipped, knowing, without question, that it was Sin's weight that made the bed sink. She rolled over slowly to face him.

"I had begun to think you weren't coming."

"I almost didn't," he said softly. "Besides, I had to wait for everyone else to fall asleep."

She scooted across the bed to be closer to him,

to lay her hand on his side. "It's been such a long day," she said tiredly.

"I know." Sin let her snuggle against him, as he hadn't last night. "But you did find time to make soup for *Daniel*."

With her face hidden against his chest, she smiled. He was jealous. Not in a million years would he admit it, but he was jealous. "Well, he did get shot on my account, bless his heart."

"Yeah," Sin admitted grudgingly.

"A bowl of soup seems precious little thanks," she murmured.

"Just don't go painting your pretty pictures around Cash," Sin warned. "He's a hard man, and he doesn't do anything for anybody without a damn good reason."

"Don't curse, Sin," Eden murmured.

"Just . . . be careful."

She draped an arm around Sin and made herself more comfortable against him, slipping her foot between his denim-clad legs. "I'm am excellent judge of character," she whispered. "Ethel was an exception, I admit, but I think Daniel is a very sweet man, beneath all the hostility."

"Sweet?" Sin said in disbelief. "Cash?"

Eden smiled and closed her eyes. A man who would be so protective of a friend, as Daniel was for Sin's sake, had to have a sweet streak. She was tempted to tell Sin, here and now, that she loved him madly. He wasn't ready to hear it again, though. Not yet.

She melted against him, drifting toward sleep, expecting him to either release her or roll her onto her back and make love to her. He did neither, but continued to hold her.

"I like it here," she whispered when sleep had

almost claimed her again, "in your arms. Here I am warm and safe, and nothing evil or ugly can touch me."

She fell asleep knowing Sin would disengage himself from her as soon as consciousness left her, that he would leave her here alone in the bed. Only sex, he said. If she was too tired to make love, he surely had no need of her.

But when she woke, hours later, Sin still held her.

Chapter 21

In the four days following Ethel's capture, the nights began to turn cold. Nate and Rico transported Ethel to the Ranburne jail, turning her over to Sheriff Tilton. Jedidiah made plans for the trip to Georgia, a trip Eden had yet to agree to, and Sin touched her whenever he got the chance.

They kissed in the tub and slept entwined. They kissed in the kitchen and by the river. They didn't speak of love or of marriage, and as long as Jedidiah was around they continued to be either hostile or indifferent to each other. Sin didn't think Jed would take it well if he knew they were sleeping together until the time came for her to leave, and Eden . . . Well, she had to take care of Sin before she could take care of Jedediah. She wasn't yet certain how to do that.

She was afraid any mention of permanence would ruin what they had, and since what they had was so beautiful she wasn't ready to take that chance.

Cool autumn rain had fallen for two of those days. The rain was needed, and she found she liked the constant patter of rain on the roof and the windows of the hotel. Sin said sometimes there were violent storms that shook the town to its roots, but this rain was gentle and steady.

She sat back in the tub, reveling in the feel of warm water on her skin. For tonight's bath she'd splurged and added some of her best rose-scented bath oils. Fragrant steam drifted up and tickled her nose.

The children were asleep, Rico and Nate were having a drink in the saloon, and Jedidiah was playing poker with Sam Sanders and Baxter Sutton and someone else whose name she'd already forgotten, in the back room of the general store. Apparently Baxter's wife, Rose, didn't have anything against a friendly game of poker, as long as it didn't take place in the saloon.

Opening her eyes, she looked at Sin. He sat on the floor and leaned against the wall, one leg cocked up, one stretched out and almost reaching the tub. He'd made love to her right there against the wall, once, in a way she'd not thought possible until it had happened. Her heart leaped and her core tightened at the memory.

He looked at her so hard her heart leaped again.

"Jed is talking about taking you out of here next week, whether you want to go or not," Sin said softly.

"Oh, is he?" She tried to sound lighthearted, but the fact of the matter was, she'd have a difficult time fighting both Jedidiah and Sin, if they decided it was time for her to go.

"Yeah. He says we should move before it gets too cold, and he's got a good point. You don't want to be sleeping in the back of a wagon once it turns cold."

The past few nights had offered a taste of what was coming. Last night she'd placed her hands on the windowpane in her room and felt a cold jolt that cut to her bones. "So you agree with him?"

He didn't answer.

"Do you still think"—she casually splashed water over her chest—"that it's necessary for me to leave?"

Again he didn't answer, but he did move slowly from his place against the wall. Each movement was reluctant, hesitant, but he ended up sitting beside the tub with one hand in the water. "Are you ready to go?"

"No." She held her breath and waited for the "It's just sex" talk. She didn't get it.

"I thought I would be tired of you by now," he muttered, reaching out, slipping his hand beneath the water to touch her side. That hand slid slowly up to cup her breast. He didn't look her in the eye, but watched the play of his hand on her flesh.

"You're not?" she whispered.

He took a deep breath and exhaled slowly. "No," he admitted. "But it won't last. We're too different, Eden."

"Different is good." She reached out to touch his face. "I like different. Sometimes it seems like you and I were made for each other. When I lie beside you and put my head on your shoulder, it feels so much like *my* place. I know a peace I've never known before. When we make love, I know you're the only man I ever want to touch me that way." She stroked her hand down to his neck.

"Maybe different hearts fit together the way bodies do."

Sin looked at her as if he wanted to agree, as if he wanted what she said to be true. There was a hint of skepticism in his eyes, though. He stroked her skin, from breast to navel. "You feel slick."

She grinned. "It's the bath oil."

His hand dipped lower to delve between her legs, to gently stroke her in a way she'd never even imagined before marrying Sin. She parted her thighs and allowed him to touch her, leaning forward to meet him halfway, for a kiss. How could he have a single doubt? Didn't he know how much a woman had to trust a man to offer herself so willingly and without fear?

"Well, we do have one thing in common," she said when he pulled his mouth from hers. She glanced at the door. "Since you finally put that latch on the door, why don't you join me?"

She didn't have to ask twice. He quickly shed his clothes. When he was naked, she moved forward so he could sit at the back of the tub, then positioned herself in his lap. The water lapped dangerously close to the edge, and the ends of his long hair floated on and fell beneath the surface of the water.

"How could I ever get tired of this?" she asked, settling herself more comfortably against him, sending a small wave of water splashing onto the floor.

Sullivan sat at the top of the stairs, just outside the room where Eden slept. He couldn't join her, not until the others were in for the night and snoring behind their own closed doors. Maybe even then he should stay right here.

What he'd said was the truth; he should be tired of Eden by now. He should be ready to send her packing, eager to get her out of town.

But he wasn't, and the words she'd whispered tonight came back to haunt him. *Maybe different hearts fit together the way bodies do.*

She'd be sound asleep by the time Rico and Jed and Nate returned. He didn't want to wake her, didn't need to. What he needed was to lie beside her and hold her, to memorize the way she felt sleeping in his arms, to listen to the way she breathed, the way she occasionally murmured in her sleep. He'd never thought to need such a thing from a woman, had never imagined he could get caught up in such simple pleasures.

Rico was the first to return, trudging up the stairs with a tired smile on his face. He didn't have to ask how everything was. Sullivan's relaxed posture against the banister at the top of the stairs was enough to tell him that all was well. He muttered good night, passed Sullivan and started down the hallway, and then did a quick about-face.

Sullivan glanced up.

Rico cocked his head and his smile widened. "*Dios.* You smell like a woman."

"I do not." True, the smell of the rose-scented water was still in his nose, but . . .

"You smell like a particular woman who has a fondness for roses."

"It's your imagination," Sullivan said. "Or bad whiskey distorting your mind."

Rico folded his arms over his chest and narrowed his eyes. His grin did not fade. "Your hair is damp, just on the ends."

Sullivan searched for and discarded an explanation.

Bending over slightly and unfolding his arms, Rico reached out to barely touch Sullivan's forearm. "And your skin is as soft as a baby's butt."

Sullivan jerked his arm away from the grinning kid. "It is not."

"Well, perhaps not, but it is very . . . soft." He sniffed again. "And rosy."

Sullivan sighed. He had never been able to get much past Rico, anyway.

"Smoke a cigar," Rico advised. "Splash on a little witch hazel. If you smell like this when Jed gets back, there will be hell to pay, and I for one am too damn tired to lock horns with Jedidiah Rourke tonight."

When Rico was in his room, Sullivan lifted his forearm to his nose and took a deep whiff. He didn't smell anything more than a hint of Eden's rose-scented water, even though his clothes had been thoroughly doused in it when water had splashed from the tub and onto the floor. The shirt was almost dry by now, and a few spots on his jeans were barely damp. Maybe the odor was there and he just couldn't smell it anymore. He could change his clothes, but if the scent was on his skin and in his hair there wasn't much to be done for it tonight.

He would've thought that anyone as much a lady as Eden would be prim in bed, that she would be shy and reserved and prudish when it came to sex. But she wasn't, not at all. She laughed and cried and moaned. She reveled in her own pleasure and his, and found a new wonder in every time they came together.

Even more amazingly, so did he.

He didn't have any witch hazel in his room, but he did have a cigar. That ought to do the trick. He'd smoked half the pungent cigar before Jed came plodding up the stairs, the grin on his face telling Sullivan that he'd come home a winner.

Jed didn't mention the fragrance of roses as he passed.

Jed paced in the lobby, again and again rehearsing his lines in his head. When he thought of chickening out, he reminded himself that it was his brotherly duty to . . . to do this. He stiffened his spine and wished he was fighting *banditos* again.

The children hurrying down the stairs took his mind off his troubles. Momentarily, anyway. Millie was bright and her smile was amazing. And as for Teddy, well, the kid needed some time, that's all.

As the kids approached, he lowered himself and offered his cheek for a kiss.

He didn't get one.

Millie pursed her lips and looked him square in the eye. "Teddy said you don't like Pa . . . I mean, Mr. Sullivan. He said you're trying to make Mama go back to Georgia." She stared at him accusingly, and so did Teddy.

"Well . . . that's not exactly . . ."

"I heard you," Teddy said softly.

Jed rose to his full height of six-foot-three, which should be enough to intimidate a couple of nosy kids. It apparently wasn't, since they continued to stare accusingly up at him.

"Georgia is a fine place, and the both of you will be better off there." He nodded his head once in emphasis.

Millie's lower lip trembled. "I like it here. I don't want to go back."

Jed bit back a curse as he narrowed one eye. He'd always been a sucker for blond curls and that quivering lower lip, even when Eden had been little and he'd been no bigger than Teddy. Well, he thought, glancing at the dark-eyed boy who glared up at him, he had likely been *born* bigger than Teddy. The important thing was, he could not let a little girl, Millie *or* Eden, make him veer from his path. He knew what was right and that was that.

Millie headed for the dining room, and Teddy stepped boldly forward.

"If you make my sister cry," he said in a soft voice, "I'll make you sorry."

Jed did not like these kids making him feel guilty! "Oh yeah?" he asked with a glare. "What are you gonna do, kid?"

Teddy curled his fingers together and lifted the pathetically small fist. While Jed eyed the less-than-threatening fist with a grin he could not contain, Teddy kicked him in the shin.

"Jesus, kid!" he yelped, reaching down to rub his stinging shin. "That hurt!"

Teddy ran to join Millie as she reached the dining room, placing his arm around her shoulder and comforting her in a low, reticent voice.

Jed was about to follow, to give the kids a piece of his mind, when Eden called, "Good morning" from the stairway. He turned to watch her descend with a warm smile on her face.

Sullivan was just a few steps behind.

She had never seen her brother so nervous. Once the children had gone to school and Jedidiah had ordered Sin to bed, since he'd taken the night watch, he called her into the lobby and instructed gruffly that she sit on the sofa. Once she was settled, he sat beside her.

"I rode to Ranburne and sent out a few telegrams," he said. "I know lawmen all over the West, and one of them is bound to know where the Merriweather boys are and what they're up to. As soon as I get word that they're in jail somewhere or else have been spotted halfway across the country, you're headed home." He nodded his head as a firm and dictatorial ending to his statement. *No arguments,* the nod said.

"What if I don't want to go?" she asked softly. "Teddy and Millie are doing well here. I'd hate to make them leave their new home and their new friends."

He rolled his eyes and, for some reason, reached down to rub his shin. "They can make friends in Georgia or . . . or you can leave them here. I'm sure there's a family or two around who wouldn't mind . . ."

She punched her brother on the arm. He flinched. "I will not leave them here!" she snapped. "The last thing either of them needs is to be abandoned again."

"Then . . ."

"And that old crone Miss Hyter is still teaching in the Spring Hill school. Can you just imagine how she'll treat Teddy? *If* she even allows him to attend school there. He has mixed blood, Jedidiah. He won't be welcome in Spring Hill."

"Then leave him here," Jedidiah said through gritted teeth.

"I can't."

He sighed and took her hand, an unusually tender gesture for the big man. "I've gotten off the subject. Before we leave town . . ." He lifted a silencing finger when she opened her mouth to argue with him. "Before we leave town, I have to make sure of one thing."

Eden waited patiently, watching the color rise in Jedidiah's face, feeling the constant movement of the hand that held hers. She'd never seen him so nervous before!

"I know you thought you and Sullivan were married"—he didn't look her in the eye—"so I won't lecture you."

"Thank you," she said dryly.

He did snap a censuring gaze to her, before dropping his eyes again. "It was just the one time, so it's unlikely that there are any . . . that you are . . . I mean, it's not likely that the first time . . ." His face was now beet red. "Damn it, Eden, are you pregnant?"

The question surprised her, but it shouldn't have. Of course, Jedidiah didn't know that she and Sin had been together many times after that first night, that it would be a miracle if she *wasn't* carrying a baby.

And yet, she hadn't given it much thought. When they were together there was just her and Sin, her love for him, his need for her. But a *baby*. "I don't know," she whispered.

"Well, when *will* you know?"

"I'm not . . . sure."

Jedidiah snapped at her. "Well, you damn well should know!"

"Don't curse," she snapped back. "And how exactly am I supposed to know?"

Impossibly, he turned redder than ever. Even his ears, almost hidden in a mass of unkempt curls, turned a bright red. "I'm not going to tell you. You . . . You need to talk to another woman."

"I don't know very many women in Rock Creek,

and I certainly know none that I'd feel comfortable having such a discussion with."

Jedidiah scratched his scruffy beard as he thought, and when he had the answer she saw it in his eyes before he said, "Mary. Reese's wife. She has a baby." His color returned to near normal. "You've met her, right?"

"Yes, but I don't know her all that well. Certainly not well enough for the conversation you're suggesting."

Jed nodded his head, pleased with himself. "She'll do just fine."

"What if I am?" Eden asked in a soft voice. "What if there's a baby?"

Jed narrowed his eyes and his neck tensed. He even flexed his hands. "I'll beat the snot out of that . . ."

"You will not!" Eden interrupted, horrified. "I asked a serious question and I want a serious answer. If there is a baby, what will happen?"

Jedidiah narrowed his eyes. "Like it or not, you'll have to marry Sullivan for real."

She could just see it—Jedidiah demanding that they wed again, probably with the barrel of his shotgun shoved against the groom's back. She wanted Sin, but not that way. He would never forgive her and besides . . . She wanted him to choose her, to ask her to stay. She wanted him to come to her without obligation.

"Oh, Little Bit," Jedidiah said with a pat to her hand. "I'm sorry. I know you don't want to marry that . . . that mongrel." He'd taken her sudden sadness for a reluctance to be trapped into marriage with Sin, but the real dilemma was she didn't want Sin to be trapped into marriage with her. She wanted him to choose. "Damn it, right now I want to pound that son of a bitch into the ground."

"Jedidiah," Eden said calmly. "What happened was not entirely Sin's fault. I wanted . . ."

He leaned back in obvious horror. "I don't want to hear this."

She couldn't help but smile. "Sometimes I think you forget that I'm a fully grown woman."

He looked her up and down. "You call this fully grown?"

"I'm twenty-four years old!"

He sighed deeply. "I swear, I look at you sometimes and I see a twelve-year-old with pigtails and a collection of raggedy dolls and maimed pets."

"I'm not twelve anymore," Eden said softly. "And even though I don't look fully grown to you, I am certainly old enough to make a few decisions for myself."

"You're not safe in Rock Creek, and I won't have you staying here, you hear me?"

Now was the perfect time to tell him about Sin, about the fact that they were husband and wife, whether he thought Nate's ceremony was sufficient or not. Perhaps she should even tell him that if she wasn't carrying Sin's child it wasn't for lack of trying.

"Now Jedidiah . . .", she began calmly.

Rico came bounding down the stairs, landing in the lobby with a smile on his face. "I am starving. Is it too late for breakfast?"

"Of course not," Eden said as she stood, relieved that confessions would have to wait for another day. "Eggs or flapjacks?"

"Flapjacks," Rico said without hesitation. He joined them with a wide smile on his face. "You certainly do smell nice this morning, Eden.'' He leaned in and took a deep breath. ''Roses?''

''Yes. Last night I splurged and got into my rose-scented bath oil.'' She remembered the evening and her own smile bloomed.

''Interesting.'' Rico flashed a wide, knowing grin.

Eden glanced down at her brother, and at Rico, and to the stairs that led to the rooms above—including the room where Sin slept. She liked these people. She liked this place. She *would not* leave. Her mind was made up.

Jedidiah just shook his head in dismay. ''I'll bring Mary by this afternoon.''

''Marvelous,'' Eden said as she headed for the kitchen to make Rico's flapjacks.

Jedidiah might not realize it yet, but she could be every bit as stubborn as he was!

Chapter 22

Eden did like Mary, very much, even though they had not spent much time together. She'd always trusted her instincts where people were concerned, and she was rarely wrong. Poor Ethel was the exception.

Mary held her baby girl, little Georgia, as the two women sat in the dining room, tea and cake on the table before them. Eden thought that if she was going to ask Mary such personal questions, she should at least offer refreshments.

For a while they talked about the kids, Millie and Teddy and the baby, as well as the school in Rock Creek. Eden was happy to tell Mary that she was more than pleased with the education the children were receiving.

"I have been meaning to come over for a purely social visit and to properly welcome you to Rock Creek," Mary said. "I'm so glad you're here. We don't have enough women settling here. I know it's a harsh place, but in order to grow a town needs women."

"Jedidiah doesn't want me to stay," Eden said softly, unnecessarily stirring her tea. "He thinks it's not safe."

"Rock Creek is more than safe enough, as long as James and the other boys are about," Mary said with a smile. "Who would dare go up against them?"

Eden slapped her hand against the table. "That's exactly what I told Jedidiah and Sin."

"Sin?" Mary asked with skeptically raised eyebrows.

"Sinclair Sullivan," Eden clarified. Her eyes fell, as they had often thus far, on the baby Mary held. What a delicate, beautiful child! She found herself hoping that she was carrying Sin's child, no matter how much a baby would complicate matters. "We were married, shortly after I came to Rock Creek."

Mary's eyes widened. She looked truly shocked. "I didn't know that."

"Nate performed the ceremony, late one night. We thought it was sufficient, but Jedidiah . . ." She sighed. "Jedidiah has other ideas."

Mary nodded understandingly. "Brothers often do."

Eden took a deep breath. While she was enjoying this conversation very much, it wasn't the purpose of this particular meeting.

"My mother died a long time ago," she began by way of explanation, "when I was just ten, and I find myself rather ignorant in some respects. I am uneducated in the matters of marriage and men, most especially," she added with a hot flush to her cheeks.

Mary pursed her lips and shook her head. "It's

a crime that we keep our young women ignorant of such important matters.''

"Could I ask you . . .'', Eden began shyly, "a few questions?''

Mary smiled. "You can ask me anything at all. I was rather ignorant myself, not so long ago, so I sent off to Boston for a collection of enlightening pamphlets.''

Eden took the opportunity to ask the pertinent questions, and Mary told her more than she'd ever wanted to know about semen and the uterus. Obviously, the woman had once been a teacher, as her husband was now. No detail went untold, no question unanswered. She didn't blush once.

"You're welcome to borrow the pamphlets, if you'd like,'' Mary finished.

Eden shook her head, certain she now knew more than she'd ever need to know.

"Exactly how will I know if . . . when . . . I'm carrying a child?'' Eden asked, now that she knew in excruciating detail how babies were made.

"When your monthly flow stops,'' Mary said, without hesitation.

Eden felt the blush rise again.

"Also, you may be unusually tired, have an increased appetite, and many women suffer from nausea in the first few months.'' Mary raised her expressive eyebrows once again. "Have you been ill?''

Eden shook her head.

"Tired? Hungry all the time?''

She shook her head again.

Dauntless, Mary lifted her chin. "When was the last time you had your monthly flow?''

Well, by this point there was little reason to remain shy about such matters. "In San Antonio.

Millie and I were there for several days, purchasing the wagon and horses and obtaining a map. That was . . . That was about six weeks ago.''

Mary nodded knowingly. ''Are you usually regular or have you been late in the past?''

''I've never been late before,'' Eden whispered. ''Never.'' Six weeks. Why had she not even thought of it until now? Six weeks! A small smile crept across her face.

''Congratulations,'' Mary said softly.

''It's too soon to be sure, isn't it?''

''Perhaps.''

''I'd rather not tell anyone just yet,'' Eden said, leaning across the table and lowering her voice even though they were all alone in the dining room. ''I want to be positive.''

And she wanted Sin to love her first. She wanted him to ask her to stay *before* he knew about the baby. Her heart did an unpleasant little flip in her chest. What if he didn't?

Sullivan had allowed Rico and Nate to keep an eye on Eden during the day, telling himself it would be too telling to trail after her twenty-four hours a day. Much as he'd like to. He wanted her; he needed her; there were even times when he thought he loved her. But he wasn't sure that was enough, for her or for him.

He reclined on the bed in his room, deeming it the only safe place for the moment. Occasionally he heard Eden's voice drifting through the hotel, her laughter teasing him at unexpected moments. It would be selfish of him to ask her to stay, to say to hell with the rest of the world and ask her to remain his wife.

He heard booted footfalls running up the stairs, and something in the step cautioned him. He sat up quickly, and was swinging his legs from the bed when Rico threw open the door.

"Someone is coming," he said. "Two riders."

He bounded out of the room and down the stairs, Rico right behind him. Sullivan knew he and Eden were the only ones who'd recognize the Merriweather brothers.

Nate and Eden waited in the lobby. "Get her upstairs," he ordered without looking at Eden.

"I don't want to hide," she said softly.

At the sound of her voice he had no choice but to turn and meet her eye. She was afraid, but not in a panic. Her cheeks were flushed slightly, but her eyes were dry and her mouth was firm.

"For me," he whispered.

She nodded without another word and headed for the stairs. Nate started to follow, but she shooed him back. "If I'm in my room and the Merriweathers are on the street, I don't see why I need a guard." She looked over her shoulder. "You might need him, Sin."

Nate joined Sullivan and Rico, and the three of them stepped onto the boardwalk and into the street. He saw and recognized the Merriweathers. They rode slowly, casually, down the street toward the hotel. The sight of Curtis and Will Merriweather riding so calmly into town gave Sullivan a chill. Eden was right; they should know better; they should be frightened, not cocky. The brothers dismounted just north of the saloon and casually tossed the reins over a hitching post.

"Good afternoon, Sullivan," Curtis said with a crooked smile. "What a surprise to find you here. How's that pretty little wife of yours?"

Surprise? He didn't buy it, not for an instant.

Curtis waved his bandaged hand in the air, wiggling his fingers. "It's almost healed, see? I don't hold any grudges against that pretty little lady of yours. As a matter of fact, I'd like to thank her." His eyes narrowed. "A man ought to be prepared for whatever misfortune befalls him. While my right hand was injured, I learned how to shoot with my left."

"Want to give it a try?" Sullivan asked. "Here and now, Merriweather. You and me." The man would never have a chance to touch Eden.

The saloon door swung and Jed stepped onto the boardwalk. He assessed the situation quickly and aligned himself behind the brothers, his rifle held confidently in both hands.

Curtis's smile disappeared, once he was surrounded. "I did a little investigating, and I heard all about you and your pals, Sullivan. I'm not completely stupid. Do you think I'd ride in here without an ace up my sleeve?"

Sullivan didn't like the gleam in Merriweather's eye, or the new smirk on his brother Will's face.

"We'd be a couple of fools to come to Rock Creek without a plan, without a little assistance."

Sullivan's heart leaped to his throat, but he didn't dare turn his back on Curtis to search the street for this *assistance*.

Curtis nodded to the hotel and his smile drifted back. "I'd like you to meet my brother Jacob."

Sullivan turned around, just in time to see a man drag Eden from the hotel entrance and onto the boardwalk. She didn't fight as he pulled her onto the street, holding her body before his as a shield, pointing his revolver into her side.

"Jacob is my older, meaner brother, and when he found out what you two did to us, how you shot our brother George down in cold blood, he wanted to be a part of our rightful vengeance."

"Let her go," Sullivan said, his eyes on Jacob.

Jacob's answer was to push the barrel of his weapon against Eden's ribs. Her eyes widened and locked onto his, and he could see her terror. See it? Hell, he *felt* it to his bones.

Jed sidled away from the Merriweathers, his gaze riveted on Eden.

"Jed," Sullivan said, his voice low and calm, "stay where you are."

"That's my sister . . .", Jed began.

"That's my *wife,*" Sullivan interrupted, taking a step forward.

He didn't look back, but the familiar sound of Jedidiah Rourke working the lever of his Winchester was a small comfort.

Sullivan took a few steps across the street, toward Eden.

"Hold it right there," Jacob said, "unless you want me to splatter the lady's guts all over the street."

Obeying without question, Sullivan stopped. Eden's eyes were still latched to his, as she looked to him for comfort and assistance and courage. His gut twisted. He didn't know if he could give her what she needed.

For the first time in his life, he was in battle and didn't know what to do. If he moved forward, Eden might be shot. If he didn't move forward and do something, she might be shot.

"It'll be all right," he said, trying to assure her.

* * *

Much as she wanted to believe Sin's confident assertion that everything was going to be fine, she didn't. Her heart beat so fast she was sure the man who held her could hear and feel it.

And all she could think about was Sin and the baby. The baby he didn't even know about.

Sin's eyes told her, too clearly, that he was every bit as scared as she was.

She didn't think she could be more frightened, but when, out of the corner of her eye, she saw Millie and Teddy walking home from school, she knew she was wrong. She kicked back, her heels making contact with Jacob Merriweather's legs. "Let me go," she muttered.

"Eden," Sin said in a calming voice.

She wasn't the only one who'd seen the children. Jedidiah lifted a hand and whispered to the man at his side. Nate, his weapon still drawn, walked away from the Merriweathers. After one step, he started to run, smoothly and seemingly without effort or frenzy.

The children came to a dead halt in the road. Millie frowned, obviously confused. Teddy dropped his books and screamed, "Mama!" He started to run toward her, but Nate scooped him up easily.

Curtis Merriweather waved his gun in Nate's direction. "Bring them damn kids over here, too, you hear me?"

Eden's heart leaped. Surely Nate wouldn't do as Curtis asked! Ignoring the wiggling boy in his arms, he slipped his gun into its holster, smiled at Millie, then unceremoniously scooped her up as he had Teddy and dashed for the nearest building, the general store.

Angry, Curtis Merriweather fired a wild shot at Nate and the kids. Eden's heart stopped even though she could tell by his wild aim that the shot would go far wide. That shot, and the way Will took aim in the same direction, was the only invitation Rico and Jedidiah needed. Jedidiah's rifle popped into position and he fired at Curtis. Rico moved so quickly she wondered at first what he was doing, but when Will let out a surprised whoosh of air at the impact of a thrown knife plunging into his chest and crumpled to the ground, she knew full well what he'd done. Will and Curtis Merriweather were dead, and Sin had not taken his eyes off of her, not for one second.

Jacob's arms tightened around her, and he wheezed in her ear. "I'll kill her, and then I'll kill you."

"No, you won't," Sin said calmly, taking another step. "She's the only thing keeping you alive."

He fingered the handle of the six-shooter he wore, and she wondered, briefly, if he would try to draw and get off a shot. Jacob's head was unprotected, as he peeked over her shoulder. She could see Sin consider and then almost immediately dismiss the idea.

"I'll drop my gun," he said, lifting the six-shooter from his holster with two unthreatening fingers, "and you let her go."

"No," Jacob said with a shake of his head. "But you toss that gun aside anyway." He emphasized the order with another fierce poke at Eden with the gun barrel.

Sin obediently dropped his gun. "Let her go and take me instead. One hostage is as good as another, and her brother's back there." He nodded to the rear. "He won't let you out of town with her as a hostage, but he won't care what you do with me."

Jacob did, at least, seem to consider the possibility. His arms loosened a little, and a confused hum filled her ear.

The saloon door swung, and Daniel, limping, wearing only a pair of black trousers, stepped onto the boardwalk. A pistol hung almost casually from his hand. There was nothing threatening about his pose. "Sullivan," he called calmly, "step aside."

"No!" Sin looked horrified. More frightened than before. He advanced on the last remaining Merriweather. "A trade." A hint of panic crept into his voice. "You let her go and I make sure you get out of town."

The gun pressed into her side wavered. "Don't come any closer."

"It's the best deal you're gonna get," Sin whispered.

"Damn it, Sullivan!" Daniel shouted, his pose of indifference disintegrating as he sidled cautiously down the boardwalk.

Sin took another step forward, and the gun that had been pressed against Eden's side turned on him.

"You stay back!" Jacob ordered, as he shifted his weight so he could better control the weapon that was now shakily aimed at Sin.

Daniel's arm popped up so fast his movement was a blur to Eden. She could see one dark eye narrow as he took aim. Sin dropped to the ground and rolled toward her as the gun fired. Almost simultaneously, Jacob fired.

The world went black.

Eden crumpled and fell to the ground, blood on one shoulder of her white blouse and splattered across one pale cheek, her eyes closed, her body limp.

"Eden?" Sullivan whispered, gathering her into his arms and pulling her away from Jacob Merriweather's body. With trembling fingers he brushed the flecks of blood from her cheek. Shadows surrounded them, fell over Eden's body and his. He looked up. Of all the men present he saw only one. His eyes fell on Cash, who stood there half naked, favoring his left leg, his revolver hanging from his hand.

"You shot her," he said hoarsely. "You son of a bitch. I told you no. I knew that shot was too risky."

"I did not shoot her," Cash said indignantly. "I fired one bullet and it found its intended target, there"—he gestured with the gun toward a motionless Jacob Merriweather—"just above the left eyebrow. I believe Eden fainted. The blood is Merriweather's."

Eden stirred and opened her eyes. Immediately, she threw her arms around his neck and held on tight.

"Did he shoot you?" she whispered against his neck, her breath so warm and soft Sullivan had to close his eyes and savor it.

Eden's hands rapidly skimmed over his shoulders and chest, over his sides and thighs. "He came out of nowhere," she said as she searched. "Before I could scream he clamped his hand over my mouth, and then he dragged me out here, and oh, Sin, I was so afraid he would shoot you."

Rico went down the street to check on the kids and Nate. Cash turned to Jacob Merriweather to admire his handiwork, and Jed spread his legs wide and took a stance of defiance.

"This is why we're getting you back to Georgia

as soon as possible," he snapped. "And get your hands off of Sullivan! It's obvious he hasn't been hurt. You've already checked damn near every square inch."

"I'm not going anywhere," Eden said confidently.

"No, you're not," Sullivan agreed, and then he kissed her, a soft kiss to make sure she was still warm and breathing. He had never been as afraid as he'd been when he'd turned to see that gun against her side. He wasn't about to let her leave. He couldn't. "You're not going anywhere."

"No, I'm not," she whispered.

"You belong here, with me."

She smiled and nodded.

"I love you," he said softly.

"I love you, too," she whispered with a smile. "But you already know that, don't you?"

God, yes, he knew it. She'd told him. She'd shown him in a hundred ways. He kissed her again.

"I've been hornswoggled," Jed said softly. "You two aren't on the outs at all!"

"No, we're not," Eden admitted as she took her mouth from his. "We're married. We love each other, and if you don't like it you can just . . . just . . . Well, you can learn to keep your opinions to yourself."

Sullivan helped Eden to her feet, holding on to her as if she might break if he let go. They were both still a little weak in the knees.

"I can't believe you fooled us all with that . . . What you did was treachery, pure and simple. All this time we thought . . ."

"Speak for yourself, Jed. You were the only one who was blind enough to be fooled," Cash said with a smile as he stepped away from the body of

Jacob Merriweather. "Remember how you told me a few days ago that Eden was cleaning the tub? I almost busted a gut trying not to laugh."

"Why?" Jed asked with a frown.

"You see . . ." Cash began.

"Daniel!" Eden gasped. "Don't you dare."

Cash grinned. "Well, maybe there are some things a brother shouldn't hear about his little sister."

Nate and Rico joined them, telling Eden, when she asked, that the children had been told all was well, and they would remain in Rose Sutton's care until the bodies were removed from the street. She thanked them for being so thoughtful of the children's delicate sensibilities.

"I need to see Millie and Teddy," she said. "To give them a hug and tell them everything is fine. But I can't do that until I change out of this blouse." She wrinkled her nose and plucked at the bloodstained shoulder. "I don't want them to see me like this. It would just upset them, and I'm sure they're already distressed enough by this episode. Goodness, did you hear Teddy scream?"

Eden shuddered as Sullivan draped his arm over her shoulder, and together they turned about. She slipped her arm easily around his waist and leaned comfortably against him. The shaking stopped almost immediately.

Rico grinned widely as Sullivan led Eden toward the hotel. He muttered something in Spanish, and for once no one told him to translate, and Cash didn't bellow at him to speak English. Nate didn't seem to pay them much mind at all, but he did seem quite pleased with himself.

Jed lifted his arms in frustration. "Is there anyone here," he bellowed, "besides me, who was hornswoggled into thinking these two were . . . that they didn't . . . that they hadn't . . ."

"Not me," Nate said. "I married them, remember? I knew it would last."

"I forgot you're the *wise* one among us," Jed said tersely.

Rico continued to grin. "If you would take your head out of the sand long enough to take a good look at the people around you, or perhaps to take a nice long smell . . ."

"I think I like the sand," Jed said, but there was surrender in his voice.

Sullivan and Eden walked toward the hotel and left the others quibbling. He couldn't hold her tight enough, couldn't touch her enough. When he thought of how close he'd come to losing her . . .

"Hold it right there!" Jed hollered as they reached the hotel doorway.

Together, he and Eden turned to face the furious man.

Jed shook a menacing finger. "I guess if she had to marry one of us, it might as well be you. It could've been worse," he said, glancing at the men around him. "She might've married Rico, or Nate, or"—he shuddered—"*Daniel.*"

"Well, thank you, I think," Sullivan said.

"Is this your way of giving us your blessing?" Eden asked with a dimpled smile.

Jedidiah Rourke actually blushed. "I reckon," he mumbled. He waved a dismissive hand. "You go change out of those clothes, and I'll go check on the kids. If you're all going to stay here, I need to . . . mend a few fences with my niece and nephew."

"We'll be there in a few minutes," Sullivan said as he turned Eden about and they walked away from Jed.

"I was so scared," she said as he led her up the stairs.

"Me, too." Truth was, he'd never been so scared in his life.

When they reached the second-story hallway, she stopped, took his hand, and laid it over her belly, just beneath her navel. He knew what was coming even before she said, "Mostly I was worried about him. Or her. Our baby."

His fingers brushed against her still-flat belly, where his child, their child, already grew. "I shouldn't be surprised."

"No," she said with a smile. "You certainly shouldn't."

A baby. He should be terrified. He should be concerned about the blood of his father and the blood of his mother running through another body, and how he and Eden were going to make it when they were so different and always would be, but at the moment he was oddly happy.

"Did I thank you?" she whispered, "for saving my life, that is?"

He shook his head. "I don't believe you did."

She came up on her toes and kissed him, her lips soft and yielding, the caress deep and undeniably loving. "Thank you, Sinclair Sullivan," she whispered as she reluctantly took her mouth from his. "What would I do without you?"

He brushed a strand of pale hair away from her face. "You'll never have to know."

"Good," she whispered, kissing him again, much too briefly. "I suppose I should thank Daniel, too, and Rico and Nate and Jedidiah, of course," she said softly. "They were all wonderful."

Sullivan arched his eyebrows slightly. "You can't

thank them the way you thanked me,'' he insisted. ''Make 'em soup.''

''I do make very good soup,'' she said with a smile.

How had he survived this long without that smile?

''I meant what I said out there.'' He slipped his arms around his wife and lifted her off her feet. ''I do love you.''

She laughed lightly and tilted her head back. ''I knew it before you did, Sinclair Sullivan.''

''Yes,'' he whispered as he gently spun her around. ''Yes, you did.''

Chapter 23

The Merriweathers had been disposed of less than a week earlier, and Sin was already packing his saddlebags. Eden tried to stay calm.

"How long will you be gone, do you think?" She sat on the edge of the bed and watched him pack.

"Not long," he said. "I have a few things to take care of. A few loose ends to tie up."

How many days was *not long*? Two? Ten? Thirty? "You're going to Webberville," she said softly.

Sin lifted his head and smiled at her. "Yep."

Eden had to bite her lip to keep from telling him, at least *asking* him, not to go. "It's that damn hat," she muttered. When Sin lifted surprised eyebrows at her unexpected curse, she muttered an even softer, "Sorry."

She'd told Daniel she would become the woman Sin needed, if that's what it took to keep him. Could she do it? If he needed to ride off on occasion, to one troubled place or another, could she stand it?

Yes.

"You know," she said more calmly, "I still want all of you, but I'd rather have a little piece of you than all of anyone else in the world. If you need to go, go. I'll be waiting for you when you get home."

He gave her a look that said he'd never doubted it, but there was nothing possessive or selfish about that look. It was warm and confident and told her all she needed to know. It told her he loved her.

"I'm going to rename the hotel," she said, changing the subject so she wouldn't cry. "Jedediah's going to help me paint a new sign to replace the old one."

"Does he know this yet?"

Eden shook her head. "No, but he won't mind."

"What are you going to name it?"

She looked deep into his eyes. "Paradise."

Paradise. He thought about the new name for Eden's hotel all the way to Webberville, a trip much quicker on his horse and alone than it had been in Eden's crowded wagon. *Paradise.*

What had Eden said? A long time ago, it seemed like, she'd said she'd rather live in the most desolate place on earth surrounded by people she loved than to live alone in paradise. She'd also supposed that the exact opposite was true of him. Maybe she was right, or at least had been then. Now . . . Hell, he missed her already. He missed the kids. He missed his own bed.

And he'd only been gone a few hours.

He camped out that night, slept on the hard ground. When he dreamed, he dreamed of Eden and the baby she carried. If it was a girl, he decided, he wanted to name her Fiona. The world needed a happy Fiona Sullivan again, he figured.

The next afternoon he arrived in Webberville. No one would take him by surprise this time, that was for goddamn sure. They weren't expecting him, so he had time to glance around as he stepped through the bat-wing doors. Almost immediately, he spotted the men who had ambushed him, his hat hanging behind the bar like a kind of trophy . . . and something else that drew his attention away from it all.

Eden looked up at the new sign, red paint on a white background standing out against the weathered boards of her hotel. PARADISE.

"It looks good, Mama," Millie said, shielding her eyes with her small hand. "Very pretty."

"Yeah," Teddy said. "I like it."

The streets were crowded, but then it was Saturday afternoon and people from visiting ranches filled the streets and streamed from the businesses along Rock Creek's main thoroughfare. As soon as she hired one or two girls to help her, she might start opening the hotel restaurant for meals in the evening and on Saturday afternoons. There appeared to be lots of hungry people out there.

"Papa's coming," Teddy said softly, his eyes turned to the end of the street.

Eden turned to watch the black stallion making its way slowly down the street. Sin had been gone less than a week, and she'd missed him so much she hurt with it. How would she stand it when he left again?

She would, she reminded herself. She would do whatever she had to do.

Sin wore his accursed hat, the one he'd been compelled to go back to Webberville and fight for, and underneath that hat his long strands of hair were missing. She squinted against the sun to see more clearly, but it did not help. He might've pulled his hair back, she supposed, but he'd never done that before.

He had another surprise in store for her. A child with pale brown hair peeked warily around Sin's side as he pulled up to the hotel. He helped the kid to his feet before dismounting and tossing the reins across a hitching post. He took the child's hand as he came to Eden with a smile.

"This is the lady I told you about," he said, "Eden Sullivan. Eden, this is Rafe. He's going to be staying with us."

Rafe looked terrified, as if he expected an argument. He held on to Sin's hand and stared up at her with big green eyes. The sun made his hair look like honey, and it was as fine as spun silk. He probably wasn't much older than Millie.

She gave him a smile. "Well, I'm glad to have you here, Rafe."

"You are?" he asked suspiciously.

"Of course," Eden said, her voice leaving no room for doubt.

Millie and Teddy had to vie for Sin's attention, Millie springing up until he caught her, Teddy standing close until Sin dropped to his haunches.

With Millie still in his arms, Sin looked Teddy in the eye, man-to-man. "You been keeping an eye on things around here, like I asked you to?"

Teddy nodded. "Yes, Papa." His eyes got wide. "Uncle Jed is teaching me to shoot a rifle," he added with unconcealed excitement.

Jedidiah and Teddy had spent a lot of time

together in the past few days. Teddy didn't glare at his new uncle anymore, and had even confided to Eden once that not all uncles were bad.

"He is?" Sin asked.

"Yep. I have to be able to defend my sister with something other than the pointy toe of my boots. That's what Uncle Jed says. He said I'm a natural marksman." And then something wonderful happened; Teddy smiled. "I'm glad you're home."

Sin ruffled the hair on Teddy's head, not making a big deal out of the smile, and he offered his cheek when Millie leaned forward to kiss him again.

Eden had to do something, otherwise she was sure to cry, right there in the middle of the street. "Teddy, why don't you take Rafe upstairs and show him where he'll be staying. In the room with you two, for now. In a few minutes I'll fix our travelers something to eat. Do you like custard pie, Rafe?"

"I don't know, ma'am," he said softly. "I never had any custard pie."

"That is an injustice that will soon be remedied."

Sin rose slowly to his feet and readjusted the hat on his head. The three children headed into the hotel, leaving Eden to stare up into his face. She'd worried incessantly for days, but in the shadow of the hat she could see no bruises, no cuts. He looked perfect, in fact.

"Got my hat back," he said sheepishly. "And my rig." He jangled the well-worn holster and plain six-shooter that hung low on his hips.

"And I suppose the fine men of Webberville just handed them over without a fuss," she said.

"No, ma'am. I had to kick some ass to get my hat back."

She put a finger on his jaw and turned his head

this way and that. "Looks like they didn't touch you."

"Not this time." His smile faded. "That's where I found Rafe. His mother used to work upstairs, but she died a while back. The kid was sweeping the floor when I got there, cleaning up after a bunch of drunks."

"That's terrible," she whispered.

Sin opened his mouth, closed it again, shifted uneasily on his booted feet. "Hell, Eden, I couldn't just leave him there."

She smiled and wrapped her arms around his neck. "Of course you couldn't."

He gave her a belated kiss hello, in spite of the fact that people passed all around. Neither of them cared. When she pulled away, Eden reached up and grabbed his hat.

"Let me get a good look at this hat that's worth so much trouble."

She didn't look at the hat after it left Sin's head. He'd cut his hair. Short. A barber somewhere between Rock Creek and Webberville had given him a crisp, neat, very ordinary haircut. She reached up to touch the strands above his ear.

"You cut your hair," she whispered.

"Do you mind?"

She shook her head. "It's very handsome, but . . ."

"I don't need it anymore," he interrupted. "On the way back from Webberville it kept blowing in my face, and getting hot against my neck, and I wondered why the hell I'd kept it long all these years."

Eden raised her eyebrows skeptically.

"Besides," he said, "the haircut goes with the job."

Oh, he was going to leave again! She took a deep breath to calm herself. "What job?"

He pulled a telegram from his pocket. "You are looking at the new sheriff of this fine county. The governor's appointed me to the office until we hold a special election and make it official."

"Sheriff Sullivan," she said with a smile. He wasn't going to leave her, after all. He wasn't going to come and go like a nomad. He was going to stay.

He leaned down, placing his handsome face close to hers. "Did you really think I could ride away from you and be content?"

"I did wonder . . ."

"Well, stop your wondering, Mrs. Sullivan. I'm home to stay."

Sin put his arm around her shoulder and they walked toward the hotel entrance. He glanced up once and studied the new sign.

"Paradise," he muttered as they stepped into the shade of the boardwalk. "You got that right."

If you liked SULLIVAN, be sure to read RICO by Lori Handeland, the next in the *Rock Creek Six* series, available wherever books are sold in November 2001.

Although Enrico Salvatore's friends call him "The Kid," Rico is a man through and through—and one who can't resist a lovely woman's charms. Lily Jeanpierre, the main attraction at Rock Creek's saloon, is Rico's kind of beautiful, and her voice rivals an angel's. But while Lily won't deny the powerful attraction between them, she won't admit that it's anything but desire. Rico can't forget the bond his parents shared, and he's determined to prove to Lily that true love is possible—even when a dangerous secret from her past forces him to risk a lifetime in her arms to prove it. . . .

COMING IN NOVEMBER 2001 FROM
ZEBRA BALLAD ROMANCES

__MY LADY RUNAWAY: The Sword and The Ring
by Suzanne McMinn   0-8217-6876-X $5.99US/$7.99CAN
Elayna knows that she and Graeham may still have a chance for a future if
only she can discover the truth about the shocking past that haunts both their
families. But first, she must convince her stubborn knight that she will risk
anything to escape the fate that awaits her—and that love is the only thing
worth fighting for. . . .

__RICO: The Rock Creek Six
by Lori Handeland   0-8217-6743-7 $5.99US/$7.99CAN
Rico is a man who can't resist a woman's charms. Singer Lily Jeanpierre is
beautiful, and her voice rivals an angel's. Rico hasn't forgotten the special bond
his parent's shared, and he's determined to prove to Lily that true love is
possible—even when a dangerous secret from her past threatens their chance
of a lifetime together.

__CHILD'S PLAY: Dublin Dreams
by Cindy Harris   0-8217-6714-6 $5.99US/$7.99CAN
Rose Sinclair is shocked when her dead husband's mistress arrives with three
children in tow—and claims that they are now Rose's responsibility! One of
the children claims another man is his father. Sir Steven Nollbrook, a successful
barrister. Steven insists that the child isn't his—but as Rose discovers Steven's
secrets, she vows to show him that love can be as simple as A.B.C.

__HER LEADING MAN: The Dream Maker
by Alice Duncan   0-8217-6881-6 $5.99US/$7.99CAN
For Christina Fitzgerald, film acting is a surefire way to earn money to get into
medical school. At least she has intellectual producer Martin Tafft to talk to.
Then an accident on the set forces Martin to take the male lead, and Christina
gets a taste of his kisses. Now all she has to do is convince him that he would
be perfect for another role. . . .

Call toll free 1-888-345-BOOK to order by phone or use this coupon to order
by mail. *ALL BOOKS AVAILABLE NOVEMBER 01, 2001*
Name _____
Address _____
City _____ State _____ Zip _____
Please send me the books I have checked above.
I am enclosing $ _____
Plus postage and handling* $ _____
Sales tax (in NY and TN) $ _____
Total amount enclosed $ _____
*Add $2.50 for the first book and $.50 for each additional book. Send check
or money order (no cash or CODs) to: Kensington Publishing Corp., Dept. C.O.,
850 Third Avenue, New York, NY 10022
Prices and numbers subject to change without notice. Valid only in the U.S.
All orders subject to availabilty. NO ADVANCE ORDERS.
Visit our website at **www.kensingtonbooks.com.**

Discover The Magic of
Romance With

Jo Goodman

Embrace the Romances of
Shannon Drake